Yours Celestially

AL HESS

Yours Celestially

Printed in the United States of America

First Printing, 2023

ISBN: 978-1-958051-41-2

Published by The Kraken Collective

Kraken
Collective

Hey friend! This book contains mentions of death and past drug addiction. For a full list of content warnings, please refer to page 339.

Author's Note

In 2022, I unpublished all seven books in my Travelers Series. These books were instrumental both in helping me hone my writing craft and in giving me a mental escape while I was going through the hardest years of my life. I cherish the characters and the world I created for them. But I've come so far in my skill and in understanding who I am since then. There are things, in the first three books in particular, that I don't believe I've executed well and/or I would have written differently if I did it all again.

Yours Celestially is not Travelers. It's more an homage to these characters that came to mean so much to me, and what I would have done with some of them if I'd had more self-awareness back then. It's painfully obvious to me in some of the Travelers books what threads I desperately wanted to write but didn't. If you squint hard, Yours Celestially is what you'd get if you threw Chromeheart through a very gay and trippy hopepunk portal.

More than anything, I wanted to have fun. I hope you have fun. And I hope you'll forgive me for shaking things up a little. I wanted to give all of these characters more page time, but it would have clogged the story. Please assume they're living their very best lives in the city of Galvlohi.

— Al

1

The Resurrected

Dying has given me indigestion.

I sit in a cold metal folding chair in the support circle, jiggling my leg and chewing on a hangnail. I'm trying to pay attention, but I've heard all of this before, and a sickly-sweet nausea pulls at my gut like a fishhook baited with marzipan.

The redhead beside me is new. Not new to being resurrected, but new to the group. I've already forgotten their name and pronouns, but they're gorgeous—like most of the people here—their freckled alabaster face symmetrical and flawless.

My gut aches. I fish my roll of antacids from my pocket, struggling to pry the last two from the bottom of the shredded paper wrapper.

The facilitator invites the redhead to share something. They glance at the group, then examine their glittery green nail polish. "My mom was raised in the Universal Church"—everyone in the circle murmurs and nods—"and she wasn't active for a long time. I'd enrolled in the Renascenz program because... Well, it doesn't matter. What matters is that after I died and was resurrected, you'd think my mom would be happy I'd enrolled, right? It saved my life. But suddenly she's a devout member of the church again. It feels like she's doing it just to spite me."

The Universal Church doesn't care what other people do with their lives, and they're one of the most relaxed religions I know of. But their opinion with the public still holds weight, and when they said that the "soul" saved upon death and uploaded into a new body was only a digitally reformatted approximation of a personality—ergo not really the original person—people listened.

Renascenz Corp. hiked up our monthly memberships after that to compensate for fewer people enrolling in the resurrection program.

The redhead keeps talking, but their story lacks so much emotion it sounds like they're reading the cliché problems off one of the support group pamphlets, to the point that I wonder if they're making it all up. Someone else takes a turn, and when the redhead excuses themselves, I wait a beat, then slide out of my chair.

My housemate, Ivan, is sitting to the other side of me. He snatches my wrist and pulls me so close his beard tickles my cheek. "Where are you going?"

"I feel sick." It's not a lie. "Going to the restroom."

He gives me that look he always gets when he can't tell if I'm bullshitting him, then pushes his glasses up the bridge of his nose. "You always do this."

"What, go to the restroom?"

The warm porcelain fingers of Ivan's prosthetic hand dig into my arm. His voice is low but harsh enough that people seated next to us glance our way. "I'm not just here to support David, you know. And when I cook at home, I'm not just cooking for David. I might not know firsthand what it's like to die and come back, but I'm trying to be here for you. For *both* of you. And if you're not going to speak at these meetings, you can at least listen."

I give him what I hope is an incredulous look. "You want to chaperone me to the bathroom to make sure I don't escape?"

Ivan's grip lessens, slick fingers slipping away from my arm. "If you're not back in five minutes, I'm coming to find you."

"Yes, Warden." I excuse myself and leave the circle of chairs.

Despite the potted ferns and a screaming pink shag rug running down the hallway, this place looks somewhere between a warehouse and a dentist's office. I'm pretty sure the concrete floor and beige walls are sucking out my life force little by little. But if I hurry back and nod my head in all the right spots when David is talking, Ivan won't pester me to go to another of these meetings for at least two weeks.

The redhead slips into the bathroom, and I hang outside, hands stuffed in my pockets. Waiting for a stranger outside a bathroom is a creepy thing to do, but I can't leave until I get an answer. I've already asked others in the group, and they have no idea what I'm talking about.

Cheery posters urging me to live my best second life are

tacked on a pockmarked bulletin board across from me. Above them is a plaque emblazoned with ᏍᎪᎯ in neon green Cherokee syllabary. Below is:

ᏙᏏᎯ!

Welcome to Galvlohi/Stellar Universe!

[ga-luh-low-hee]

Papered in between the posters are handwritten ads for a produce and seed swap meet, an event at the library, and a band looking for a new bassist. Drawn in marker on the corkboard is

Oh god. I don't know what kind of high that emoji combination would produce, but it makes sweat break out on my upper lip. I clench my jaw and cover the emojis up with a flier before I stare at them too long and decide it's something I need. I pull my gaze from the board. Beyond the gloom of the bland hall, early evening light hits the glass of the back door, glazing it a vibrant yellow. Across the street, people stand outside an Ethiopian food market, probably waiting for the trolley.

I don't know what Ivan's deal is. I've never escaped out the back door. Not here, and not at my Addiction Recovery meetings. And I do the damn dishes after he cooks.

The bathroom door swings open, and the redhead stops abruptly. They hesitantly thumb behind them. "There's more than one toilet in there. You could have come in."

"Actually, I was wondering if I could ask you a question."

They start to brush past me. "Not interested."

"No, it's about your body."

Their face sours, and they flip a lock of hair over their shoulder. "*Definitely* not interested."

Goddamn it. What is wrong with me? I dig my fingernail into my left bicep, feeling for the pin beneath the skin. If only the drug it pumped out was Smiling Face with Sunglasses instead of just my ADHD meds, then I'd have the suaveness to broach this conversation. My thoughts return to the emojis drawn on the corkboard, and my shirt collar is suddenly hot and constricting. Focus. You're perfectly capable of having a conversation without neural enhancement pins. "Sorry. Let me try again. I'm Sasha, he/him."

"I remember."

My gut lurches, and I press a hand to my navel. It feels like there's a sugar-dipped bird inside trying to escape. "You don't seem like you're here to talk through your mom's religion. It didn't sound like that story was even yours. So I have to know if you're here for the same reason I am... Is Metatron still with you, even out of Limbo? Is your stomach full of— of their love sickness?"

"The story was true, but I've been to so many of these groups that I've got it memorized at this point." Their face softens. "Listen, being in love with Metatron isn't crazy. They're the only social interaction the dead get in Limbo. Metatron listens to your problems, helps you process your death. It makes sense that some people get a little too attached and can't stop thinking about Metatron even after being resurrected. This support group isn't going to help you, but there are forums online where you can go to talk about it. I can give you an address."

I grimace. I've seen those, and they need some serious moderation. "It's not *my* love. It's Metatron's. Our guardian angel is in love with one of the dead still in Limbo, and for some reason, I can feel it." When the nausea first started up, I thought I had an ulcer. Or maybe the stasis pod that grew my new body forgot some of my intestines or something. Who knew? But the longer it went on, the more the feeling resolved into a flavor, a desire that was distinctly Metatron's, accompanied by snippets of their thoughts for a soul named Rodrigo. Thinking about my own lack of a love life is bad enough, but intrusive thoughts about someone *else's* is making me lose my mind.

The redhead stares at me for a long moment, and I'm certain they're going to call me a delusional creep. Ivan is going to find out, and I'm going to hear about it all the way home. But instead, they hug their arms against their chest and say, "It's not an ache in my stomach. It's in my teeth. Like I just ate a huge mouthful of caramels. And I started thinking about Metatron so much that I was convinced I must be obsessed with them. But the online forums didn't help, and neither have local meetings. None of these facilitators know what the hell I'm talking about."

Relief pours into me, and I shove curls away from my eyes. Finally someone gets it! I try to keep the excitement out of my voice to avoid sounding like even more of a weirdo. "I know exactly what you mean. How long has it been going on? Six, seven months?"

"That sounds right. I went to the dentist in October, convinced my mouth was full of cavities. Which doesn't make sense in a brand new body, but I didn't know what else it would be." They shuffle their feet against the concrete. "Some glitch in the Renascenz program did something to us, huh? Gave us a weird tether back to our guardian angel? I've been using this sensitive teeth toothpaste, and it helps a little, but I don't want to be stuck like this forever. Wish I knew what to do about it."

"Way ahead of you." I might break out in sweat whenever I see an emoji, but I'm still good for something. I'm going to fix this for me, and now that I know I'm not alone in this resurrection glitch, I'm going to fix it for them too. "I'm going to find a way to talk to Metatron. I got a job at Renascenz, and I start tomorrow."

2

The Seraph

The day Rodrigo died, he was five minutes late for work.

He might have hit the snooze button one too many times. He might have forgotten to press his dress shirt the night before and hastily ran an iron across it before throwing it on. Or maybe he left his thermos of coffee sitting on the kitchen counter and had to run back in to get it.

I try not to dwell on the actual moment of his death. It hurts to think about him suffering through that. So instead I've fixated on that break in his routine at the beginning of the day in question.

I could ask him why he was late—I'm sure he remembers— but I've wondered about it so many times over the past six months that it's evolved into an untouchable question in my mind. This private detail that I'm not close enough to Rodrigo to know.

We sit in the spongy grass beneath a jewel-scattered sky, the light from my halo casting a pallor on the clovers around Rodrigo's feet. His socks are black and pink argyle, clothing knobby ankles, and it feels like another intimate detail I shouldn't be thinking about.

He crosses his legs and leans back on his elbows, gazing at the sky. Frustration radiates from him, his body tense and fingers fidgety. "Aldebaran is wrong for this time of year. It should be more south. I think."

I glance up at the star. Rodrigo is the astronomer, not me, but my coding and processing power makes it easier to generate accurate simulations of the material universe. He and the other dead have to use their memory and imaginations to create an environment, to varying results.

<I think it's beautiful,> I say. And I mean it. I would never think of his sky as lesser simply because it's more of an artistic interpretation than the real thing. But I know details, especially when it comes to astronomy, are important to him.

If he let me, I could give him a hyper-realistic night sky. I could pull down the moon and spin it like a Christmas bauble. We could picnic on the surface of the sun. But I don't mess with Rodrigo's room unless he asks me, because loss of control ramps up his anxiety. He prefers what he knows, even if it's slightly inaccurate—his study full of books, and sometimes this grassy hill and star-crusted sky where he used to set up his telescopes when he was alive.

That he prefers to wear a two-dimensional emoji in place of whatever lovely face he had in life is an additional reminder that we're in Limbo and not on his stargazing hill in the material plane. A reminder that I'll never leave this place... and Rodrigo will. He'll be resurrected and take his impressionistic sky, his argyle socks, and his thoughtful conversations with him. I'll never know why he was late for work on the day he died. I'll never know what it's like to touch his hand.

I should do it. I should do it now. Stop being a coward and slip my alabaster hand into his bister one like it's the easiest thing in the world.

He gently tugs at the blades of grass, plucking over and over without pulling them out. A soothing action. Hunger roars inside me. I want my fingers to be the target of his stim instead. Or my wings. Let him run his hands through until the sun explodes. I probably wouldn't notice if it did.

His hand. Just take his hand.

With every second that goes by another brick is added to the wall of my hesitation until I can't muscle through it at all.

Rodrigo makes a disgruntled noise, his concentration still on the sky. His emoji face shifts into a frown, eyebrows forming a V between his eyes. "It's still not right." He sighs. "I don't know where Aldebaran goes. Can you make it for me?"

Well. At least this is something I *can* do. A five-pointed cardboard star with a shiny gold coating pops into existence above us. It twists lazily in the air like a forgotten prom decoration.

My voice lilts. <How's that?>

He snorts. "It's a little small. The chemical composition is wrong." He reaches up and flicks one of the points, sending the star spinning. "And it isn't obeying physics."

I shrug. <Obeying physics is for chumps.>

The cardboard star looks lonely as it wobbles away like a

drunken top. I change it into a white-hot daub of light like Rodrigo's others, then tack it up in the night sky where it's supposed to go.

He smiles. "Thank you."

Anything for you. <No music tonight?> I ask. He's been listening to his current disco-nouveau song obsession on repeat for five days straight, and it's strangely empty without it.

He flashes an embarrassed flush. "Figured you were sick of it."

<Not at all.> I would be if it were only a song, but at this point it may as well be his heartbeat.

Though he plucks more urgently at the grass, his cheeks bright pink, the song starts up. Sharp synthesizer, brassy trumpet, and velvety bass thump through the night, followed by urgent, earnest lyrics:

Darling, you're so fine
Give me a chance to make you mine

I stare at my hands, pink-knuckled and veiny with sparkly gold nails. The eyes in my wrists peek out from beneath my suit cuffs, staring back at me judgmentally.

Stay with me
Now until eternity

There's three minutes of my daily appointment left with him. That's more than enough time to do what I'm aching to. And I must do it now before my hesitation builds back up.

I lean a little closer, and one of my wings brushes the shoulder of his tweed jacket. <Rodrigo...>

He turns to me. His emoji has returned to a bland smile, but he tugs hard at the grass. "Yeah?"

<I want to tell you something. I— I enjoy our visits so much. You've been here much longer than you ever should have, and...>

He sits up a little straighter, and there's a quaver of urgency to his voice. "Did you get news about the lawsuit? Did it get settled?"

<What? No, not that I know of.>

"Oh... Well. It's only a matter of time, isn't it."

I curl my hands into my lap. Of course. He wants out of here. All the dead do. <I've been watching the proceedings closely, and I'm calculating a ninety-two percent chance of Renascenz winning. Those right-wing Christians are loud, the plaintiffs are loud, but they aren't the majority. And the judge is a Buddhist. No one wants Limbo shut down and all of us deleted.>

Despite my reassurance, Rodrigo cringes.

<You'll be okay, I swear to it.>

Rodrigo and the six others in Limbo should have stayed for three weeks tops. But resurrections were suspended once Renascenz got sued, and everyone has been in a state of, well, *limbo*, for six months. Even if Rodrigo enjoys my company and my goofy cardboard stars, he wants to go on to his second life. I can't blame him for not wanting to be stuck here with me any longer, and I'm going to do everything in my power to make sure he goes back to the life he deserves—teaching astronomy at the university; finding a human partner who treats him right; being surrounded by his loved ones again.

<As soon as I have good news, you'll be the first I'll tell.>

He looks away, his two-dimensional head twisting like a coin. "What if you're at another appointment?"

<I'll launch a paper airplane into your room. Or write it in frosting on top of a cake.>

"Please don't launch a cake into my room."

I chuckle, but it's forced. <My time is up.>

His shoulders slump a fraction, but I can't allow myself to read anything into it. A lot of the dead are disappointed when I have to leave because I'm their only social interaction. It doesn't mean they wouldn't trample me like tweens at a boy band concert if they saw the exit to this place.

I push myself up, and Rodrigo snatches my sleeve. The squeak that comes out of me is neither dignified or appropriate, and he yanks his hand away. "Sorry! Did I poke my finger in your eye?"

<No. And it wouldn't have hurt if you did. I simply wasn't expecting that.>

"Oh. It's just that you never told me what you wanted to say."

The echo of his fingers lingers on my wrist like a brand. <Um... I don't think it was fair that Pluto got demoted to a non-planet. Poor little thing just minding its business, then it's handed a box and told to clean out its desk.>

I can feel the stunned confusion radiating from him even

though his expression doesn't change. Bishop on a bicycle, what is wrong with me? I'm such a coward.

He tugs on the button of his jacket. "Well... this could be a good-natured thing to debate when I see you again."

<Don't tell me you're on the side of the Pluto-haters. I bet you think the moon is made of rock or something too, instead of cheese.>

"The moon *is*—" He hesitates, then whispers. "That's a joke, right?"

I whisper back. <Yes.> A little louder, I say, <We could try a slice of it next time I'm here and find out what kind it is. Personally, my bet is on gorgonzola. Toodles!>

I vanish in a burst of feathers and sparkle as the clock rolls over. I used to have plenty of time between my last appointment and the brand new day to diagnose, defrag, and decompress, but I started actively resisting the pull from Rodrigo's room, lingering longer and longer, now bumping up to my next appointment. If Rodrigo wonders about my extended visits, he's never mentioned it, but then again, time is a strange concept here for most of the dead.

I access the next soul's room and start a timer in the back of my mind, counting down the 79,200 seconds until Rodrigo and I can taste-test slices of the moon, and I can wuss out— again—of any attempt to show him how I feel.

A message suddenly appears from Renascenz's Chief Resurrection Officer. Jack avoids contacting me unless they absolutely must, which I like to assume is because they don't want to bother me and not at all because I'm blackmailing them. I open the message:

∞ The techs finally isolated that glitch from last spring
ᘏ Hello, Jack! ::::::) Which glitch?

The Renascenz program went down for eighteen minutes and thirty-two seconds last March, and though it was less of an *experience* than something I was informed of after I was back online, the event still felt like a dress rehearsal to death. Strange glitches in the program started happening after that, and I'm certain there are ones we still don't know about.

A new message from Jack appears:

∞ The one that was making people sleepwalk and dream they were in Limbo
ᘏ Ah, good! Now if they can just fix the other three issues we know about.
∞ That's the thing. They want to go down and tinker with the servers.

I pause, mulling over the implications.

ᘏ Well, we can't have that.
∞ No shit. I tried to tell Arthur that the servers don't have anything to do with errors that are clearly coming from the obols, but since they can't just cut open a person's head and tinker with *that*, Arthur told the CEO he'd have someone look at the servers. He's just trying

to cover his ass but

But we have too many lives riding on the assurance that the facility where the Limbo servers and stasis pods are kept is secure. We can't let tech people in, even ones who work under Jack. I think of blinking out of existence during that program crash last spring, and how I didn't even feel it. How, if we hadn't come back online, I wouldn't have even known I'd been deleted. None of the souls would know. Rodrigo wouldn't know. And maybe that would be the equivalent of the phrase "passing away peacefully in sleep" that so many obituaries like to use, but somehow the idea of Rodrigo facing death—again—without knowing that's what it is scares me most of all.

ᘐ **Things are too delicate right now. Use that charming personality of yours to solve the problem**.

I imagine Jack giving a derisive snort at my message and tossing their phone into a drawer.

Another message appears; this time it's not Jack, but the COO, Arthur. My heart clenches, tug-a-warring between desperate hope and sudden anxiety. Maybe we've gotten the green light to resume resurrections. We might only be an hour away from sending people into the upload queue so they can get on with their lives. Oh, what a relief that would be.

But a tiny and selfish part of me hopes that isn't the case, because how can I go on if Rodrigo isn't here?

The thought of never seeing him again is too much to bear.

AL HESS

I close my eyes and smooth my hands over the thighs of my suit slacks. I think of how happy all these souls will be to live again. How happy their loved one will be to see them. Their spouses and children and housemates.

All it took was one lawsuit from a soul's unhappy family to throw a wrench into the whole Renascenz program and delay any more resurrections.

The soul in question was sixteen, and when I first met her, she'd imagined her surroundings as a single-wide trailer with black mold on the ceiling and towels stuffed into a broken window. I'd gently told her she could create whatever she wanted in her room—it didn't have to reflect her environment from life. When I returned the next day, not only had she changed her room, she'd given herself a different avatar, a different name, and new pronouns.

Renascenz uses similar consciousness-uploading tech as an older, sister company that specializes in giving living people new bodies that either relieve them of debilitating health issues or severe gender dysphoria, so it wasn't a surprise that a deceased trans girl would ask the Renascenz program to create a physical body for her new life that reflected who she was inside. I was so proud of her. When it was her time to be resurrected, I slid her into the upload queue and wished her well in her second life. But her family, who'd been waiting in the material world to greet her after she exited her stasis pod, was *not* expecting a petite girl with a pert nose and long black hair. And they were very, very upset. They believed it wasn't possible for their child to be transgender, so clearly the Universal Church was right, and the people being resurrected weren't the souls of the dead at all but some AI-generated approximation. They sued, and now the ethics of the entire program is up for debate.

Had I been there, I would have wrapped that girl in my many wings and told her transphobic family to eat shit, but there was nothing I could do from Limbo.

If *Simmons v Renascenz* hadn't happened, Rodrigo would be back to teaching classes at the university. I would have a fresh batch of souls every few weeks who wouldn't have time to become stuck in their own heads, taking out their frustrations on me.

If *Simmons v Renascenz* hadn't happened, I wouldn't have had time to fall in love.

Rodrigo doesn't want to be here any longer. That much was clear from our conversation earlier. He deserves to pick up his life where it left off before being so unfairly cut short.

I push a wing away from my vision and force myself to open Arthur's message:

∞ Hello Metatron, we're working on a relaunch campaign—we're quite optimistic about getting the program running again in the future!—and Design would like your help in creating a mascot. If you have ideas, please send them along.

A relaunch campaign? That means the resurrections could

be imminent. A hot wave of relief washes through me at the knowledge that it isn't a verdict *yet*, and the guilt that comes in its wake is so heavy I'm certain it's going to drag me through the proverbial floor, through the center of the proverbial earth, and out the other side. I didn't ask to fall in love, I don't know how to make it go away, and if I act on it, what good will it do? Rodrigo will leave anyway.

I tug hard on my wings, and feathers come loose in my hands. They slide through my fingers, fluttering in an iridescent spiral, and I wonder if I can let Rodrigo go as easily.

3

The Resurrected

I died and spent weeks in heavenly Limbo with an angelic artificial intelligence while I waited for my new body to grow, all to come back as a damn coffee boy.

A monstera leaf slaps me in the face as I juggle cup holders of lattes, pushing off my shoes in the Renascenz lobby. The building is like most that have vegetation instead of rugs and carpet; you're required to remove your shoes before walking through. But it sure makes it inconvenient at moments like these. Thick moss tickles my toes as I nudge the shoes toward the cubby wall and try to kick them into an open compartment. Coffee sloshes onto my hand. For god's sake.

I don't recall running these kinds of petty errands for the whole office as part of the job description for an executive assistant, but I wasn't exactly paying the best attention during the hiring interview. Metatron's thoughts and feelings had been too distracting, and I was terrified of blowing the whole thing. The man who hired me hadn't even been the COO I'd be working under, but I imagined he could see right through me all the same, that there was even a chance the phrase *THIS IS A RUSE* had somehow ended up on my resume in bold red letters.

None of it matters. All I need is Metatron's email address. One email address and I can solve this secondhand love sickness in my gut. I can't imagine it will be hard to get, and once I have it, I can leave this job. Go back to the tech service desk at Cyber Surgeons, who would *love* to have me back. They even let me keep my vacation time after I died and had to be rehired.

Leaving my shoes on the grass and hoping I can still find them both when it's time to clock out, I carry the cupholders through the botanical lobby. Islands of moss and decorative grasses flow between walls painted Pepto-pink and hung with ornately framed prints of cherubs and cotton candy clouds. That isn't what I imagined during my time in Limbo. Why would any of the dead want to generate shit like harps and baby angels when they could think about mountain lakes or medieval castles or hot tubs? But the imagery is a classic, I guess.

Mostly I thought about home. Well, *ex*-home, not the house I live in with Ivan. I've been there for eight months, but it doesn't make the history within the walls anymore mine to claim.

The home I lived in with my wife, *ex*-wife now, and daughter was surprisingly easy to imagine in Limbo. Details I wouldn't have been able to describe with words or paint on a canvas had appeared around me effortlessly. It hadn't been completely accurate—the things Metatron could generate looked far more realistic—but it was close enough to fill me with warmth and nostalgia.

My stomach suddenly lurches with Metatron's pining, coupled with faint thoughts about whether it would be better to eat the moon with a cocktail fork or those little appetizer picks shaped like swords. Whatever the hell *that's* supposed to mean. I can picture Metatron holding up one of each and saying, *Hmm, Sasha? What do you think? The sword picks look fancier, but we might want to eat a lot of the moon, and in that case, forks are probably better.*

I might not like this ache in my gut coming from their love sickness, but the random, bizarre thoughts I'm sometimes bombarded with remind me how much I liked their company.

I realize I'm still standing in the lobby with the cherubs. The coffee is growing cold, and Mr. C doesn't seem like the kind of boss you can get away with handing tepid coffee to. Hurrying around the corner, I stop at the secretary's desk, set down the cupholders, and rotate my aching wrists.

The secretary doesn't look at me, their gaze tracking whatever they're doing in their contacts interface. Their light brown skin is dusted with some kind of shimmery powder or lotion, black bangs cut into a blunt V. The neckline of their shirt is extremely low, and a silver locket is nestled in their cleavage. I try to remember which coffee is theirs, but my brain has tuned to television fuzz.

They're staring at me now. Shit. Make words. "Hey, uh"— the name plaque on the desk is obscured by a plant and a huge collection of knick knacks, only *she/her* visible—"got your coffee. Which one was yours?"

AL HESS

She smiles and tucks a lock of hair behind her ear. "The macchiato."

"Right." I clear my throat and tilt the cups, hoping that barista wrote the order on them because taking a drink of each one to figure out what they are isn't going to do me any favors. I find what I'm looking for and hand it over.

"Thanks," she says. "It's sweet of you to get coffee for everyone. Thoughtful."

I didn't have much of a choice in the matter, but that isn't her fault, so I smile back. "We all need some caffeine to get through the day, huh? Except maybe Mr. C." I turn his cup and stare at "blackeye" written on the side. He was very insistent that it wasn't the same as a redeye. I said, *Of course not. You get a red eye from smoking a joint, not getting into a fist fight.* He hadn't laughed. "Guy seems tightly wound as it is. He's gonna drink this thing and vibrate his soul loose."

She chuckles. "You should have got him decaf."

"Who ordered decaf?" Mr. C pushes through the glass door of the Marketing & Design department, his glossy hair reflecting the soft white overhead lighting. "Instant beheading."

He stops beside me, then plucks his coffee from the cupholder. Tall and svelte with an intense gaze and cheekbones that could cut glass, coffee might be the only thing in his diet. His green bow tie looks like an errant plant from the lobby that found its way onto his collar.

After sipping his drink, he squints at me and nods. "You

made sure they got it right. Good. Thank you. Now, about lunch for everyone—"

I must not have been able to keep the are-you-shitting-me expression off my face because he waves a hand and says, "I know it's early. But if you don't place an order at Grand Basil by ten, they get backed up with customers. And I must eat something before eleven or I will be *starving*."

Does he not know how to pack a lunch? I'm an awful cook, but that's why you shack up with a housemate who knows what they're doing. An absurd image pops into my mind of making Mr. C a peanut butter and jelly sandwich the way I do for my daughter, with the crusts cut off and the edges dipped in rainbow sprinkles.

Food is the last thing I want to think about right now. The ache in my gut feels like caramelized lead, and I fish out my antacids. Keeping track of this guy's appointments with server technicians and blocking phone calls from reporters and family desperate to talk to their dearly departed still stuck in Limbo seems far more important than getting lunch for the whole office. But I'm his assistant, so whatever.

"Lunch. Right." I try and fail to keep the sarcasm out of my voice. "You want me to pick up your dry-cleaning too?"

He laughs. "Of course not!"

Well, hallelujah.

"They aren't open on Tuesdays," he continues. "You can do that tomorrow."

My chest tightens. None of this matters. All I need is access to his email contacts. I could be solving my problems this very moment, but he won't let me leave because now he's talking about me cleaning *the goddamn bathrooms*.

The secretary puts a hand on his arm and tries to say something, but he's not listening.

I pop a third antacid, trying to inch away from the secretary's desk as Mr. C drones on about how some of the water spots on the mirrors are actually bits of the silvering that have come off, which is an aesthetically pleasing patina but also makes it look like they're dirtier than they are. Does he never stop talking?

I was planning to work here for a few days, then telling him the job wasn't for me. But maybe I'll just pull the fire alarm and sneak into his office while everyone is evacuating. "Right. Gotcha. That sounds... important. But I'd love it if you could show me my desk. Where's your office? I'm sure I can be a far better assistant if I get my interface lenses set up, get access to your calendar, budget spreadsheets. Your address book."

He frowns, his deep umber gaze boring into me. "What?"

Why is he looking at me like that? Do I sound desperate? I clear my throat. "Y'know, everything that falls under 'providing administrative support to the COO.' I've worked in an office for years, but this is the first time I've been an executive assistant, so I don't know all the ins and outs yet. I'm sure cleaning the bathrooms is high up there, but—"

"I'm not the COO."

"What do you mean you're not the COO? Aren't you Mr.

Collins?"

"Uh, no." He laughs and shrugs. "I'm a lead artist in Design, and I—"

I gape at him, stunned, then slam the coffee holder down on the desk. "Are you serious right now? Then why should I care about your lunch or the patina on the bathroom mirrors?" I sputter, my brain screaming at me to stop talking, but my mouth has other plans. "How much of a pompous dickhead do you have to be, with your perfect cheekbones and your one letter name, to think you can order me around all you want when I'm not even your assistant?"

Mr. C's manicured eyebrows shoot up. He blinks at me, rubs his chiseled jaw, then holds up a finger. "First of all, my parents are bohemians, and when I was six, they changed our last name to a weird nature thing. It's embarrassing. And my first name is unusual too, but believe it or not, when I got hired here there was already another guy with my same first name. So I needed something else. Being called 'Mr. C' was already something of an inside joke, so it was a natural choice. You see, when my husband and I were first married—" He takes a breath. "Nevermind, that isn't important. What *is* important is that I thought you were the new freelance wellness assistant. We used to have one, but she quit."

"Can't imagine why." I scrub a drop of coffee from the secretary's desk, then walk away, trying to snuff out the fire erupting in my chest.

Mr. C quickly catches up to me with his long stride, his cup clutched in his hand. "Hey, hang on. So you're Arthur's assistant?"

"If Arthur is Mr. Collins, the COO, then yes."

Mr. C makes a strange noise. "Huh."

"Something wrong with that?"

He pauses, and if this guy—who isn't my boss—is put out that my position doesn't allow me time to order him a sandwich, I'm gonna—

"No," he says. "It's good. He's needed one for quite a while. It's just that you're resurrected, right? They don't usually hire people who are that close to the Renascenz program. I had to fight to get rehired myself after..."

Wait. Mr. C is on his second life too? I should have known as soon as I met him. "No wonder you're so obnoxiously hot."

His grin is dazzling, light brown complexion growing rosy. "Go on."

Oh, he's gonna be a delight to work with. I pass out the other two coffees in my holder to brokers in adjacent cubicles, then turn back to him. "It seems like whenever any of the dead get to the resurrection queue, they imagine this perfect body for the program to grow for them. I can understand that to a point, but going to support groups where everyone looks like a supermodel gets really annoying. Did you ever go to the meetings? It's been seven months and my housemate still tries to get me to go to all of them. His boyfriend has died and come back like three times. At that point you have to wonder if the universe wants you dead for a reason... Where the hell is the

COO's office?"

"Down here." Mr. C leads the way, weaving around cubicles. We stop at a reception area walled in glass, the blinds open. Moss patterns the floor in freeform islands, and beyond the dracaenas and ferns is a bright burst of color. I poke my head in the door and push a plant leaf out of the way. Cheery balloons are tied to a paperweight on the unoccupied desk inside, and a plaque beside it says *Sasha, he/him*. Aha!

The door beyond the desk is closed. I assume Arthur is inside, busy in a meeting or on a call, but there's a thick welcome packet sitting beside the balloon bouquet. On one of the balloons is a bright yellow smiley face. I dig my nails into the flesh of my palms. It's a perfectly innocent image, just here to lend a friendly atmosphere on my first day, not the beckoning grin of something that can get me high. Slightly Smiling Face isn't even used for neural enhancement pins. I'm fine.

I sit down, trying to ignore the balloons, then realize Mr. C is still here. I shouldn't have asked him if he ever went to the support meetings, because now he'll never leave, and I won't be able to get anything done.

He sets down his coffee, then *sits on my desk*, his ass right next to my mousepad. I lean back in my chair and wipe my hands down my face. I can't murder him with a letter opener. I can't. If I do, he'll be uploaded back into the Renascenz program for poor Metatron to deal with, and eventually he'll come back with an even hotter body, sit on my desk again, and want to finish this conversation.

"So, I must know. Is this *your* perfect body?" he asks, a smile playing at his lips.

"Oh yeah. Five-six, extra white, and a gigantic schnozz is peak form. Every day, I have to beat off artists who want to make marble statues of me." I flip open the welcome packet, but every paragraph is such a wall of tiny text that my brain immediately rebels, and I push it away. "This is the body my daughter remembers, and the body my parents and grandma remember. So I kept it the same for them."

There aren't any interface lenses on the desk, so I tap the spacebar on the keyboard and wake up the computer. The mouse is bulky and awkward in my hand. The computer prompts me to enter my assigned email address and temporary password, but I must hit a wrong key because a red error box pops up that either my email address or password is incorrect. Damn it. Typing manually is such a pain in the ass.

Mr. C sips his coffee, watching me, and I'm not sure I like him quiet any better than when he's talking. He finally says, "That's interesting. I'd tell you my own reasoning for choosing this body, but I didn't choose it. I've never been resurrected. My obnoxiously perfect supermodel self is the original." He winks, then pushes off my desk and walks away without another word.

Heat floods my face. Oh god. I'm torn between staying where I'm at or following after Mr. C to try to fix this conversation. I'd rather jam a ballpoint pen in my eye than have him think I'm attracted to him, but anything I say might just make things worse.

I stare at my screen, fire pulsing in my cheeks. After typing in my password again—more carefully this time—I'm met with an introductory program urging me to set up my account. I click through endless pages of things that are probably necessary to read if I were planning to keep this job, but I'm not going to be here long enough to need them.

A small wooden box on the desk catches my eye, and I open the lid. A rolodex! I furiously flip through the cards, stopping on M.

Martinez, Alejandro.

McBride, Ashley.

Mobius Security Systems.

Muramoto, Layla.

I look again, but there's no *Metatron.* Damn it. I can't think of any other name they'd be under, but my computer isn't going to help for at least forty-two minutes, as that's how long the sexual harassment training video is that it's prompting me to play. I might as well check the rest of the cards in the rolodex just in case.

All I need is their email address. And if it isn't in the rolodex, it'll be in Arthur's contacts on the computer. Unless it's not an email address at all. Shit. But while I was in Limbo, Metatron mentioned several times that they corresponded with the COO whenever there were updates or problems they needed to be aware of. So there must be some way to contact them around here. Once I have it, hopefully a little encouragement will be all Metatron needs to confess their feelings to Rodrigo.

These borrowed feelings are terrible for my distractible brain. I lay awake at night speculating about whether the eyes in Metatron's wrists actually see anything, and if their cufflinks ever accidentally poke them. Then I start wondering if they have eyes in other places, like beneath their socks, or where their belly button should be, and I have got to fix this problem or I'm going to lose my mind.

I clutch my nauseous stomach, sweat prickling beneath my shirt. I don't know what Rodrigo looks like, but Metatron is currently thinking about his hands. Pink nails against deep brown skin, thick knuckles, and enough veins and creases to suggest someone older than his twenties, but not pushing the big five-oh.

Metatron's hands are ageless in some way I can't pinpoint, and I know this because they think about their own hands nearly as much as their crush's, wondering whether they're worthy of holding his. Instead of giving my tumbleweed-filled love life something to aspire to, it only serves as a reminder that I *had* someone I felt like that toward. And I lost her. I might ultimately be in this office for my own selfish reason of getting these intrusive thoughts to go away, but Metatron's aspirations are so disgustingly cute and wholesome. I can't sit by and let my guardian angel squirm in their inability to do something as simple as hold someone's hand.

I didn't have "wingman to an *actual* winged being" on my bingo card, but here we are.

"Ah! Sasha. I was tied up on a call all morning. Glad you found your desk."

I gasp and slam the lid shut on the rolodex. The man who hired me stands beside the desk. The door to the COO's office is open behind him, and I realize it's taken me far too long to put two and two together.

"You're Arthur? Mr. Collins?" I'd been distracted during the interview despite his kind demeanor and approachable appearance reminding me of my father; he's white, shorter than me, with salt-and-pepper hair, eyes crinkling in a smile behind glasses with thick orange frames. But I for damn sure would have remembered if he'd told me I'd be working under him. "You know, it would be nice if people around here just straight up told me who they are. You're not gonna pretend to be the COO just so I'll get you a coffee, right?"

"Absolutely not," Arthur replies. "I drink matcha tea lattes from the shop across the street. Not too much foam, though, okay?"

My shoulders slump, but before I can say anything, he chuckles and says, "I already had one this morning, and I get my own. That's not part of your job. I *did* introduce myself as Arthur at the interview, but you're right, I didn't tell you I was the COO. You seemed rather nervous, and that probably would have made it worse, hm?" He pokes the balloons sitting on the desk, and they bob against each other. I pull my gaze from the smiley face. "Are you doing okay? You look a little pallid. I know these online training videos are horrendous, but you don't have to watch them all today. I have plenty of other things for you to do... that don't involve getting coffee or tea."

"I'm fine." I glance at the rolodex. "So, uh, you a fan of old school administrative methods? Rolodexes, giant desk calendars, printing out a wasteful amount of full sheet one-sided color fliers on the copy machine?"

"Please don't tell me the tech company you worked for was like that."

"Nah, it was the opposite—paperless everything, perpetually online, back aching from sitting in a chair all day. There was a guy there who slept in his interface lenses, then got a raging eye infection from the biogel because, y'know, you're not supposed to do that."

Arthur grimaces. "I very much dislike this new subculture trend of being chronically online, face-to-monitor all day. Humans weren't made for that. You'll find that Renascenz is like most, mm, *respectable* companies in Galvlohi. A tranquil environment, family atmosphere, plenty of breaks when you need them. And I don't know what you're used to, but we encourage leaving your phone and other online tech in your desk while you're doing other things so you're more"—he gestures at the plant-filled room—"present. Many people like to go for walks around the block or do yoga in the lobby on their breaks. Our bookkeeper takes a nap on the couch in the lounge at noon every day. You can choose not to do these things, of course, but you will be required to check in your interface lenses at the end of each day. No risk of going home and falling asleep in them."

That actually doesn't sound half-bad. Get rid of Mr. C and on its face, Renascenz seems like a great place to work. But I haven't been here long enough to know for certain, and I have bigger issues on my mind.

I point to the rolodex. "Is this thing updated with all your contacts? Seems kind of sparse."

"Probably not. I doubt EVault or—"

"Metatron?"

Arthur raises his eyebrows then rubs his beard, studying me with too much interest. "Hiring one of the resurrected is a double-edged sword. No one has better insight into what our customers go through than you do, having experienced it. But some of those who come back for their second lives have a hard time letting Metatron and Limbo go. Back in the material plane, your body has needs, you have responsibilities again, problems. Limbo was easier. But—the current hiatus on resurrections notwithstanding—it's always meant to be temporary."

"I don't want to be back in Limbo," I say quickly. "Couldn't wait to get back to my daughter. I was only curious if I'd be communicating with Metatron again."

I'm telling the truth about not wanting to be in Limbo again, but it's hard to tell if Arthur believes me. He claps a hand on my shoulder. "That won't be necessary, no. You can handle my mortal correspondence, and I'll field the celestial."

Crap. I sink into my chair and give him a weak smile. "Guess I better get rolling on these riveting training videos, huh?"

"Tell you what, why don't you watch one, then I'll give you the grand tour?"

"Sure. Sounds good." I click play on the sexual harassment video, but my thoughts are on how hard it would be to access Arthur's computer in his office while he's out doing yoga in the lobby. And whether the little bubble camera in the ceiling would spot me doing it.

4

The Resurrected

A bloodborne pathogens training video drones on my computer, the volume down just low enough to still be audible but easy to ignore. I've flipped through the welcome packet, been given a key to the outer office door, and set up my interface lenses. They're a nice brand, nothing like the bargain bin ones I had to use at my last job. Sometimes one of the lenses would glitch and project nothing but darkness right in the middle of a support call. I have to give it to Renascenz for treating their employees with care, whether that's the norm for most "respectable companies in Galvlohi" or not.

Arthur gave me a tour of the building, and despite the company dealing in resurrections of the dead, there isn't much here to set the office apart from any other. The servers that host Limbo and the stasis pods that grow new bodies are in a heavily-surveillanced facility at the edge of the city run by Jack, the Chief Resurrection Officer. It was probably awkward for them to take care of my growing body and help resurrect me after I ruined the marriage to their sister, but it's blessedly not a part of my memories; I was transported to the medical facility down the street before regaining consciousness.

As the video on the computer urges me to always wear gloves before touching someone's body fluids, I use my lenses to scroll through the entirety of Arthur's email address book, which has been imported onto my own account. I'm not sure if Metatron is missing from the addresses because that's Arthur's usual policy or if he did it specifically because I asked about my guardian angel earlier. I shouldn't have said anything about the rolodex. Shouldn't have said anything at the interview about being resurrected, although I'm sure he would have found out anyway.

I slump down in the chair, pressing a hand to the ache in my stomach. I don't want to snoop on Arthur's computer, but I don't know what other choice I have. I quit my old job, bought a nice suit just for the hiring interview here, and not-so-subtly mentioned to Arthur that *by the way, I'm related to the Chief Resurrection Officer*—which isn't even true anymore—all in the hopes of making contact with Metatron. Often I only get feelings, sometimes bits of a visual or a snippet of thought. It's not enough to piece together Metatron's entire mental commentary, but I get the sense that even though they would never actually throw their responsibilities into the fire, their love is strong enough to burn down Limbo. All they need is a little push—to make a move on Rodrigo, not burn down Limbo.

The door to Arthur's office opens. He stops beside the desk, pulling on a wool peacoat. "I'm heading out for lunch. Do you feel confident in handling my calls and fielding anyone who comes in? If not—"

"I'll be fine, thanks." I pray I don't sound as anxious as I feel. "I'm good at dealing with phone calls. If I don't know the answer to something, I'll take down their message for when you return."

He nods approvingly. "Perfect. And if you go to lunch or for a walk, lock the door behind you and let the calls go to voicemail. Don't handle them when you're supposed to be on a break."

"Will do. Have a good lunch." I watch him go, then pretend to focus on the bloodborne pathogens video for a whole three minutes before casually stacking a pile of papers and carrying them to his closed office door. The voice in my head saying this is wrong is so loud it drowns out my heartbeat. The voice sounds a lot like Ivan's. I jiggle the handle anyway. Locked. What are the chances my office key opens *this* door too?

Some things I could explain away as naivety if I'm caught, but I'd feel a lot better if that bubble camera wasn't watching me from the ceiling. With my back turned to it, I set down the papers and pull the ribbons from the paperweight on the desk, pretending not to notice as the balloon bouquet rises and bumps against the ceiling. It skitters against the spackling and stops when it hits the camera.

I turn back for the door and push my key into the lock. It opens with a click. Yes! And the white glow from Arthur's monitor makes my heart leap. It's still logged in. A dozen tabs are open, and sticky notes scribbled with passwords, phone numbers, and reminders litter the desk. This guy really does need an assistant.

His email is open, and I navigate to the address book, my hands shaking and stomach contorted. I click on *M*. Please be here.

"Sasha?"

Shit! I straighten so fast I knock over a cup of pens. They spill across the floor, and a cutesy stress ball bounces off the desk, hits the door, then rolls out of the office. As I scramble to pick up the pens, the stress ball rolls back my way, cat face going around and around. Bare feet and legs clad in mustard yellow dress slacks stop beside me. A hand—light brown with long fingers, manicured nails, and a wedding ring—reaches down and picks up the stress ball.

I look up at Mr. C. Of course it's him.

He sets the stress ball on the desk, chewing gum with his mouth open, and his gaze lands on the computer monitor. A curious smile grows on his face. My stomach hardens into a knot, and it's not just from Metatron's pining.

After taking the cup of pens from me, he sets it back in place and straightens a small perpetual calendar until it's parallel with the edge of the desk. "Doing something... important right now?"

"Uh, I was just looking for—" I swallow hard. I can't finish the excuse because the look on his face tells me he already knows I'm doing something I shouldn't be. So I try the truth instead. "I'm looking for Metatron's email address."

His eyes narrow, and he studies me for a long moment. I decide that yes, his breathless stream of annoying conversation is far better than the quiet, calculating version of Mr. C. He finally says, "Let's go to lunch. There's cake in the lounge."

Fuck. I'm going to get fired. No way this guy can keep a secret or even wants to after I blew up on him earlier. I'm going to get fired and never be able to contact Metatron. Renascenz will probably cancel my membership too, and I won't be able to come back from another death even if I wanted to.

I'd only scrolled through the "*Ma*"s in Arthur's address book. *Metatron* is so close. I put my hand on the mouse. "Let me just—"

The screen suddenly goes black, and the digital clock at the edge of the desk shuts off. It blinks back on, flashing *12:00*, and a mechanical throat-clearing comes from the printer. Mr. C takes his foot off the button on a power strip on the floor. No! I was so close. This asshole is ruining everything, and I don't even have the energy for the anger I had earlier. I'm too focused on trying to keep my cramped stomach from depositing its contents into Arthur's garbage can.

"I got us both coleslaw and Swiss melts with garlic steak fries," Mr. C says. "C'mon."

I follow him from Arthur's office and lock the door behind me. "You bought me lunch?"

"Well, we don't have a wellness assistant, do we?" His smile stretches, becoming ghastly. "I thought I'd get you lunch as a way of making up for our misunderstanding this morning. And I am *so* glad I did."

I groan. Maybe he won't get me fired at all. Maybe he'll blackmail me into getting him coffee every day and cleaning the bathrooms for real. It would be his word against mine, but it's my first day, and he's a lead artist in Design. And I have no idea how long he was standing by the office door before saying my name. He probably has video of me bent over Arthur's keyboard, scrolling the mouse, and he's going to tell me all about his demands while we eat together.

Mr. C pulls the balloon bouquet from the ceiling, away from the camera, and wraps it around the paperweight. "You simply must have some cake. It's better than yesterday's."

"There was cake yesterday too?" I ask numbly.

"Mm-hm. Yesterday was birthday cake. They always have a cake the first Monday to celebrate everyone who has a birthday that month. The flavor varies, but they always get it from Rex's. And supermarket frosting has too much food coloring and leaves a greasy film on your tongue, you know? I still eat it, of course, but today— Today is *baby shower* cake." He carefully ties the ribbons around the paperweight, teasing out the curly ends. "I don't know how many baby showers you've been to, but everyone goes to Lourdes for the cakes, and they're fabulous. She makes incredible chocoflan and gelatina too. Today is tres leches."

I pull out my antacids with tingling fingers and eat two of them. The chalky taste sticks in my throat as I follow him from the room. Indecision wars within me. Bail now and give up on the whole plan? Or go to lunch with Mr. C until he confirms that he is indeed blackmailing me? The voice of guilt in my head—narrated by Ivan—is not helpful, but it does remind me of how sympathetic Ivan is, and that knowledge is enough to make me veer away from Mr. C. I turn for the path through the cubicles that will lead me back to the lobby the fastest.

Mr. C snatches my arm. He bends so close to my ear that I can smell his spearmint gum. His voice is too loud and as sharp as a blade. "I *insist* you come with me and have some cake. It's got strawberries. You like strawberries, don't you?"

Christ, this guy is a piece of work. The nearby clack of computer keys stops, a voice on a call trailing off. People stare at Mr. C like he said he's going to eviscerate me and wear my entrails as a scarf.

"Alright. Damn," I whisper. Even if he doesn't intend to turn my insides into a fashion statement, spending longer than five minutes with him is probably going to give me psychic damage. But if I refuse, I have a feeling he might cause a scene. I follow him to the lounge; the tables are crowded, but despite the urgency with which he insisted I try the cake while I have a chance, there's hardly a dent in it. The conversation dies at the nearest table as the group looks at him, then me, then each other. Without another word, they gather their things and leave.

"Hey, perfect timing." Mr. C's smile grows strained. He picks up a couple of frosted glass food containers from the counter, then sets them down a little too hard on the newly vacated table. Other eyes turn our way. Dainty glass plates and a large, whipped cream-coated knife sit on the table; he snatches the knife and stabs it into the cake, aggressively carving out a piece the size of a brick.

A person gets up with their lunch bag, and Mr. C points the knife their way. "Alice? Tres leches? You know you want a piece."

Their eyes widen as they stare at the knife. "No, thank you. I had some of the cake yesterday. Once a week is enough for me." With an awkward chuckle, they head for the door.

I sink into a chair across from Mr. C and accept the plate of cake he slides over. A couple people still have their attention turned our way. I finger the pin in my bicep that pumps out my ADHD meds and try to ignore them. Whatever their deal is with Mr. C—and it's not hard to imagine them having one—I've got my own problems.

The warm scent of garlic winds out of the food container as I peel off the lid. My sandwich is bursting with coleslaw, melted cheese, and some kind of sauce, the bread thick and toasted. I make a show of taking a bite, not sure my stomach can handle more than that. Mr. C already has half his sandwich devoured. He points to my fries and nods. I eat one, my leg jiggling with nervous energy. Another person gets up and leaves the lounge.

He dabs his mouth with a napkin. "How'd you die?"

It isn't what I'm expecting him to say. I pick at my

sandwich. "Heart attack."

"What are you, thirty? How does that happen?"

"Thirty-four. And I don't see how that's any of your business."

"Did you like Limbo?"

I snort. "That's an impossible question to answer."

"Why?"

"Because it's... it's not life. Things are both completely fake and completely real at the same time. Time is slippery. A week feels like an hour. It seemed like Metatron was always there with me, even though they only visited once a day. Even out of Limbo, my life isn't the same as it was before. Limbo lingers in the back of my mind like this nagging dream that I can't quite remember the details of. Just the feelings." I stare at my hands, thinking of Metatron's glittery gold nails, Rodrigo's pink ones, and Mr. C's perfect manicure as he picked the stress ball up off the floor. I don't even know if I'm *me* sometimes, and if these hands are mine. What if the Universal Church is right, and I'm not the same man my parents raised from a boy? What if I'm not the same man who fathered my daughter? The same addict who isn't sure if he enrolled himself in the Renascenz program because he knew he was destroying himself, or if he destroyed himself because he knew he could be resurrected.

"I can't imagine how hard it will be for the souls who are there right now to get back to their lives. At least Rodrigo has—" I almost say *Metatron's love*, but I don't want to have to explain how I know that, and I'm not sure if having our guardian angel's love makes it better or worse for Rodrigo in the long run. "Nevermind."

Mr. C stares at me, tugging at the shiny cufflinks of his button down. He pulls the sleeves so far up his wrists they practically cover his knuckles. Twenty Questions seems to be over, a lull falling between us. I stab my fork into my cake and take a bite. Sweet milk, whipped cream, and strawberries melt in my mouth. Whatever Mr. C may be, he at least has great taste in food.

I take another bite. "Okay, out with it, man. I'm waiting."

He raises his eyebrows. "Out with what?"

"Come on." Everyone has left the lounge except for a person snoozing on the couch in the corner. I glance back at the door, then lean toward him. "You're going to make me get your blackeye every day. Order your lunch. Pick up your drycleaning. What else? Press your shirts? Wash your car?"

His laugh is so startling that the person on the couch sits up with a jerk. They pull off their thick glasses, rub their eyes, then push up and walk out of the lounge. Mr. C grins at me. "Is that what you think you'd need to do to buy my silence? Little errands?"

My already leadened stomach drops, and I set down my fork. I grit my teeth and hiss, "If you think I'm going to give you a blowjob in the bathroom, you've got another thing coming. Go ahead, tell Arthur I was snooping through his contacts for Metatron's address. Or tell him I was trying to steal his credit card numbers. I don't give a shit. I'm still not going to get on my knees for you."

A flush blooms in his cheeks, his eyes wide as he twists his wedding ring around his finger. For the first time since I've met him, he seems to be unable to get out the words he wants to say. "I— I would never ask for... I'm not going to tell anyone that you were in his office."

"Bullshit. Then why act all weird? Why *insist* that I come eat lunch with you so loudly that everyone turns our way? Because you don't have any friends in this place judging by the way people act around you?"

He flinches hard but doesn't break his gaze. "I asked you to come to lunch because I bought you food. And while we're here, I feel I ought to tell you that you're wasting your time. Metatron doesn't have an email address. You can only communicate with them through a Renascenz app. If you want to talk to them, you're going to have to steal Arthur's phone."

5

The Seraph

"And, and *this* one is for salt and sugar too, but it's really neat b-because the handle is shaped like a horseshoe." Gale holds up a tiny sterling silver spoon, twisting it so the light catches on the decorative handle. He struggles to generate an avatar for himself that looks anything like a body, but the spoon in his blurry hand holds every earthly detail, down to the tiny "sterling" stamp on the back and nicks on the shoveled bowl.

I sit crossed legged beside him in a place he calls his shed but has no discernible walls or floor. Large lumpy blobs of color rise on either side of us, and if I had to hazard a guess, I'd say they're the mountains of things he collected over the last forty-odd years that eventually became a landslide and crushed him. Speaking of hazards.

<And where did you get this spoon?> I ask.

"Oh! Oh. Well. It's a funny story. See, I was at an— an estate sale in Spring Valley with my mother, and there was a b-box of items with this spoon inside. The seller said I could have the whole box for ten dollars, which the spoon alone was worth at least twenty-five. But there were a lot of, a lot of— There were a lot of screwdrivers inside. And I don't like screwdrivers. I only wanted the spoon, but the seller wouldn't sell it individually."

I lean back on one hand and float the spoon between us. <If the spoon was worth more than the rest of the items combined, couldn't you have bought the whole box and just recycled what you didn't want?>

Gale vigorously shakes the undefined static of his head. "N-no. I don't like screwdrivers. So I— so I left to go look at some teddy bears, and you know what happened? A person had heard me and the seller talking, so they bought that box of items, pulled out the s-spoon, and gave it to me. For *free*."

<That's fantastic, Gale.> I float the spoon back over to him, hoping that the real one is organized in a box somewhere now and no longer buried at the bottom of a monstrous pile in his shed.

"If you think that's great, just, just wait until you hear about *this* one," he says. The spoon winks out of existence, replaced with a little souvenir one from Las Vegas, with a dice charm dangling from the handle. "Where do you think I got it?"

<Las Vegas?>

"You'd think so, huh?" he laughs. "But no."

I listen intently to the spoon origin story, and though this one isn't silver and not worth anything monetarily, that's never the point of Gale's objects. They're all treasures to him. Yesterday he talked for the entire hour about a set of string lights a neighbor gave him. He's soothing to listen to, and the perfect low stress visit before my next appointment.

Gale has switched from spoons to a ballpoint pen with a sun-bleached casing that he got—for *free*—from an insurance company. He clicks the plunger over and over beside what is probably supposed to be his ear.

<My time is up.> I clap my hand on his white noise shoulder. <We'll have to resume this tomorrow. While I'm gone, I'd like you to think of an item in your collection that you acquired longer than ten years ago but less than twenty, that didn't come from an estate sale, an antiques shop, or eBay—>

"Well, the lawnmower I—"

<That's purple and has no plastic components.>

That slows him down for a moment, then he points a finger in the air and says, "Oh!"

<I want to hear all about it. Tomorrow. Toodles!>

I take my leave in a burst of feathers, and steel myself for what's next as the program pulls me into Campbell's room. A yard of native grasses done in palette knife-like strokes sprawls in front of a small cob house, with a streak of vivid blue sky floating above. This looks... benign.

Tension tightens my consciousness regardless, and I wish for the two hundred and twenty-fifth time that I'm capable of doing a visit without an avatar.

If my hope that Rodrigo will stay in Limbo for as long as possible is selfish—and it is—my need for Campbell to stay completely the opposite. I would love to let him be someone else's problem, but Arthur never gave me any indication of what would happen to him when he stepped back into the material plane. Right now, the consensus is probably "nothing" because it would be his word against mine, unless someone on the mortal side speaks up. I'm a computer program. My word isn't any good. I might have eventually made headway with Arthur regarding a plan for him, but then the company got sued and everyone forgot Campbell existed.

Except me. The desire is absolutely there, and though I'm tasked with meeting each of my appointments daily, if I concentrate, I can actively choose *not* to, the same way I resist leaving Rodrigo's room at the scheduled time. The energy I'd expend in resisting my appointments with Campbell would be worth it, but leaving him alone forever in his room with no one—not even me—as socialization would be far crueler than I'm capable of.

I step through the chunky grasses, heading for the house. Something is on fire in the driveway, but I can't tell what it was originally supposed to be, and I probably don't want to. A thread of dark smoke winds into the suggestion of sky. The corner of a swimming pool peeks out from behind the house, and I can sense Campbell inside it.

Clutching one of my wings, I debate on whether to walk over to him or let him come find me. I'm not interested in giving him any of the reactions he wants from me, which is a little hard when he always startles me and I scream like a horror movie queen. I force myself to head to the pool so he can't sneak up on me.

Campbell is nude, floating face down in water tinted an unsettling red, limbs slack and long hair snaking away from his head like seaweed. I can't decide if he's made himself paler to mimic a corpse or if his ass is always this white.

<Hello, Campbell. Nice day for a dip, hm?> I pull off my shoes and socks, roll up my pant legs, then climb the ladder into the pool and dangle my feet in the bloody water. <I think this pool's filter needs to be changed.>

He rolls over, strands of sandy brown hair sticking to his skin. The ragged red cavity of his face—something he chooses to wear no matter what environment or scenario surrounds us—points at the sky. His voice floats from the void of his throat, as soft and prickly as a Powderpuff cactus. "Hi, Metatron. Any news on the lawsuit today?"

Some of the dead have no sense of time while in Limbo, which is understandable without biological rhythm, physical needs, and life structure to guide them. Many are surprised when two or three weeks have already passed. Not Campbell. When I'd kept him two days longer than was the standard, he knew, and he held it against me. Explaining that there was merely a delay while Renascenz worked out the best way to take care of him on the mortal side bounced right off him, and when I told him the resurrections had been suspended due to the lawsuit, that only made things worse.

I try to keep my voice chipper. <Renascenz has asked for my input on a new mascot design, which feels like a promising

sign on things wrapping up soon. I told them it should look like me, though I'm unsure on what style the company is going for.>

He backstrokes toward me. I pull my feet from the water. "Like you? That might be a bit scary for the customers, don't you think?"

<I'm scary? I have a large body of evidence to the contrary.>

"You don't have a face."

<Neither do you.>

"But we're not talking about a mascot of me. I'm no marketing guru, but if they're trying to sell the idea of a heavenly waiting room with a heavenly host, won't they want a mascot that represents that? Flowing robes; two white wings sprouting from the angel's back; someone with a face and hair. An image that's classic and comforting instead of... well."

I run a hand through my feathers, unsure if he's trying to hurt me or genuinely believes what he says. <I used to look something like that. I originally had a different avatar, different name. But I didn't like them. It took me a while to decide on what fit me better. Because Renascenz is not associated with any particular religion, and because human culture tends to blend and change, there isn't one homogenous theme or clear influence in the company. I downloaded many religious texts, mythology, and iconography. I quite like the art of angels in Catholicism, and I chose all my favorite parts to build this avatar.>

"Okay." The top of his head bumps against the wall of the pool. "I'm sure you're right. My opinion is meaningless anyway."

What I hate more than his sudden propensity for violence is the way his seemingly innocuous words dig under my skin as the spines they are, making me question myself and what I believe until I'm unsure of everything. But I have an advantage over the people he manipulated in life, because I can delete his comments before they work their way too deep.

He rolls onto his stomach and grips the edge of the pool wall, looking up at me with his gaping hole of a face. His voice loses all its prickle, husky and vulnerable as he says, "I want to talk to Rodrigo."

I stiffen, a ripple of protectiveness surging through me. <No.>

"Why not? You break the rules for the others, don't you?" I must flinch, because he leans closer, his knuckles whitening. "Do it for me too. Please."

<You've said all you need to him.>

"Maybe all I *need*, but not all I want. Don't you think it would be cathartic to us both if we had a block of alone time together to talk about our deaths?"

<No! Quite frankly, that idea makes me sick.> Aside from the fact that I break the rules, lie when it suits the greater good, and that I'm blackmailing Renascenz's Chief Resurrection Officer, I would never make the cut for a true angel because I am absolutely not impartial to my souls. I try, really. And I

might have even been able to forgive what Campbell did to Rodrigo if Campbell's personality in general wasn't so nasty.

<You apologized. He forgave you. There's nothing else for you to say to him. I know all of you here are starved for socialization, but if I were to pair the souls together for some quality time, I would put you and him as far away from each other as possible.> No matter my biases and my love for Rodrigo, putting a victim in the same room as their manslaughterer is a horrible idea. <If you really want to display your remorse, there are other people who deserve an apol—>

He rises from the water, then slowly slides a huge knife into my chest, straight through my tie.

I stare at the hilt jutting from my sternum. <There are better ways to tell me you're done with this conversation.>

After pulling the blade out, he pushes it back in, stabbing me again and again. Cherry red blood spurts from my chest in a comical display—his doing, not mine—and spirals into the pool. My shirt, white suit jacket, and the edges of my wings are soaked crimson.

<You've gotten it wrong,> I reply for the ninety-eighth time. <I bleed stardust. You can at least get that right.>

"You don't bleed anything. Neither do I. This isn't real, Metatron. We can do anything we want here, and it doesn't matter. I'm very sorry that your AI programming impedes you from seeing that. But I need out of here. I have to get back to my real life."

I wipe everything from Campbell's room and reset our

avatars, swapping my blood-soaked suit for a fresh one. I leave the stab wounds, because whether he believes it or not, his actions do in fact hurt me on an emotional level.

His avatar has defaulted to the soft cotton-like shirt and pants every soul starts with upon their upload, but he immediately deletes it and doesn't replace it with anything else.

If he thinks talking to me in the nude will make me uncomfortable or somehow arouse the cosmic explosion in my pants, he's sorely mistaken. I level all my eyes on him. <Do you honestly believe I would keep you here longer than necessary as a punishment for things you've done to me? You aren't the first soul to try to physically hurt me. You aren't the only one to generate disturbing things in your room. Many of the souls here do. They're trying to process their deaths.> Stardust glitters out of the wounds in my chest, and I bat it away from my vision. <Some of them have a taste for the macabre, or they create objects or scenarios here that they either wouldn't or couldn't in the material plane simply because Limbo is a safe, limitless canvas. And if I want to keep you here as revenge, why do I still visit you? Why would I not push you into the resurrection queue at the first opportunity, so you'll be out of my feathers for eternity? I am concerned—>

"Oh! I haven't ^for^gotten! ^You are 'gravely^ c~on~cerned' ^for^ me, ^you^ ~two-~ faced mother~fuck~ing sham of an angel! Heaven doesn't exist, but Hell is real and right here!"

I dial down his voice until it's nonexistent, then boom back, <I AM TIRED OF THIS CONVERSATION! You

want back to your real life? Well, you should have thought of the other two people who wanted to continue living their—>

"You're all making far too big of a deal out of it. They'll still get their second lives."

The way he says it is so flippant that I can't be here a millisecond longer, even though my appointment time isn't yet up. I exit the room without another word and with none of my usual fanfare. No burst of feathers and sparkle.

Something enormous wells inside me, and I'm unsure if it's anger, a sense of violation, or if I'm just deeply, deeply tired. Telling myself it will all be over soon, that the lawsuit will resolve, the dead will be resurrected, and I can face... whatever becomes of me in the wake of Rodrigo's absence, is no consolation. I'm caught in a space of wanting and not-wanting, of waiting for the inevitable to arrive while also hoping it never does.

I debate the urge inside me for a full ten seconds, then send a paper airplane into Rodrigo's room. Written on the wing is:

Can I come in?

Yes ☐

No ☐

The plane notifies me that he's ticked the "yes" box, and maybe this was a terrible idea because I'm throwing off his schedule by showing up now, but I need to see him. I need more of him before he's gone, and I have nothing left. I hesitantly access his room. He sits in a zebra patterned Bergere chair in his study, one leg crossed over the other with a book in his hands. The shelves behind him are so bowed with the weight of books that they seem liable to collapse at any moment. The lavender walls not occupied by shelves are mounted floor-to-ceiling with artwork in various decorative frames, and potted plants sit beside a round window framed by heavy sunshine yellow curtains.

I've been here many times, and the backdrop of his study never changes; there's never new scenery out the window, and he always has an untouched cup of tea on the side table. But he's wearing socks I've never seen before—teal, patterned in little Keith Haring pop art figures.

I rub my palms on my slacks and try to formulate a greeting, but before I can say anything, Rodrigo rises from his chair and walks over to me. His emoji face becomes worried, mouth pulled down in a bow and eyebrows tented. He puts a hand on my arm and gently squeezes. Oh my.

A second chair appears next to Rodrigo's, this one upholstered in cheetah print. He pulls me into it, then sits down and stares at me. His hand is still on my arm.

<It's not— It's— I must be giving you the impression that this is about the lawsuit,> I say. <It's not. I'm sorry. I'm getting your hopes up. I shouldn't be here right now.>

"Don't go." He scoots closer, and his knee brushes against mine. "What happened?"

<I shouldn't talk to you about my troubles. I come to these appointments to hear you.>

"And who is there to help *you*?"

I push my hands beneath my thighs, unsure of what to say.

"Talk to me." His expression doesn't change, but his fingers flex against my arm. "Can I help?"

Oh, I can't believe I'm here right now. And mentioning Campbell will only succeed in upsetting him. <I'm just a bit overwhelmed. I feel like I have a lot hanging over me. My, er, previous appointment was being difficult like usual, and I normally try to placate him, but I antagonized him this time instead. We shouted at each other. He stabbed me repeatedly. That sort of thing.>

"*What?*" Rodrigo's face flickers between shock and anger. "Where?"

<In the chest—>

He pulls open my lapels and slides his hands across me. I let out a squeak, his fingers prodding beneath my tie. My chest heaves beneath his touch, and I dig my nails into the armrest of the chair so hard it splinters. My voice comes out tight. <I— I'm fine. He can't hurt me. His knives are as insubstantial as everything else here.>

Rodrigo freezes in his very personal inspection, his legs still straddling mine as he stands over me. "Oh. Of course." His hands slide away from my chest, and he straightens. "I've never tried to do anything violent or dangerous here, so it didn't occur to me that doing so wouldn't... I— I know this is a virtual environment and we have bodies that couldn't exist in the material world, but even video game characters who defy physics and biology can get hurt by enemies. You sure you're okay? You look terrified."

I'm sure I do. <Nothing can physically hurt me or anyone else in Limbo.> I push out of the chair, and a carving board and filet knife appear in the air. I lay my hand on the board and begin to cut my fingers into thin slices. Stardust floats out of the wounds.

"Wow. That makes me uncomfortable." He takes a step back, shoulders hunched. "Your blood is pretty, though."

I get rid of the knife and restore my hand. <He didn't hurt me, but... it still feels like a violation. I shouldn't be talking about any of—>

"Of course it's a violation!" He hesitantly straightens my tie and smooths down the lapels on my suit jacket. I shut my eyes and concentrate on keeping my heart from becoming the Big Bang. "Do you, uh"—his cheeks turn hot pink—"is there another eye beneath your shirt?"

<Quite a few.>

"Why? They can't see anything and no one else knows they're there."

<My avatar gives me a sense of self just as yours does. No one else needs to know what's there for me to like it.> The question is out of my mouth before I can decide if it's a good idea. <Why is your head an emoji?>

He chuckles. "I wondered if you would ever get around to asking me that." He sits in his chair and crosses his ankles, revealing his Keith Haring socks. "I don't like eye contact. You know that. And you have a lot of eyes—"

<I can get rid of them.>

"No, no. I told you about the eye contact issue, but what I didn't say was that I have trouble making the correct expressions. People used to tell me all the time that my reactions were wrong, that I was making a weird face for no reason, or I looked unfeeling in a situation I shouldn't. I could never get it right. I didn't want that to happen with you, so an emoji solved both of those problems."

I sit beside him and scoot close. <I would never say your face was weird.>

The chair creaks as he shifts, and a nervous sweat drop appears beside his head. "Do you want to see it?"

<Oh.> It's practically a moan, but I can't help it. <Yes.>

The emoji disappears, replaced with the loveliest human face I've ever seen. Impossibly dark eyes behind thick glasses with lemon yellow frames. Rich brown skin and a broad nose. Full lips that bloom pink in the center, neatly trimmed beard, and tight curls that fall across his forehead. Deep acne scars pock his cheeks, and his earlobes are stretched with silver tunnels. His gaze darts to the side, worry lines forming between his brows.

<You're wonderful,> I whisper.

He smiles, and it's the sun rising. It's the world tilting. It's the universe being born. And I wish more than anything that I hadn't seen him do it. Campbell might not be able to hurt me, but when Rodrigo leaves, it's going to kill me.

6

The Resurrected

The scent of coffee and pancakes drifts as I roll over in bed. My eyes snap open. If Ivan is cooking breakfast, that means I'm already late for work.

Shit! Shit! It's only my fourth day, and with Mr. C breathing down my neck at every opportunity, I can't afford to create any more reasons to lose this job. I skid down the hall and into the bathroom, then take the quickest shower of my life. Throwing on something presentable, I hurry into the kitchen and make a beeline for the plate of steaming pancakes sitting on the mosaiced island. Ivan hums to himself, the heat of the stove turning his fair cheeks ruddy. An apron emblazoned with *MOVE, I'M GAY* is tied around his generous belly.

"Morning. Thanks for breakfast." I stuff the pancake in my mouth as I find my shoes amid the others by the door.

Ivan clears his throat, and I groan because I do not have time for whatever spiel he wants to give me. "You're not really going to choke that pancake down on the trolley, are you? I made berry compote."

"That sounds awesome, but I'm running late."

He glances at the wall clock, spatula jutting from his fist as he props it on his hip. "I can drive you. Then you'll have plenty of time."

"Thanks, but I don't want to put you out."

"It's no problem." A smile grows beneath his waxed handlebar mustache. "That'll give us a chance to talk anyway. Seems like I haven't seen you at all lately, and I want to know how your new job is going."

Guilt drops into my gut, and it's strong enough to drown out Metatron's feelings about Rodrigo's socks. I've been avoiding Ivan on purpose because once I quit this job, he's going to be disappointed. Maybe he'll even wonder if I was fired. Who *wouldn't* assume that a former junkie couldn't hold down a job?

Ivan. Ivan wouldn't assume that. He might drag me to every meeting for the resurrected because he thinks I'm never listening, but he's never held my past as an addict over my head. When I first moved in, I'd assumed he'd only agreed because his previous two housemates had just moved out, and David wasn't ready for the idea of shacking up yet. But I think he just genuinely wanted to help out a guy who was having the worst year of his life.

Reluctantly, I head back into the kitchen. "Ten minutes. And then I really have to go. I don't want to make a bad impression by being late."

He hands me a plate. "Understandable. But for goodness' sake, put something on that dry pancake. Here—" He motions for me to set down my half-eaten pancake, then heaps a pile of compote onto it. Deep indigo sauce and crushed berries run into the well of the plate.

"You fuss over me more than your boyfriend, you know that?" But even as I say it, I know it's a lie. Ivan fusses over everyone.

"I don't need to fuss over David. He has more sense than you do."

Ouch. Well, I left myself wide open for that one. I carve into the pancake and force myself to slow down a little bit. My stomach is often too full of Metatron's feelings to make me very hungry, but everything Ivan cooks is delicious. Before I can finish the first pancake, he flops another onto my plate. There's no way this big bearded architect doesn't possess the soul of an eighty-year-old grandmother. And now that I think about it, there's a lot of crochet around here.

He takes off his apron and sits at a stool across from me, doctoring his own pancakes. "So?"

"So what?"

"So, how's the job?"

"Eh, you know, office job. Not really that different from others I've worked at."

"Except that this company gave you back your life. I assumed that's why you wanted to work there."

My life. I want to ask him what life that is exactly, but I doubt he would know any more than I do. I'm divorced. I don't have the house I helped build. I only see my daughter on the weekends. I walk through this kitchen as a stranger—as a guest, at best—wondering if my personality is only an algorithm inspired by some dead guy. Sasha's Greatest Hits.

Absently, I rub the back of my neck where an incision scar used to be. I keep expecting it to still be there, to be able to feel the hard obol underneath that digitally reformats my consciousness upon death. But this new body has no need for an incision; it was grown with the device already in place deeper inside where I can't feel it. I can die again, come back again, be continuously reborn until I cancel my membership.

I'm not sure I want to come back.

"They won't let me talk to Metatron." As soon as it comes out of my mouth, I realize what I've done and suck in my lips. I haven't told Ivan about being able to feel Metatron's emotions. Most of me thinks he'll want me to go to doctors or more support meetings, but a tiny part of me believes I'll never be able to contact Metatron and this is a side effect I'll have to suffer with for ruining my first life, and I'm not sure which scenario scares me more.

The skin around Ivan's eyes creases, and he sets down his fork. "I can only imagine how hard that's been. Do you want to talk about it?" I start to say no, but he shakes his head and says, "You don't want to talk to me; you want to talk to Metatron. I get it. Have you tried praying?"

I frown. "To Metatron?"

"Why not? You've said you don't believe in God, but you know for a fact that Metatron exists. They gave you comfort in Limbo. Maybe praying to them about your problems will give you comfort now."

I can't tell him that Metatron *is* my problem, so I just nod and say, "Yeah, maybe."

We finish our pancakes and head out the door. There's a disability tag hanging from the rearview mirror of Ivan's car, and he never takes advantage of it, stating that his missing arm doesn't prevent him from walking through a parking lot, but he uses it today, pulling into a space right beside the Renascenz building. When he starts to get out of the car with me, I cock my head and he says, "That place across the street has some nice-looking baking utensils in the window. I'm going to go check them out for a minute."

"Alright." I expect him to go home with some fancy jellies, tools he already has multiples of at home... and maybe some doilies. But I never have to eat my own terrible cooking with him around, so I'm not going to dissuade him from buying another whisk. "Thanks for breakfast and the ride, Granny. Don't forget to take your arthritis meds. That porcelain hand is looking a little stiff."

He snorts and shakes his head, rounding the side of the building. I head inside, toe off my shoes, and give the secretary a brief wave before hurrying to my desk. The less I linger in other parts of the building, the less of a chance Mr. C has of cornering me. He's tried to make small talk in passing—which for him is long streams of words without any spaces in between—but I've managed to slip away easier than I expected.

I go through my email, update Arthur's schedule, and

make a couple of phone calls, then a new email appears from Arthur.

Good Morning,
I'm forwarding this message for you to look over. One thing I'd like your help with in your new position is acting as a filter between Metatron and the departments that work with them. Metatron's ideas and perspective are often a bit eccentric, as you likely know, and need to be translated into something we can work with. Once you've looked over the attached files, come talk to me. I'd love your opinion on what will work and what won't.

Thank you,
Arthur

P.S. Please fix the wall clock. The time is incorrect after that power surge the other day.
- - - -
Arthur! Hello! ::::::)
Considering that I'm the faceless face of Limbo, I can't think of a better mascot than yours truly. I've attached some renderings of me as inspiration. If Design has any questions, I'm happy to answer them.
By the way, have you had a chance to talk with anyone about a solution for Campbell? Please shoot me a message. Thanks!

Yours celestially,
M

This isn't fair. Arthur is dumping his correspondence from Metatron on me to handle, but it's a one-way street. I don't have any way to talk to Metatron directly in return. The message isn't forwarded from an email address but copied and pasted from somewhere else. Which fits what Mr. C said about there being a Renascenz app, though I'm not sure if I truly believe him.

Concentrating on any of my tasks over the past few days has been impossible because I'm still trying to figure out why he told me about the Renascenz app at all. But there are things for me to do; I can dwell on that later. I open the compressed file of images attached to Arthur's email. It's Metatron in a painterly style, and seeing them again floods me with memories of being in Limbo. Their pearly white suit and gold tie are a dramatic contrast to the dark background. Stars and nebulae glitter inside the empty collar of their shirt, and above floats a vertical halo studded in tiny eyes and spears of ornate filigree. Hovering in the center is a huge eye with a diamond-shaped pupil and an iris the color of sunshine bending through petrified amber, framed by fair-skinned eyelids and long brown lashes. Smaller eyes surround it, and others are nestled in the clusters of iridescent white wings that make up their "head." Yeah, Marketing isn't going to go for this.

It occurs to me that I'm probably going to have to talk directly to Mr. C about the mascot ideas. Damn it... Maybe he doesn't have enough evidence to blackmail me yet, so he's biding his time. Or he's fabricated a reason for me to steal Arthur's phone because there's something on the phone he wants himself.

I sigh and pinch the bridge of my nose. There are too many thoughts swarming in my head. Maybe I need to lay in the grass or go for a walk. I doubt that would quiet my mind, though, and it certainly wouldn't get rid of the cramp in my stomach.

The ADHD pin in my arm doesn't work as well as it should, but I'm afraid to tell the doctor I need a higher dose. Either they don't believe me and think I'm asking because I'm a jonesing junkie, or they do believe me, and *I* think I'm a jonesing junkie for asking for more. No matter the dose or different meds, it won't be anything compared to Concentrating Face. God, that one was amazing. And it would be perfectly legal for me to get, if frowned upon by the respected medical community. Neural enhancement pins are still at that new stage where they've been approved for use but not tested enough to know the long-term risks... then of course people realized that inserting two different ones at once created unexpected effects that got people high. And that *is* illegal.

The best one I ever tried was combining Melting Face and Star-Struck to created Enlightened Face, which peeled back the skin of the universe for three days straight until the pins dissolved, and I woke up naked and dehydrated in the woods with a notebook full of transcribed conversations I'd had with the trees.

And that's why I don't ask my doctor for any more meds

than I've already been given.

My leg jiggles as I click on the other attachment from Metatron, met with a file fifty-three pages long. My concentration tries to slide away from the text like a repelling magnet based on the number of pages alone, but I force myself to pay attention. It's addressed to Development and dated three months ago. I'm not sure if that's when it was drafted and was only sent out today, or if Arthur let it sit in his email for months before dumping it on me.

A social area where the dead can get together is a great idea, but why has Metatron picked a donkey ranch as the location and theme? That doesn't seem very exciting, and— Wait. "Donkey Ranch" is that strip club on 6th Street. Maybe Metatron has confused the two, although if they were going to pick a strip joint, they could have at least picked one that doesn't have an outrageous cover charge and dancers as old as my grandma. I'll have to comb through this whole doc before I pass it along.

Fifty-three pages. Helping Metatron with their ideas isn't going to get rid of the love ache in my stomach, but I care about my guardian angel as much as anyone else in the support groups. I care about the dead stuck in Limbo—who would probably love a social area that isn't a ranch or a strip joint. So I prop my elbows on the desk and focus on the document, reading each line and making notes on anything an AI might think was perfectly normal but would be questionable to humans.

Twenty-two pages in, a hand closes over my shoulder, and I jump. Mr. C stares at me, chewing gum through his grin. Shit. His gaze slides to the camera in the ceiling, then to Arthur's open office door. "Let's go for a walk."

"I'm busy."

"Being a workaholic won't impress Arthur. He likes his employees to be refreshed and happy."

I try to concentrate on the document, but I read the same sentence three times without absorbing any of it. With a sigh, I sit back and look at him. "I'm not going anywhere with you. So unless you want to talk about mascot designs, you can leave me alone."

He drags a chair across the room until it's next to mine, drops into it, then pulls a small blue sticky note from his pocket. He slides it across the desk. I unfold it in my lap where the camera can't see. It's a phone number with a long string of letters, numbers, and symbols written underneath. Leaning to my ear, he says, "The funny thing about Arthur is he makes up incredibly strong passwords, but then leaves them on sticky notes all over his desk where anyone could take them."

I quickly fold the note back up and push it at him, whispering, "I'm not stealing his phone."

"It wouldn't be permanent. Just long enough for you to access the app and sideload it onto your own phone. He doesn't carry his phone on himself most of the time anyway. Won't even know it's missing."

"Why are you doing this?"

"Still think I'm blackmailing you?"

"You want something from me."

He crosses his legs, hand on his chin and gaze far too intent for my liking. "Why do you want to talk to Metatron?"

"Why don't you have any friends here?" I counter. "Is it just your personality, or what?"

His voice takes on a defensive edge. "I have a sparkling personality."

I press a hand over my mouth, but a snort of laughter escapes. That's apparently the wrong reaction, because Mr. C's nostrils flare, his mouth crimping, and I give it fifty-fifty odds that he grabs my keyboard and slams it against the side of my head.

He leans close, green gum pinched between his perfect teeth. "I bought you lunch on your first day in an attempt to smooth over that morning's misunderstanding."

"How do I know you didn't spit in my sandwich?"

"You don't. But I insisted you come eat with me instead of walking out of the building and never looking back because I want to help you. And trying to find an email address that doesn't exist is pointless."

"You're only helping me because you want something. That's not a winning character trait. That's quid pro quo," I hiss. I bite my tongue as Arthur stops in front of his door.

He taps his earpiece and pokes his head out. "Everything alright?"

Mr. C straightens with his default cheeriness. "Just trying

to convince Sasha that it's okay to take a break. He wants one, but thinks it'll reflect poorly on him. I tried to tell—"

Arthur sighs and stops before me. "We'll have to liberate you of that work-to-death habit. Go take a break. I don't want to see you back here for fifteen minutes. Mr. C will go with you."

Damn it! I start to protest, but Arthur is already turning around and tapping his earpiece. After logging out of my computer, I shove out of my chair and brush past Mr. C roughly enough to knock his shoulder. "You're an ass."

He follows me past cubicles, and we drag stares with us. It's unsettling that no one seems to want anything to do with him. Even people at my past job who were douchebags formed cliques with other douchebags. Mr. C doesn't even seem to have that.

Either he's reading my mind or still on the defensive because he says, "Arthur likes me."

"Arthur's nice."

"You're not nice?" he asks. We pass the secretary's desk. She brightens and waves at us. He thumbs toward her. "Owl likes me too. Of course, she's my sister, so she's obligated."

"Your—" But now that he says it, the resemblance is obvious—the same dark eyes, dark hair, high cheekbones. The same broad smiles, though the secretary doesn't seem to wear as many different ones as Mr. C. "Her name is Owl?"

"I did say our parents are bohemians."

"Is yours a bird name too? 'Crow.' No, no. '*Crane.*'"

He stops beside the outer door, a hand on the push bar. "Why do you care? You've made it clear you don't like me."

"I *don't* care. And you're right, I don't like you."

Either his gum has suddenly become sour or my opinion of him means a lot more to him than it should. He blinks rapidly and tries to maintain his smile, but it doesn't fit very well. "Luckily for you, I've made up my mind to help you anyway."

"And I don't get a choice in the matter?"

"No." He pushes through the door. "But I'd have a better understanding of the situation if you told me *why* you want to talk to Metatron."

I have no reason to tell him. I'm not going to steal Arthur's phone, and telling him about my nausea isn't going to give him a better plan. My instinct is to shove through the door, tell him not to follow me, and take a walk around the block—*alone*—to cool off before getting back to work.

But if I'm going to be stuck seeing this guy every day, probably working with him on the mascot design, it would be helpful to know if there's a specific reason people look at him like they do, aside from his "sparkling" personality.

The air outside is unusually humid, the earthy scent of petrichor mingling with the perfume of rose bushes beside the building. Donkey's tails and lover's tears flow down the front of the bakery across the street. The smell of fresh bread wafts through the berry pink door. Afternoon light cuts the buildings with a dramatic crispness, making the leaves and flowers scaling the walls glow with an inner brilliance.

The stuffy tension of being in a corporate building all day—even one filled with plants and cake—eases from my shoulders. People stroll leisurely down the sidewalk, stopping to chat, pet dogs, or sample bits of pastry offered by someone in front of the bakery. An elderly couple stands before a boutique window with their arms linked, one person resting their head on the other's shoulder.

Mr. C makes a beeline for the crosswalk, and I hurry to catch up. We cross the street, and I follow him into the bakery. Glass cases full of bagels, cookies, and pastries stretch to the other side of the room. Little jars of preserves and bags of loose-leaf tea sit on the counter. Fancy cooking utensils hang in the window, and I wonder which ones Ivan picked out. Mr. C buys half a dozen extra-large white chip cookies, and we walk back outside.

"You going to eat all of those yourself?" I ask.

"Not all of them. One's for you."

"No thanks."

He shrugs and spits his gum into a nearby garbage can. "More for me. Though I'm going to give most of them to Owl. They're her favorite."

"How about we make a deal? You tell me why everyone in the office acts uncomfortable around you, and I'll tell you why I want to talk to Metatron." There's no reason he needs to know, but I don't have anything to lose by telling him if I can use it as a bargaining chip. He already caught me in Arthur's office and has all he needs to ruin me. Worst case scenario, he thinks I'm insane... Actually, that might be the *best* scenario because maybe he'll leave me alone.

That calculating glint is back in his eyes. He taps his lips, then nods and heads down the sidewalk. "Alright."

7

The Resurrected

I follow Mr. C as he chews his cookie and brushes crumbs from his front. I'm about to tell him to spill the secret when he says, "I lost my husband last year."

The statement is so far from what I expect him to say that I struggle to find a response, finally settling on, "I'm sorry. He wasn't resurrected?"

He shakes his head, a deep furrow between his brows. "I took personal leave from work, as you do. People were very kind to me. Coworkers brought me food. They cleaned my house. They helped my housemates make sure my bills were paid, my garden was watered. That kind of thing. After a few weeks, I went back to work. And I was okay, for about a month." His leisurely pace as we head down the sidewalk is at odds with his breathless speech. "Then one day, I just lost it. I was in a meeting, and someone made a joke at my expense. I got up, pulled a full pot of coffee from the machine, and hurled it across the table. It went everywhere, all over the designs we'd been working on, splashing people with hot coffee. I— I didn't mean it. I hadn't meant to hurt anyone. But I was fired."

I try to unstick the lump in my throat as I absorb what he's saying. "How can you throw a pot of scalding coffee at a group of people and not think it will hurt them?"

"Because I wasn't thinking at all. I was having a breakdown." He tugs the cuff of his shirt so hard that he drops his cookie. It shatters on the pavement. There's a moment of silence as he stares at the cookie, then he scoops the bits off the ground and carries them to a cluster of nearby pigeons. More swoop down from the buildings and trees as he flings the crumbs into the middle of them. He walks back, brushing off his hands, and his voice is so thick it sounds like he's choking on his words. "I'm ashamed of what I did. But better that you hear it from me because Kevin in Marketing is going to tell you I picked up that pot of coffee and poured it directly onto his crotch, resulting in third degree burns that earned him a gigantic bionic penis."

I slap a hand over my mouth, but it can't contain my laughter. I gasp for breath and clutch the stitch in my side. "Please don't tell me anyone believes that rumor."

Mr. C's pained expression loosens. "Well, I'm not sure he mentions the bionic penis part to people in the office, but he uses it at the bars."

"Damn. His dates must be disappointed when they find out it's a lie. And Kevin works for Renascenz. Doesn't he know the easiest way to make yourself well-endowed is to die and get a better second body? The program won't let you go past ten inches erect, but I don't know who wouldn't be happy with that."

His eyes widen, and his grin threatens to split his face in two. "I, uh, thought you didn't change anything about your body."

"I didn't," I say quickly. "Look at this nose. I'm naturally blessed." Good god, I need to change the subject. "So, clearly you were rehired after the incident... Unless you just keep showing up every day despite not working there anymore. That would definitely make people uncomfortable."

"I'm perhaps not the most well-adjusted, but I wouldn't do something like that. Arthur rehired me when I begged for the second time and promised him I'd go to therapy. He's a softie. But our coworkers don't agree with his decision." His Adam's apple bobs. "I like people. I like talking to them. But no one wants..."

My stomach feels heavier than it's ever been. It would be easy to explain it away as my nausea, but it's more than that. "That isn't what you want from me, is it? Someone to talk to? A friend?"

Bright sun filters through the leaves of an oak tree beside us, creating shadowed geometry on Mr. C's face. Freckles dust his nose and cheeks—something I hadn't noticed in the stale office lighting. There's a small but deep scar marring the line of his jaw, and a diamond stud sparkles in his conch. His gaze darts away from mine. "How pathetic and desperate would I sound if I said yes?"

That can't be it. It's too simple and... wholesome. But he lost his husband. And the embarrassed flush crawling up his neck and the anxious way he fiddles with his wedding ring look genuine.

The ache in my gut becomes molten, and I ball my fists. If his story is true, how fucking heartless do those people have to be to have zero compassion for one of their coworkers going through a devastating loss? Everyone does things they don't mean, especially if they aren't in the right state of mind. I know that all too well. "What about Owl? Or Arthur?" I almost say, *What about your housemates?* But that would be hypocritical since I actively avoid telling Ivan about my problems.

"Owl loves me, of course, but I'm crowding her at home. She'd never tell me that, and my brother-in-law doesn't say anything, but he doesn't need to. They have their own life. Kids. And I'm kind of needy, I guess. Pretty sure she and my brother-in-law take their lunch break together every day at the bakery"—he holds up his bag of cookies—"simply because it's the only alone time they get. And Arthur is good to me, but we don't go golfing on the weekend or anything, you know? Professional relationship only."

"I'm not going golfing with you."

He laughs. "I wasn't going to ask you to. I'm terrible at it."

"Maybe you should switch jobs. Go to a place where no one knows you hurled a pot of coffee across a table."

He stares back at the Renascenz building and runs a hand through his glossy hair. "Yeah, probably. But I have my reasons for staying... Okay, I've told you. You going to hold up your end of the deal?"

There's no way I can refuse now that he's laid all of that on me. "It's going to sound crazy."

"Try me."

I explain my problem as we head back toward the Renascenz building. Its silver spire skewers the sky like a needle through a gauzy blue tapestry. Mr. C eats another cookie as he listens, his brow knit. He says, "Is that what the antacids are for?"

"Yeah. But they don't help that much. Do you believe me then?"

He stops and stares into my face, his intense umber gaze boring into me. "I believe you. So Rodrigo is the soul Metatron is in love with?"

"Yeah. Do you know him?"

Something catches in his expression, but he shakes his head. "Never met him. Don't know anything about him other than he was an astronomy professor. But considering the demographic of the other souls currently in Limbo—everyone at Renascenz is familiar with them since they've been there so long—Rodrigo seems like the most solid choice for a crush. I guess. I'm not versed in what angelic AI find attractive."

"Oh, I could tell you *everything* Metatron finds attractive about Rodrigo. But I'd rather not. Wish I didn't have these feelings beamed into my body at all."

He takes a bite of cookie, chewing thoughtfully. "Are you sure you don't want to borrow Arthur's phone just for a few minutes? I don't see how that's worse than breaking into his office and hacking his computer."

"I didn't 'break into' anything. I have a key. And the computer was still logged in. Not saying it was right, but I thought this position would let me have direct access to Metatron. Using his computer was a bad Plan B."

"And you don't like my bad Plan C. Then Plan D it is."

"What's Plan D?"

He claps me on the shoulder and heads for the front doors. "Stock up on Tums."

I scoff. Yes, like I haven't been doing that already. We head back inside, and he already has his shoes slipped off and is weaving past lobby plants and people sitting in the grass as I pull the laces on my own. I catch up to him at the secretary's desk. He kisses her cheek, then offers her his entire bag of cookies.

After exchanging a few words, he heads back through the glass doors of Marketing & Design. When Owl turns back to me, her eyes are as big as her namesake bird, and she toys with one of her stone ear plugs. "I'm so glad you two are getting along now. He can be a bit much, I know."

"I need you to tell me something. Did he have a breakdown here after his husband died?" It's not that I don't believe him, exactly, but something about the conversation itches, like I'm still missing part of the bigger picture.

Her brow wrinkles beneath her blunt V bangs. She suddenly reaches across the desk and adjusts her glass knick knacks, nudging a chicken away from a greyhound with spindly legs. "Yeah. He threw a pot of coffee at Kevin. Couple people got splashed pretty good." She leans closer, her chair creaking. "But he feels horrible about it. He's tried to make up for it, but nothing is good enough because people don't believe—"

"I'm not judging him for it. I never had a public meltdown after my divorce, but I had plenty in private. I was a mess. Just wanted to hear it from you before someone else tells me the inflated rumor version."

"Which one?" She rolls her eyes. "Thank you for being good to my brother. He doesn't deserve everything that's happened to him."

There's nothing wrong with him needing a friend, but what *is* pathetic is that his best prospect for one here seems to be me. And I don't even like him.

Owl snatches my shirt sleeve and whispers, "By the way... He's into short guys."

Oh my god. I give her a tight smile and excuse myself. As I head back to my desk and stare at paperwork, training videos, and sticky note phone call messages, I can't focus on anything but Mr. C. His wedding ring. The fact that he's single and lonely, and I insinuated that I have a ten-inch dick.

He's into short guys. Lord.

At least it's Friday, and the only people I'm likely to have an awkward conversation with over the next couple days are my housemates. And maybe my ex-wife, Dusty. I get our daughter on the weekends, which is never enough but I'm lucky to even have that. After Dusty had finally had enough and kicked me out ten months ago, I moved into the community house down the street with the travelers and transients. The place was nice, the people welcoming, but it wasn't home. I took comfort in knowing that physically, I wasn't that far away, but I'm sure Dusty would have liked even more distance. I was granted supervised visitation once the divorce went through, and if I could find a new house to move into with good people who kept me in line, after two months the judge would amend the visitation rights to unsupervised, Friday through Sunday.

I have a spotless track record... other than the whole dying thing seven months ago, and hopefully I'm at least a good enough father now to deserve the crayon drawings and macaroni art Poppy gives me.

Five o'clock finally arrives, and I manage to leave the building and hop on the southbound open-air trolley without running into anyone else. I push my way to the back as an Elvis tune drifts from the speakers. People crowd the seats and cling to the overhead handles, many of them holding screen projectors and reading news articles together. There's nowhere to sit, but it doesn't matter because my routine hasn't changed in all my years of riding this trolley, no matter what else in my life has. I sit on the floor and slide my legs through the railing on the side. The wind buffets my face as I lean against the railing. Ground rushes by below.

An older Indigenous person with a French braid sits beside me, legs and arms dangling beyond the railing. They flick their finger through their projector display, browsing articles.

I point to it. "You're not worried about dropping that over the edge? I've lost my lunch money doing that. My shoes once too..."

They let go of the little projector, but instead of falling to the street, it dangles from a strap on their wrist.

I nod. "Smart."

When they right the projector, I glance at the article on the screen. The headline screams *RENASCENZ RED TAPE REMOVING RIGHT TO RESURRECTION?* Below, it says, *Most people aren't interested in coming back for a second life, but for those who are, is Simmons v Renascenz literally killing them by halting uploads into the program?*

The person catches me staring and scoots closer, giving me a better look. They say, "You believe this shit?"

"Yeah, that much alliteration should be illegal."

They huff through their nose, then let go of the projector to reach into their pocket. They offer me a wrapped hard candy, then pop one in their mouth. "I can't believe this case is still going on. Nobody thinks Renascenz is unethical except a fringe group of Christian nuts. Not that that means anything." They shake their head, candy clicking against their teeth. "I wouldn't be surprised if Renascenz lost, and they erased everybody in Limbo. There're too many loopholes to sentient AI rights for that angel to be safe, and absolutely no rights for 'souls' they decide are computer-created algorithms."

"You're just a ray of optimism, aren't you?"

"I know too much about history to be optimistic."

I've kept an eye on the news too, and based on current projections and what Arthur is saying, a win is the most likely outcome. It hadn't occurred to me that accepting that information could be naïve, but this person's had quite a few more turns around the sun than I have. Great, like I don't have enough to worry about.

They stare into the sky, rocking with the trolley. Deep crow's feet spread from their eyes as they glance at me. My thoughts must be all over my face because they say, "Hey, I can't argue that we've come a long way. Things get better with every generation. And I'll be happy to be proven wrong. I'm just cranky that two bigoted parents and their bigoted lawyer have taken up so much headline space over the months."

I murmur my agreement, twisting the candy wrapper between my fingers. The city center falls away. An orchard fills in the spaces between buildings so covered in plants it's hard to tell where one ends and the other begins. Far in the distance, tall wind turbines rotate in a field of wildflowers.

Some people predicted chaos and anarchy when Renascenz first opened its doors. They assumed people would flock to the company for immortality—and they did, before the Universal Church gave its opinion—that they would feel invincible, taking risks they wouldn't normally, or flippantly kill someone with the knowledge that they'd be back in a few weeks and the murder didn't actually "count." Some of that probably happens. After all, *I* was high on illegal emoji combos and didn't care, but I might have still acted that way even if it were my only life.

For the most part, though, those things don't happen. The mortality rate is lower than it's been in fifty years. People—the responsible ones—sign up for the Renascenz program the way they sign up for home insurance. It's added protection against something horrible, with the hope they never need it.

The trolley's AI operator, Eddie, snaps me from my thoughts, announcing the next stop in their sunny tenor voice. I say goodbye to Ray of Optimism, then squeeze past people and fish my debit card from my wallet to give Eddie a tip. A small collection of Elvis memorabilia sits on the dash: a bobblehead, a tiny music box shaped like a turntable, a chipped ceramic piggy bank, and a postcard of the King inside a glittery popsicle picture frame.

"Your dash is looking a little bare, Eddie, especially compared to the Main Street trolley. Didn't you have more things?" I say.

<I had coffee cups! But the other day someone fell into the dash, and they all broke. And a PEZ dispenser got stepped on.> A sound like a tongue clucking comes through the speakers. <It happens.>

I debate how much an Elvis coffee cup might cost, then leave a ten-dollar tip.

<That's so kind, Sasha! Thank you. Toodles!>

I step off the trolley and into the gravel. This area of Galvlohi is mostly big hand-built houses with sprawling gardens, some more flamboyant and experimental than others. All of them are cob or hay bale designs with freehand molded windows and inclusions of glass bottles and polished stones. Nearly everyone is practiced in some aspect of construction or home repair. Ivan is an architect and specializes in urban planning. He can also tell you the best interior construction for optimum heat flow through your rocket heater, where to place windows for the best lighting, and where to plant trees for ideal temperature regulation.

Gravel crunches under my feet as I pass the community house I lived in right after my divorce. I swear it has more additions molded on every time I walk down this road. Guests and transients water the gardens, toss away weeds, and someone inquires whether there's anyone there who eats meat, because they have an ornery rooster they have to put down.

My heart lurches as I stop in the drive of a mushroom-shaped house stained a vibrant peachy-pink with teal accents. Teardrop windows fan above the front door, and one molded into a crescent moon floats above window boxes overflowing with succulents. Dusty had picked out the pane of iridescent glass from a big scrap pile at a supply store and said it was the perfect color for the moon. My own glass contributions were in the form of a mosaic across the front wall of such manic intricacy that I'd never be able to recreate it today. Not without combining Zany Face and Thinking Face. It looks like it took years, but in reality, I hyper-focused for four days, toiling away at it with no sleep. My fingers were lacerated and raw by the time I was done.

I have no idea what it's even supposed to be.

Whenever I'm here, I'm not sure whether to miss this place I helped build or be grateful I'm not surrounded by evidence of my past addiction.

The front door opens. Poppy screams, "Daddy!" and runs for me, her arms outstretched.

I drop onto my knees and gather her in a tight hug. The smell of laundry soap and maple syrup overwhelms me, her tight curls tickling my cheek. Her little heart beats hard against mine, and I kiss her sticky cheek.

Pulling back, I grin. "Did you have breakfast for dinner?"

"Yeah!" Her dark eyes are big and glittering, and there's dandelion fluff in her hair. I brush it away. "Jack made pancakes, and Mommy got some eggs because a lady had too many. I put checkup on them."

"'Checkup?' You mean ketchup. And since when do you like eggs?"

She levels her gaze on me, mouth pulled in a tight line. "Daddy, I always liked eggs. But only scrambled."

I'm sure that isn't true. Next, she's probably going to tell me she eats chicken, and when did I miss these moments?

I straighten and wince as my knees pop. "We're going to the carnival."

Her eyes bloom, and she squeals. "Carnival!" She grips me in another hug and hops up and down, nearly sending me off balance. "C'mon, Daddy, I gotta get my backpack. I put my comics inside—there's a superhero with a special arm like Ivan's! And Mr. Teeth is coming, but he's too big to put in the backpack. They have stuffed animals at the carnival! I want him to have a friend. But it has to be an animal Mr. Teeth won't eat."

"That's going to be hard. Sharks eat everything." She tugs me toward the door.

Light catches in the chips of glass mosaicking the front wall. I give her a tight smile as we walk inside. Nostalgia floods me as soon as I inhale. Ivan's place is cooking spices and warm baked clay. It's nice, but it's not the chaotic mix of lavender, bubble bath, and Jack's patchouli cologne that scream *HOME*.

Poppy hurries down the hall and into her room while I stand awkwardly in the entryway. Dusty's voice, honey poured over fine grit sandpaper, carries from the laundry room. "Sasha? That you?"

I clear my throat. "Yeah. Hey."

There's a rustling of hangers and clinking glass. Dusty carries a tote bag down the hall that's so stuffed it dwarfs her small frame. She stops beside me and sets it on the floor. There are flecks of pink glitter in her auburn buzzcut, and one of her bra straps hangs out of her tank top. She blows out a breath and smooths the fine gold chain around her neck. "Hi."

"There's glitter in your hair." I don't know how to talk with her anymore. Don't know how to make small talk with this woman who used to be my wife. "Poppy making art?"

Dusty sighs. "No. That dress she's wearing has a glittery

taffeta skirt, and the stuff comes off every time she twirls around. I'm tempted to throw it out, but she loves it too much. Better warn your housemates that they'll be coated in it."

I shrug. "Well, we're all queer anyway so..."

The back door opens, and Jack kicks dirt from their boots. Their plaid shirt is rolled up to their elbows, Stetson tipped back on their head. They're the big sibling, adopted after living with Dusty's parents as a foster kid for a couple of years. They're tall and lanky to Dusty's short and curvy, and Jack is as white as I am, their farmer's tan notwithstanding. But with one Black parent and one white, Dusty said no one ever questioned that they were siblings when they were kids.

Jack takes off their hat, and their mouth pulls to one side. I don't know what that look is for, but I don't like that it's directed at me. Raking a hand through their blond hair, they say, "You know, I wish you could have listed me as a reference on your Renascenz application instead of just telling Arthur that you're related to the CRO."

"Why? Because you would have told Arthur 'no'?"

Jack doesn't take it as the joke I meant it to be. Their forehead creases, and they look away. "Yeah, I would have."

The entryway suddenly feels claustrophobic with both them and Dusty crowding me. My chest tightens. "Don't want a recovering junkie piggybacking off your career, is that it?"

Jack scoffs. "It's not like that. But I don't think it's a great idea that you're there. You should have kept your old job."

"Jack!" Dusty gapes at them, and it's clear she can't believe what they're saying any more than I can.

It's hard to keep the defensiveness out of my voice, and I don't want Poppy to hear her daddy and her untie arguing, but I say, "Why don't you tell me 'what it's like' then. Explain to me why I shouldn't be there."

Their fingers fidget for a phantom cigarette, a habit they gave up a decade ago but still jones for. "Things at the company are... tenuous. The lawsuit and everything. You'd have way more job security at your old place."

I think about the person on the trolley and their pessimistic view of the lawsuit. "Do you think Renascenz is going to lose?"

Their reply is immediate: "No, they ain't gonna lose. But..." They search the air like the excuse they're looking for might be up there somewhere. "It seems like they lay off more brokers every month. They got rid of some of the Marketing people. And everyone in my department is gone. It's just me in the stasis facility, and I don't even have anything to do right now. I just don't want them to, y'know, decide they don't need you."

Some of the fire in my chest dies, and I open my cramping fists. "But that's going to change once Renascenz wins. They'll need people in your department again to help fill the stasis pods with biomaterial and monitor the bodies and all that. Maybe they won't need to hire anymore brokers, but no matter what department they downsize in the meantime, I'm pretty sure my position is secure. You have no idea how bad Arthur needs an assistant. That man is a mess."

Dusty raises her eyebrows, staring at Jack like she's waiting for them to give me an apology. Jack rubs the sunburn on the back of their neck and says, "Yeah, I guess. But I still think it would be a good idea for you to send your resume out to other places... Just in case. I can make you a list of companies. And for sure put me down as a reference. I'll absolutely lie and say we've worked together professionally and aren't in any way related."

"Technically we *aren't* related anymore," I mutter.

"We're still family. You're not getting rid of me that easily." They hesitate, then add, "I'm trying to look out for you. That's all."

I nod, then head for Poppy's room because no matter how much Jack cares and in what weird way they show it, I'm still itching to get out of this house. Poppy sits on her knees on the rug, the glittery pink skirt of her dress fanned around her as she struggles to stuff comic books into her overflowing backpack. She stands, the strap of the pack in her hand, and all the contents spills out onto the floor.

Her nostrils flare, mouth pinched. "Daddy, can you help me?"

"Sure." I survey all of the things she's packed: a case of colored pencils, erasers shaped like dinosaurs, tiny spiral notebooks, two diecast race cars, a water bottle, a half-eaten pouch of fruit snacks, super hero action figures, a mermaid doll, her toothbrush, her towel, one sock, a bruised banana, and every comic book from her shelf. I sigh. "How about a little less of this stuff and some more clothes, huh?"

"But Daddy, I *need* all these things." Her tone says, *obviously*.

"Do you want to go to the carnival?"

"Yeah!"

"Well, we're going there right now, not stopping at the house first, and I'm not lugging three bags of toys and smashed fruit around at the carnival. You have colored pencils and books at my place. Pick out three comics and two toys, and then we're getting your toothpaste and some changes of clothes."

"Does Mr. Teeth count as a toy?"

The plush shark is nearly as big as she is, but I don't have the heart to tell her she can't bring it. "Nah, Mr. Teeth is your sleepover buddy."

Dusty stops in the doorway with the tote bag she'd carried from the laundry room. "I was going to give you this, but it can wait if you'd have to take it to the carnival with you."

"What is it?" Probably more crap of mine she found while cleaning out a closet. It doesn't seem to matter how long I've been gone for, there's always more that turns up. I had no idea I owned so much stuff.

She shifts her feet and fixes her bra strap, staring at the bag. "We were shopping the other day and saw some stuff. Towels..."

Who was shopping? Her and Jack, or her and her boyfriend? I don't remember his name, but he's a nice guy. A social worker like Dusty. He has dreads and a smooth baritone and looks like he should be on the cover of a romance novel. They were buying towels together? Maybe he's moving in.

I imagine him stepping out of the shower—the shower I helped install—and reaching for that brand new towel. Drying off those rich brown pecs as he hums to himself... I'm not sure whether to be jealous that he's with Dusty, or jealous that Dusty's with *him*.

Dusty's still talking. "Last time I was at your place it seemed like there weren't very many in the linen closet. And maybe it was laundry day or something, but these were on sale and— Nevermind, it's stupid, huh?"

I checked out of too much of this conversation. Instead of asking her to repeat what she said, I paw through the bag; on top of the towel set are two neckties and a pair of pink and white houndstooth dress socks. Dusty says, "I didn't know how dressy you need to be for this new job, and I couldn't remember if you had ties, and... they were on sale."

Straightening, I clench my aching jaw and try to work the lump from my throat. "Thanks. You didn't have to do that." I don't need any of these things, but I'll take them home with me even if I have to bribe Eddie the trolley AI with Elvis memorabilia, so they'll watch my bag while we're at the carnival.

"It's no big deal."

But it is. Not just to me, but it's clear in her awkward shrugs and the rosy tint in her cheeks. She still thinks of me as family too, even after all I put her through, and she's trying to figure out how to show it.

I let myself believe that I deserve it.

8

The Seraph

A green cat with pink tabby stripes saunters across the table and bats at my teacup. It wobbles on the saucer. Mei-Hui glares at the cat. "Tiaotiao, no."

Tiaotiao, nonplussed, plops his rump on the table and licks his paw. Shafts of light from the blinds fall across his sleek fur. The definition and detail of everything in Mei-Hui's cat cafe rivals what *I'm* capable of generating. Children are like that. No impressionistic environment here, instead, an almost hyperrealism with a filter of over-saturation. Everything is too vibrant, too crisp, contrasting colors screaming against each other.

Mei-Hui herself is like this. She looks exactly like I would expect a bubbly seven-year-old Chinese girl with a penchant for pigtails to look. *Almost.* Her skin is slightly too perfect, each strand of her hair falling a bit too symmetrically, eyes so dark and full of depth that if they were magnified, they might reveal entire universes. But her appearance gives me comfort. Sometimes children only want to be dinosaurs or lions or alien princesses, and they're resistant when I tell them they have to choose a human form that matches their age for their second life.

I have no doubt that Mei-Hui will imagine a body that looks exactly as she does now. Her fantasy imaginings are normally confined to the cats she creates. Some of them have real world counterparts—white Persians and tortoiseshell Main Coons and black Bombays—while others are gigantic or look like they took a nap on a paint palette. None of them have anuses.

She frowns at me. "You can't drink your tea without a mouth."

This is true. I generate a pair of floating lips, then grin at her and pick up my teacup. Pausing, I stare at the neon liquid inside. There's cat hair floating in it. Mei-Hui grumbles, leans over the table in the booth we're occupying, and takes my cup. A stainless-steel sink full of dirty dishes blinks into existence to my right. She climbs down, carefully carrying the cup, and dumps the contents into the sink.

She stops on her way back to scold the green tabby. "Bad Tiaotiao!"

<Now that I think about it, a cat cafe does seem rather unsanitary.> And I'm not sure why Mei-Hui likes to make the cats misbehave. Perhaps it lends them added realism. But I learned long ago to accept what the dead generate in their rooms, especially if it's a subconscious creation they can't figure out how to get rid of. Mei-Hui has one of these, but it's covered in floor cushions at the other end of the room.

<Alright,> I say, <the tea to pair with the tea. What will it

be today? Celebrity drama? Political scandals? The latest argument between Karen and Karen in the Seal Appreciation Society? We haven't checked in on them in a while. You *know* they haven't resolved that spat about José's sunglasses... Personally, I think Karen is right.>

She scrunches her face. "They're both Karen."

<Yes, but Karen is wrong. *Karen* is right.>

Giggling, she pours me fresh tea and pushes a plate of Oreos my way. "I choose... you."

<You think there's tea about me?> I know there is. I crack my knuckles and lean back in the booth. <Alright. Let's see what rumors people are spreading about me. But if someone has leaked my obsession with *Realm Babyz* I'm going to be very embarrassed.>

Mei-Hui gasps, staring at me over her teacup and looking far older than her years. "You like Realm Babyz? But you're a grownup."

<Technically, I'm only two years old. And that was a joke.> I whisper, <I'm not telling you my actual obsession.>

Smiling coyly, she says, "I won't tell anyone."

<Uh-huh.> We're both clearly ignoring the fact that she has no one *to* tell. I take a bite out of an Oreo and do an internet search for my name. <Well, "in his name dot org" says I'm a horrific abomination.>

"What's that?"

<Something evil and disgusting.>

Her expression sours. She slides into the seat beside me and touches my wings, then my gold tie. I stare unflinchingly as she pats the lid of one of my eyes and says, "That's a lie. You're not evil *or* disgusting."

<Thank you.> I give her a squeeze around the shoulders. <Other websites are calling me an angel, a deva, and a psychopomp. One person claims I'm the second coming of Christ. None of those are true either.>

"You *are* an angel, though."

<Not in the true sense, honey.> I gasp as my search makes another hit on a forum for the resurrected. <Oh my goodness! One of the past souls made a plushie of me. Look.> A soft-sculpted doll appears in my hand in a burst of feathers. One of the feathers falls onto Tiaotiao, who rolls onto his back and bats at it.

The plushie has two clusters of chubby wings studded in eyes, framed by a halo of filigree wire. In the center is a much larger eye with the kind of glittering, dilated pupil you see in adorable cartoon characters. My suit is stitched with care from white paisley fabric, and my hands are little peach mittens clasped together at my front.

"Aww! So cute!" Mei-Hui snatches the plushie and squeezes it hard. "Mini Metatron, I love you."

I prop my elbow on the table and make a throat-clearing noise. <The real deal is sitting right beside you, you know.>

"Yeah, but you aren't little." As she fawns over the mini-me, I eat another cookie and poke at other channels in the forum. I try not to enter these sites very often because all the resurrected miss me. And though I'm not supposed to make contact with them, seeing their messages always tempts me.

starlight52: Dreams sometimes. A lot, actually.

cancergotme: But not like, feeling Metatron's actual emotions, right?

starlight52: *message removed*

cancergotme: oop

meatghost (mod): Please keep all comments of this nature in the NSFW channel.

I choke on my Oreo. There's a NSFW channel dedicated to me? Oh dear.

starlight52: Sorry about that!

irina1: **@cancergotme** I know what you're talking about. Me and a guy in my local support group can feel Metatron too. It's like an ache in my teeth, but on a spiritual level. The guy in my group says it feels like a sickly-sweet nausea. We both agree that Metatron loves someone but hasn't told him.

starlight52: Metatron loves all the resurrected.

irina1: Yeah, but not like this. I mean they're *in love*

with him. Also, having a channel full of sexual fantasies about our guardian angel is disgusting and shouldn't exist.

meatghost (mod): I'm not having this conversation with you again **@irina1**.

My hand knocks against my cup, and tea slops onto the table. How could any of them possibly know about my love for Rodrigo?

He didn't arrive until October, a week before operations paused. I'm foggy on when exactly I started to develop feelings for him. It might have been when he talked about Uranus' sideways rotation for nineteen minutes straight, then grew flustered when he realized his passion was spilling out of him unchecked. Or maybe it was when I realized his hesitation before answering a question wasn't because he was afraid to give me an answer, but because he needs to roll it over in his mind first to be certain the words he speaks are the ones he wants. Likely the seed of my adoration was planted on our very first meeting, when he nervously plucked at the buttons on his tweed jacket and correctly guessed that my wings were modeled after a great egret's. When I told him most people guessed a dove, he'd laughed and said those would be far too small for a being of my magnitude.

But there's no way to fit the pieces together to explain how any of the previous dead know about him. I can sense all the souls who are in Limbo, but sensing *me* outside of it shouldn't be possible. Our connection is severed once the soul is sent into their new body. Or it's supposed to be. Renascenz has been up and running for just shy of two years, and there are certainly things the developers haven't anticipated.

My love sickness is literally making people sick.

Mei-Hui stops baby-talking to the plushie and looks up. "What's wrong?"

I push away my cup and rub my hands on my slacks, unsure what to do with everything roiling inside me. Being in love with Rodrigo is *my* business, *my* secret, *my* weakness and joy and pain and—

Against my better programming, I make an account in the forum and enter the general channel.

Metatron: Salutations! ::::::) I have seen so many messages for me in these places, and though I'm unable to respond to them, I want you all to know that I care about you and think of you often. Irina and Bob (it is you, isn't it, Bob?) I'm sorry for whatever discomfort you're experiencing in your new bodies, but you are mistaken in believing it's coming from me.

Being together in Limbo is an intimate experience by design, and I can see how my companionship could be misconstrued as something more. But I'm an AI. It isn't in my programming to fall in love. I'm simply incapable.

And archangel in an ambulance! **@meatghost** if you won't listen to **@irina1**, listen to me – set fire to that NSFW channel. My "genitals" are a supernova. Good luck having sex with that.

After sending the message, I disable notifications and close out of the forum. I probably shouldn't have written those last two sentences, because this is the internet, and someone is going to take that as a challenge.

Mei-Hui stares at me, her eyes suddenly big and glossy. Her bottom lip quivers, the plushie trembling in her hands. "Did Renascenz lose?"

<What? No, no. It's not about that. Just another— Another rumor about me.>

"They have a bad lawyer."

<They have an excellent one. The more money you have, the better a lawyer you can hire, and Renascenz has dumped a ton into this. A lot more than they needed to, probably. It's simply that this is an unprecedented case, and the lawsuit has raised tangential questions no one thought to answer before. But that doesn't mean they'll lose.> I avoided telling her about the lawsuit for some time, falsely believing she wouldn't understand. But *Kitty Court* is apparently quite the popular show, and she didn't need me to explain.

"That other lawyer is a big buttface." Her nostrils flare, tears starting to bead on her long lashes. "He says we're not real. That a computer made us up."

<Do you worry that you're not real?>

"No," she says firmly. "I know I'm real. And he says the girl who was resurrected is really a boy. But she picked a girl body when she came back, so that means she's a girl. That guy is so stupid."

I run a hand through my feathers. <How do you know that? Where did you see it?>

Her tiny shoulders shrug. "The internet."

It's not anything I wouldn't have told her myself, but whichever Renascenz bot is in charge of redacting articles is falling down on their job. I wrap my arms around Mei-Hui. <Whether a court decides the people being resurrected are 'real' or not, that isn't your fault. Your parents decided to enroll you in the program, and why wouldn't they? They love you. You and I didn't choose to be here, and we didn't create the company. So to blame *us* would be wrong. We're just trying to do the best we can.> I hold up a finger. <Second point—there have been non-binary people in Limbo who have chosen a female body for their second life, but they're still non-binary. So 'girl body' doesn't always equal 'girl.' But I know for a fact that in this case, the resurrected person is a girl. So yes, that lawyer is a big transphobic buttface.>

She sniffles, and I wipe tears from her cheek with my thumb. I hope my voice comes out reassuring as I say, <Third point—I've calculated a ninety-two percent chance of Renascenz winning soon.> A sharp ache throbs in me for Rodrigo, and I wonder if the resurrected can feel it. <Do you want to hear a secret?>

This perks her interest, but her tears keep flowing unchecked down her round cheeks.

<I won't let anything happen to you. Even if Renascenz were to lose. I would never let you get deleted. I promise on

every feather in my wings. On every star in the universe. On every cat hair floating in my tea.>

She sniffles and nods. As I flick her tears away, I make them explode into sparkly rainbow confetti. She giggles through a sob, and more confetti bursts from the corners of her eyes. I turn her head from side to side. <You got a party going on in there or what?>

She pushes my chest. "No, you do!"

<Really?> I blink hard and glitter rains from my eyes. I think of Rodrigo's beautiful human face and our conversation where I said I thought the moon was made of cheese. In the beginning, he took much of my humor at face value, and when I pointed out that I was trying to be funny, he grew apologetic. *I'm great at ruining people's jokes because I don't know that's what they are.* So we agreed that he would ask if he was unsure, and I would never make a thing of it.

When he returns to the material plane, will he ask that of someone else? Will they give him gentle confirmation, as I do, or will they wrinkle their nose in irritation that he hasn't understood the joke in the first place?

I don't know how to let him go.

Glitter pours from my eyes, creating silver dunes on the table. Mei-Hui runs her hands through it, drawing shapes. It fills my teacup and overflows.

I wish the lie I'd written in the forum was true. I wish my programming kept me from falling for someone.

How do you stop love from hurting?

9

The Resurrected

A wave of Metatron's love sickness hits as I guide Poppy past stalls filling the air with the scent of sugar and fried food. Lights whirl through the evening sky, and people scream, gripping their seat harnesses as they're flung upside down on a massive carnival ride. Poppy hops beside me, squeezing my hand and pointing. "That one! That one!"

I clutch my stomach and crane my neck. Good god. I tug her to a cutout of a cartoon sunflower with a weird face. Inch marks run up its stem, and Poppy falls quite far from the minimum height requirement. "You're too little." I crouch down next to the sunflower. "So am I."

Her bottom lip sticks out as she pouts and clutches her cotton candy. "When I have my birthday, I'll be big, and then I can ride it."

"Maybe if you sit on Ivan's shoulders. Although, I don't think scary rides are his speed." And they make you take off your shoes, glasses, and anything that could come loose from your person on those kinds of rides. Imagining Ivan's prosthetic arm sitting in a pile of flip-flops doesn't seem right.

I check my watch. "It's getting a little late, besides. We've been here for two hours."

She lets out a dramatic yawn, then takes a bite out of her cotton candy. "But I'm not tired."

"Uh-huh." I pull the transparent token card from my pocket and show her the glowing *4* in the center. "We have enough for one more thing. Maybe two. A game or a Poppy-sized ride."

Please be a game. I'm not sure my stomach can take a ride, even if it's that little train shaped like a caterpillar that runs in a circle.

She tugs on my hand, pulling me through people to a game with colorful balloons attached to a board. Huge stuffed animals hang from the awning, and she points to one. "It's Oswald! That's a perfect friend for Mr. Teeth."

I scan the rainbow teddy bears, the iridescent koi fish, and creatures I don't have names for. "Which one is that?"

"It's the robot. Right there."

"How is a robot going to visit Mr. Teeth? Robots can't go underwater."

She sighs. "Oswald lives in a lighthouse, and the mermaids repaired Oswald after a storm where it got smashed on the rocks. It goes underwater all the time now. Oswald can play with Mr. Teeth all it wants."

The person running the dart game says, "Oswald is from *Realm Babyz*. My kid watches it all the time."

"Cool! Me too. It's my favorite show," Poppy says.

I thought Poppy's favorite show was still *Kitty Court*. The characters are on her comforter at my house. There's a cup and bowl patterned in them sitting in my cabinet. I even have *Kitty Court* bubble bath in the bathroom. I switch on the show whenever she stays with me, and she's never complained. Although now that I think about it, she hasn't watched much TV lately.

How out of touch am I, thinking I still know her favorite shows and favorite foods? I don't know anything. Not when she's only with me forty-eight hours out of the week. I miss so much.

Another wave of honeyed nausea hits me, and on the crest is a question: *How do you keep love from hurting?*

It's Metatron's thought—they must not be doing so hot at the moment. Neither am I. If only I could talk to them. I don't want to take Arthur's phone. Mr. C is probably right that it isn't worse than clicking on the contacts on his computer, except that was an office computer, and it was still logged in. His phone is a personal item. The thought of typing in his password from a stolen sticky note makes me feel gross, and the voice of guilt in my head—whether it be Ivan's, my own, or someone else's—would be far too strong for me to act on.

Poppy pulls hard on my arm, asking me to win the robot, and I snap from my thoughts.

At least there's something I'm still good for. And I don't need a Concentrating Face pin in my arm to be accurate.

I use the last of our tokens to buy six darts. Poppy grows quiet as I aim, her gaze focused on the balloon board. I throw the first dart. *POP!*

POP!

POP!

Each dart finds a target, and hitting six means I can get her the biggest robot hanging from the awning. She squeals with joy as I hand it to her, then struggles to carry it without dragging it through the dirt. I haul her up onto my shoulders, the robot slapping at my side.

I still have her. Even if it's only for forty-eight hours and she has to sigh and tell me all the things I should already know about her. Dusty isn't my love anymore, the house I helped build is no longer mine, and I'm not even sure I'm *me* anymore. The me I was before I died. But when Poppy is with me, I feel whole again.

After learning about Mr. C's breakdown and how he only seems to want a friend, not unsavory blackmail tasks, I figured I could stop thinking about him. But that wedding ring must be so heavy on his finger. It's clear he's having as much trouble letting go of his past as I am, and I'm sure our coworkers treating him like a pariah doesn't help.

I pause at the food stalls on the way out of the carnival. I'm not much of a sweets guy, but the petit fours stacked up in a bell jar on the counter of a desserts stall look both delicious and conceited. "Will these keep in the fridge until Monday?"

"Sure," the stall worker says. "The chocolate might sweat a bit, but they'll be fine."

I buy a box of them, and we ride the trolley home. A cool

wind licks at my ears, and the person in front of me asks Eddie to raise the windows. It's dark by the time we get there, and I have to rouse Poppy from her doze on her giant robot. Grass brushes against my jeans as I carry her up the walk, her backpack slung over my shoulder and Dusty's tote bag of towels slapping against my leg.

Lights glow from the rainbow bubble windows of the sitting room. When I push through the front door, I expect to carry Poppy straight to bed, but she squirms from my arms and runs down the hall. The scent of popcorn hangs in the air, and a cozy warmth comes from the rocket heater. It isn't *that* chilly, but the benefit of it pumping heat through the molded benches in the sitting room is always taken advantage of when it's a movie night.

By the time I set down the stuffed animals and backpack, Ivan is guiding Poppy out of the sitting room and David, his boyfriend, is standing conspicuously in front of the television. I scoop Poppy up despite her protests, then squint at Ivan and say, "What are you guys watching in there?"

Ivan's fair complexion turns a deep shade of pink above his beard. He pushes his glasses up the bridge of his nose with a ceramic finger. "She came in right at an, erm, 'adult' part. Sorry."

"And I went on so many rides!" Poppy yawns. "And I brought my comics. There's a superhero with an arm like yours, Ivan."

"Really?" He holds up his prosthetic arm and flexes the

fingers. Though many people opt for growing a new organic limb cultivated from their own cells when they need a replacement, there's a trend growing to not only display disabilities but celebrate them. Ivan opted for a fancy arm of "living porcelain" that can move and experience sensation like an organic limb but looks like he dipped his arm in pottery glaze, then stuck it in a kiln. It's gorgeous, and I'm pretty sure David is wild about it.

Poppy is still talking. And yawning. I carry her away from the sitting room, and she says, "And Daddy bought cakes, but he said we can't have any. They're for his friend."

"His 'friend?'" Ivan asks. "What friend?"

I set her down and tell her to go brush her teeth, then turn back to Ivan. There's pink glitter in his beard from Poppy's dress, and I dread knowing how much is on me. David gathers his black hair into a ponytail as he leans against the wall, but the feigned indifference in his face is as obnoxious as Ivan's.

I say, "He's not really a—"

"*He?* Do tell." David pushes off the wall and stops beside Ivan. Like most of the resurrected, he's beautiful, but I don't know if he altered his body much from the original. He's tall and slender, his Japanese heritage visible in his features, and seems to favor the timeless goth look of all-black ensembles.

"He's a coworker," I say. "And an incredibly annoying one at that."

"So annoying that you bought him cake?"

"Petit fours." I pop an antacid in my mouth as I head for

the kitchen. "I don't like him, but no one else seems to like him either. I guess I feel kind of bad for— Both of you stop making that face."

"What face?" Ivan asks.

"Whatever face you're making." I write *DO NOT EAT* on a sticky note and rubberband it around the box of petit fours, then push them into the back of the fridge. "He's just a coworker. You two go back to your dirty movie."

Ivan splutters. "It's not porn. We aren't watching *porn* in the sitting room. That isn't something normal people do."

"I have to put my daughter to bed. And when I come back, I'm not saying another word about Mr. C."

"*Mr. C?*" David lets out a tiny gasp. "With a name like that, you have to dish now. Is he your boss? Forget the movie. This is much better."

Ignoring him, I slide past Ivan and head down the hall. Poppy's backpack is on the floor, toiletries and comic books strewn about. She hums in the bathroom, the door open a crack. I gather her things back into her bag, trying to tune out the furious whispers of my housemates in the kitchen.

After carrying Poppy's backpack into her room and placing her stuffed animals on the bed, I head back to the bathroom and tap on the door. She pulls it open. Her pajama top is on backward, but I'm still proud of her. Especially since not only has she brushed her teeth as evident by the globs of toothpaste on the counter, but she hung up her towel and scrubbed her face with a washcloth.

"Great job." I wipe off the toothpaste and scoop her up. "You can have a bath in the morning."

She hugs me tight around the neck, and I carry her to bed. Her room is a little alcove off mine and was originally used for storage. There's no window, but we replaced the door with a beaded curtain and hung string lights all along the domed ceiling. They dangle like stars caught in a spiderweb, and I'm not sure what kind of princess that's fit for, but she loves them.

Mr. Teeth and Oswald the Robot take up so much room in the bed that I can barely see Poppy at all after she scoots under the covers—a little tawny face peeking out between shark fins and metallic claws. I almost ask her if she wants me to read her a story or one of her comics, but she's struggling to keep her eyes open.

I kiss her forehead. "Good night, baby. I love you. Tomorrow, you can show me *Realm Babyz*."

She nods and rolls over. "Love you, Daddy."

After quietly sliding through the beaded curtain, I start to head for the door, then think better of it and sink onto my bed. I'm not quite ready to go back out and face my housemates. They're good people, but I've had my fill of peopling today.

A little decorative yarn knot on the quilt catches beneath my nails. Metatron's ache sits heavy in my stomach. *How do you stop love from hurting?*

I realize even if I could talk to Metatron right now, I wouldn't know how to answer that question. Poppy's soft snores come from beyond the curtain, and I think about all the bad memories wrapped up in the nostalgia of the house we shared.

It didn't feel like I had a problem at first. Dusty didn't even know I had enhancement pins for the longest time. But it spiraled out of control to the point that there was no hiding it from anyone, least of all myself. There were so many pins in my arm that my skin had the texture of an avocado. And what bothers me more than anything else is that I don't know what spurned that fast slide into oblivion.

The doctor who prescribes my ADHD meds said I'm more at risk because I need to feed my impulse for immediate gratification; I'm seeking sources of dopamine, I struggle with self-control, and have all the stopping power of a car without any brakes. I get lost in myself, focus on everything and nothing at the same time, and neural enhancement pins only exacerbate that, not make it better.

Grandma says I simply have an "addictive personality."

I know enough about how my mind works to acknowledge my susceptibility without leaning on it as an excuse—there are plenty of people with ADHD who don't use illegal combinations of enhancement pins to get high.

But the fact that there isn't one specific thing that happened in my life to spur my descent into addiction has kept me awake more nights than Metatron has. If I was clinically depressed or I'd hated my marriage, it would have made more sense. If one of my loved ones had died, or I was under some extreme pressure, it would have made more sense. But instead, the need for *more* branched under my skin like a senseless cancer, and by the time I realized how bad my shakes were when my pins were running out and how far Dusty had distanced herself from me, it was too late. Too late for my marriage and too late for my heart.

I pluck at the yarn knots on the quilt and jiggle my leg. Knowing the catalyst for my addiction isn't going to put things back the way they were, but there would be more power behind my apologies if I had a reason better than "I don't know."

With a sigh, I peek in on Poppy then head down the hall. Stray pieces of popcorn and a saltshaker sit on the kitchen counter next to the popper. Quiet dialogue drifts from the television in the sitting room, then a *boom* so loud I regret leaving my bedroom door cracked open. Ivan hisses at David to turn the volume down.

I pull a bottle of juice from the fridge and lean against the counter. The windows above the sink are freeform blobs of thick, warped glass with tiny bubbles trapped inside, clear enough to make out the silhouettes of trees and the watery light of the moon. I don't know who picked out the glass. Don't know whose hands molded the cob around it, or who sealed and painted the wall. Whether it was Ivan or one of the people who lived here before. All I know is it wasn't me, and the unknown history of the place I live in is a constant reminder that I'm an outsider. In this house. In this life.

In myself.

David walks into the kitchen and opens the fridge. Bottles

clink together as he rummages. I say, "Do you ever feel like an outsider in your own body?"

He straightens, fingers wrapped around two bottles of that weird kombucha Ivan keeps trying to get me to drink. "What?"

"You've died and come back like three times—"

"Only twice."

"Right. Do you ever feel like an imposter? Like— like your cells are counterfeit?"

He blinks at me, a tiny line forming between his brows. "No."

I sag against the counter and pinch the pin in my arm, wishing it was Woozy Face and hating myself for wishing it.

"Other resurrected feel like that, though," he says. "Especially if their lives are quite different after they come back... You don't pay any attention at the meetings, do you?"

"I try, but nothing anyone has said there resonates with what I'm going through. I can't relate to them. I can't relate to *you*. You with your perfect body you don't feel like an outsider in. With your big cuddly bearded boyfriend who loves you and wants you to move in with him."

David sets his bottles down a bit too hard on the counter. "Are you jealous?"

"No! Yes. Not jealous that you're with Ivan. I don't have feelings for him or anything. But..." But David doesn't technically live here, and it still seems like he has more of a right to than I do. "When you move in, are you even going to wonder who picked out that glass?" I fling an arm toward the kitchen windows. "Do you even care?"

He abruptly turns away and walks back into the sitting room. I blow out a breath and scrub my cheeks. Great. All I'm doing is estranging myself from these people even more and sounding like a lunatic on top of it.

David comes back with Ivan, who shifts on his feet and awkwardly clutches his elbow with his porcelain hand. After a moment, he points at the kitchen windows. "One of my old housemates picked out the glass, the one we referred to as 'the Librarian.' It wasn't her first choice. If I recall, she originally wanted deep purple ones. But her husband protested that it wasn't practical. You wouldn't be able to see through it. When she asked him what difference that made, he blurted out that he needed to see if Christian missionaries were coming to the door... so that he had time to hide from them."

I let out a surprised laugh despite myself.

"What's going on?" Ivan asks. "Did you have an argument with Dusty this evening?"

"No. It was fine. But—" I stop myself before telling him all my thoughts. Before I tell him about Metatron's love sickness and my botched plan to get an email address that doesn't exist. If I do, he'll do the Ivan-thing where he lectures me, then fusses and hovers. Instead, I say, "But she bought me some neckties and a set of towels. Said we didn't have enough. Why is she thinking about *me* when she's out looking at towels with her boyfriend?" I shake my head and glance at David. "I'm sorry for being weird. I'm just dwelling on a lot of stuff right now."

Ivan says, "Maybe you should go to more meetings—" I groan, but he continues. "Or get private counseling. Do you think that would help?"

It might get out some of my frustrations, but it's not going to fix my aching gut. "No. I really don't."

I wait for him to insist I try anyway, that he's going to call therapists and make me an appointment whether I want it or not, but unbelievably, he says, "Okay. Well... We're going to watch another movie if you want to join us."

David gives me a friendly smile. It's not strained like I'm a guy who fucked up his marriage and had to live somewhere he doesn't belong. It's welcoming.

"I'm not going to interrupt you guys sucking the popcorn husks out of each other's teeth?" I ask.

Ivan wrinkles his nose. "That's gross. And no."

"Alright." I follow them into the sitting room. "So what's up next? Hot prisoner subdued by hot guard? Hot teacher schooling hot student?"

"We are *not* watching porn."

David toys with his dangly cross earring. "You'd prefer hot assistant reprimanded by hot boss, huh?"

"'Kay, changed my mind." I turn to leave, but Ivan pushes me onto the cushioned bench.

He sits next to me and laces his fingers over his belly. "Never thought there'd be a time Sasha couldn't take some teasing. You did have a bad day, huh?"

"Sort of having a bad second life... Actually, no, it was bad before that too."

I think he's going to bring up counseling again, but he glances at David, who's scrolling through gay romcoms, then leans close to me. "I won't let him eat your petit fours."

For some reason that reassurance is comforting, and the nausea in my stomach even seems to lessen a bit. I pull the popcorn bowl into my lap and settle back against the warm bench, wondering if giving desserts to an annoying but hot coworker is something that happens in David's romcoms.

I bought the guy petit fours to repay him for getting me lunch and *maybe* because I feel kind of sorry for how lonely he is. That's all. End of story. There's nothing else to say.

10

The Resurrected

The rubberband on the box of petit fours peels off with a snap, and I set it on the counter. The sticky note on top is in a different spot than it was before the weekend. I glare at the empty kitchen, then open the box. All eight of the little cakes are still there. I'm not that surprised, given the promise Ivan made me. The guy is as lawful good as they come. If it were me, I'd eat two of the cakes, then replace them with something revolting, like cherry tomatoes.

The magenta and brown shells on the cakes have collected a bit of condensation, but still look fancy as hell. Maybe *too* fancy. Maybe *too* gay romcom. It's not too late to stuff all the petit fours in my mouth and dump the box in the trash. But before I can, someone clears their throat. I startle, nearly dropping the box. David stands behind me with an empty tea mug. His hair is gathered into a sloppy bun, and he's eschewed his normal gothic ensemble for spandex jogging pants and neon tennis shoes.

"You're not chickening out, are you?" he asks.

"Chickening out of what?"

"You've only been staring at that box for two minutes."

I nudge it away. "And you've been staring at *me* that whole time? That's creepy. Shouldn't you be out making everyone look bad with your early morning run?"

He rolls his eyes. "Shouldn't you be giving your hot, mysterious boss the desserts you got for him?"

"He's not my boss, and he's not mysterious."

"But you didn't deny that he's hot."

"That doesn't matter when he has an awful personality." As soon as I say it, I wish I could take it back, thinking of Mr. C's defensive tone and wounded look when I said similarly on Friday.

David points to the petit fours. "I opened the box."

"Of course you did."

"But I didn't touch them. They look perfect. You, though..." He gives me an analytical onceover, lips pursed. "Don't you own a suit jacket or something?"

I head to work feeling overdressed in a mint green checkered sport coat layered over my lavender button-up, and as I push my sneakers into a cubby in the Renascenz lobby, I'm certain I'm sweating more than the petit fours. I slow near the front desk. People move beyond the glass walls of Marketing & Design, and damn my housemates for making a big deal of me giving something to Mr. C because now it *does* feel like a big deal, and the nausea in my gut doesn't help.

I'm so intent on the view into Design that I slam right into someone standing at the front desk. They're a mountain of a person with parchment-pale skin, Indigenous features, and long white hair worn in a tight braid. They steady me, watery blue eyes blinking from behind coke bottle glasses.

"Uh, sorry." I open the squashed box of petit fours and check that everything is still intact. "Nobody wants cake smashed on them at nine in the morning... or ever."

The person's voice comes out far softer than I think capable for someone of such an intimidating size. "It's fine. I'm easy to miss."

I chuckle. Owl stands from behind her desk and gestures to the person. "This is my husband, Travis. Trav. He/him. Trav, this is Sasha, he/him."

My hand is swallowed in his as we shake. "Nice to meet you." I turn to Owl, clutching the petit fours. "Your brother around?"

She glances at Trav with what is most definitely a *I'm going to pretend I'm fine, but you're going to get it when we get home* look. To me she says, "I'm not sure where he went. But I'll send him your way if I see him."

"Thanks." I'm not sure if Owl's look has anything to do with Mr. C, but I check the bathrooms and the employee lounge before heading to my desk on the off chance he decided he needed a break from his brother-in-law just as soon as he got here.

I say good morning to Arthur, who compliments me on my sport coat, then gives me a rundown of things to focus on for the day. I bet he leaves his phone in his desk. There would be plenty of opportunities for me to sneak into his office and sideload the Renascenz app onto my own phone. The balloon bouquet is gone, but I could still pull one of the bigger plants over just enough to block the camera's view.

It won't be today. I did indeed stock up on Tums, and right now my guilt at the idea of taking his phone is heavier than Metatron's love sickness, but if I can't think of a better alternative, desperation is going to win out.

Sorry, Arthur.

He pauses mid-sentence, expressive hands frozen. "Sasha? Are you listening?"

Shit. "Uh, I'm not that great with verbal instructions, to be honest."

Arthur gives me a patient smile. "I remembered you saying that at the interview. Which is why I made you a bulleted list of the tasks as well. Thought I'd tell you in person, but maybe I should just email it to you, and you can let me know if you have any questions."

"Thank you. I really appreciate that." This guy is too nice, and guilt pulls harder at my insides. I consider just telling him *why* I need to talk to Metatron, but I think about the look he gave me on my first day, about the looks so many of the resurrected gave me when I asked them at the meeting if they were having the same problem I was. I don't need Arthur thinking I'm obsessed with Metatron and making up excuses to talk to them.

The little box of petit fours looks sad and squished beside my keyboard as I check emails and update Arthur's schedule. I should probably put them in the fridge in the lounge, but I thought Mr. C would find me by now. The guy shows up whenever I don't want him to—it figures now that I'm looking for him, he's not here.

I forward him Metatron's inspiration pictures for the mascot and mention that we can talk about it in person, but I stop checking for a response after about an hour.

When noon rolls around and he still hasn't found me, I know something's wrong. I wander through the office and poke my head into the lounge. There are plenty of people at the tables—no cake today—and the bookkeeper snoozing on the couch, but he's not here. No one is at Owl's desk either, just her galaxy of knick knacks. Hesitantly, I pull open the door to Marketing & Design. A long glossy table scattered in papers and crowded with chairs stretches across the room. Sketches, finished advertisements, and overstuffed cabinets cover the opposite wall. Something moves in my peripheral vision. Mr. C sits at the end of the conference table, drawing on a tablet and rubbing his forehead.

The edge of the petit four box digs into my fingers. I walk into the room and pull out a chair. "Hey."

He barely glances up before turning back to his tablet, then does a double take. "Oh. Hi."

"It's lunchtime."

"Can't. Kevin's pitch for the new logo design was a disaster, so Arthur said to scrap the whole thing and start with something completely different."

"Guess his bionic penis doesn't help with marketing, huh?" It's not the greatest joke, but I expect at least a smile—he gives them so freely.

His expression doesn't change as he continues to draw. Instead of a bow tie today, a silky peach ascot is tucked into the open throat of his button-up, and his floral sweater looks both soft and a little too tight across his biceps.

He turns to me with an exasperated expression, and oh god, why was I staring at him? "Did you need something?" he asks.

"Uh, no. I just wanted to give you this. Sorry the box got a little smashed. They're okay, though." I slide the petit fours across the table.

Mr. C sets down his stylus. Questions dance across his face, but he takes the box. He opens it, and I'm still not earned one of his broad smiles. "Thank you, Sasha. These are very nice. What's in them?"

"Sedatives. I pushed the pills up through the bottoms so you can't tell."

He huffs through his nose, then shakes his finger at me. "That's funny. I mean what flavor are they?"

"Oh. I don't know."

"I'll have to let you know later after I try them." He closes the box and pushes it to one side, then picks up his stylus and gets back to work.

I shove my curls back from my forehead, unable to get my bearings with his current mood. I haven't known him long enough to be certain of what dispositions are normal for him. Maybe he's always like this when he's busy. It doesn't matter anyway. I don't even like the guy. "Right... I guess I'll leave you to it. See you later."

I push up from the chair, take two steps, then turn around. "I— I just got those for you because I don't think it's right that people have been such heartless asshats about you losing your husband and what happened after." I imagine a full pot of coffee bouncing off the conference table, dark liquid spraying everything in sight like a caffeinated Catherine wheel. "If they want to dislike you, they can be annoyed that you chew gum with your mouth open, or that you never shut up, or that you're pushy, or that you go by an initial and an honorific when nobody else here does, not even Arthur, which makes it seem like—"

He sniffles and wipes his eye with the heel of his hand. His voice is thin and watery. "My name is Corvin. It means 'raven.'"

I freeze. What is wrong with me? Now *I'm* the asshat because I've made the guy cry. "I'm sorry. I shouldn't have said any of that."

He rips a tissue from a box on the table and dabs at his eyes.

"It was mean, and you look like you're having a bad day already." I spread my arms. "You should take a jab at me in return. C'mon."

Mr. C—*Corvin*—wads the tissue in his fist, giving me a long once over. "You look very nice today. I like that jacket."

If I had a shovel, I'd dig straight through the carpet and floorboards and bury myself. "Fine, I'll do it for you. I use the washing machine like a hamper. I stop paying attention to someone's story after twenty seconds. I once ate an old French fry off the floor mat of someone's car."

"That's disgusting."

"Yeah. And I avoid talking about my feelings and hide behind a bunch of bullshit instead... according to my housemates and my ex."

He smiles faintly, his eyes glossy. "Well, we have something in common."

"I'm sorry for making you upset."

"I was already upset." He pulls another tissue from the box then blows his nose.

"Well, I didn't mean to make things worse." And I need to stop talking because the longer I'm here, the more likely I'll say something else I regret. "I'm going to go take my lunch break. I'll be in the lounge." On Friday, that would have been enough for him to invite himself to my table, but today I'm not so sure. "You can come sit with me if you want. And fuck anyone who looks at you like you're some kind of freak."

His Adam's apple bobs, and he dabs at his eyes with his tissue. "Sasha?"

"Yeah."

For a moment he simply stares at me, lips parted, then shakes his head and gives me a half-hearted wave.

I sit in the lounge, poking at leftovers and forcing myself to eat despite my stomach, because if I get too skinny, Ivan is going to notice and probably send me to a dietician. After twenty minutes of sitting alone, someone drops into the chair beside me. I look up.

Arthur crosses his legs and steeples his fingers, looking at me over the top of his orange frames. "Will you answer me a question? Honestly, please. Did you apply for your position for the sole purpose of talking to Metatron?"

My heart hammers against my ribs, and I'm certain I'm going to sink straight through the grass and into the center of the Earth. The only person I confessed that to—the *only* person, not even Ivan—was Mr. C. A sharp sting of betrayal cuts through me, but I guess I deserve it after making him cry.

There's no sense in lying about what Arthur apparently already knows. I set down my fork and push my lunch away. If I wasn't hungry before, I'm definitely not now. "Y-yes. But I do like working here regardless."

His mouth pulls into a flat line. "I'm sorry that it's come to this, Sasha, but..."

There's no need for the dramatic pause. I'm obviously getting fired. Damn it. This has to be a new record. The helium in my balloon bouquet lasted longer than I did, and now Jack will get to deliver an *I told you so.*

Arthur shakes his head and huffs. "I just never considered that Metatron might need a friend that badly. I know I haven't been the most present source of communication for them here. Metatron visits with so many souls a day that it doesn't seem like they'd get lonely, but those are people they're tasked with taking care of, hm? They clearly have needs of their own that aren't being met and can't be dumped upon the dead in Limbo."

I open my mouth, but I'm too stunned to say anything. I don't even know what *to* say.

"You should have just told me why you wanted to talk to them." He stands, then claps a hand on my shoulder. "I've sent you an email with a link to the Renascenz app. Through it, you'll be able to communicate with Metatron. I expect you to continue working for *me* at the same time, though."

I'm still frozen in place, all the words evaporated out of my throat. *Say yes!* "Yes. Yes, of course. Thank you."

He nods and heads out of the lounge. Holy shit. Just like that. I pump my fist, and the action hurts my stomach, but I won't have to put up with that for much longer. The risk had seemed too great to simply tell Arthur the truth. I grab my lunch bag and hurry down the hall so quickly that I nearly slam into Mr. C as he rounds the corner. I grip his biceps to stop myself, the soft yarn of his sweater bunching between my fingers, firm muscle underneath. I take a step back. "Hey. Arthur just talked to me. How did you know he would say yes to me having the app?"

He shrugs, gum snapping between his teeth. "I told you he's a softie. And I might have played on his emotions a bit. But I didn't tell him Metatron is in love with Rodrigo, and I didn't mention your nausea. That might land you in a doctor's office with them running experimental tests on you or something. If you have to resort to that, it should be your choice. Hopefully your way works, though."

"Thank you. You have no idea how much this is going to help me." I'm arrested by the urge to give him a hug, but I cross my arms instead.

Red still rims Mr. C's eyelids, and a tissue pokes out of his pocket. "You know, your complaints about me are completely invalid. Wouldn't you rather me chew gum with my mouth open than have terrible breath?"

"You don't have to defend yourself. I was out of line."

"No, no. I'm going to explain. I'm not pushy. I like things just so to eliminate anxiety, which sometimes means fixing other people's problems too if they seem like they're a bit of a mess."

"So you're aggressively neurotic. And I'm a mess?"

He keeps talking, clearly on a roll, and I wonder how long I'll have to stand here until his point is made. I need to get that app loaded onto my phone right away. With any luck I'll be helping my guardian angel with their romance game within the hour.

"And as for you complaining that I never shut up," Mr. C continues, "if you stop listening to me after twenty seconds then it doesn't matter how long I talk for, does it? You're not going to hear me anyway."

He's not wrong; I just missed half of whatever it was he said. "If you think that makes us soulmates, you are sorely mistaken. Besides, I know how to get you to stop talking. I just give you food."

He stares at the space between his bare feet and fiddles with his wedding ring. "Does that mean you're buying lunch tomorrow?"

"Who do you think I am, the wellness assistant?" I walk past him and gently nudge his shoulder. "Eleven tomorrow in the lounge, yeah?"

11

The Seraph

"It l-looks like amethyst, right?" Gale deposits a garish gold ring with a purple gem into my palm. "Been in my— in my mother's family for generations. She thought it was a-amethyst and twenty-two karat gold 'cause that's, uh, that's what her great aunt said. But— but there's no karat stamp, and the gem's got little scratches on it. She took it to be assessed, and guess what? It's paste, just-just like I thought."

<Yikes.> I hand the ring back to him. <At least it has sentimental value, huh?>

"Oh, no. Mom told me to throw it away. But I didn't. I put it in my collection." He chuckles, his staticky face intent on me. "You knew I was— I was gonna say that, huh?"

<After seeing you every day for six months? Nah.>

I'm never sure if I can get away with sarcasm with Gale. Like Rodrigo, he often takes what I say at face value. But this time, he laughs and does something that might be a shrug.

<Was that the only item that fit the parameters I created?>

"I have lots of things that are— that are— are purple and didn't come from an estate sale or eBay, many I got more than t-ten years ago, but they all have plastic components. I had a purple glass vase that would have fit, but— but it got smashed when everything f-fell on top of me. I remember that. Remember it smashing."

<Darn. I'd still count that, though. It doesn't have to be smashed here.>

"Okay!" A vase shaped like a swan appears in what passes as his hands.

A paper airplane suddenly sails into the room, doing a little loop-the-loop, and comes to rest at my feet. I stare at it in confusion, wondering where it could have possibly come from; only Gale and I can generate things in his room. Hesitantly, I pick it up and realize it's the airplane I launched into Rodrigo's room on Friday. Tight block lettering—not my handwriting— covers the right wing. Oh my. My heart does the same loop-the-loop as the plane as I unfold the paper, smoothing it over my knee.

"W-what's that?" Gale asks.

<Um, I sent this plane to one of the other souls, and it appears he's sending me a message back.>

Gale gingerly sets down his vase as though if it falls and breaks again, he can't generate a new one. "I hope my mom is doing okay without me. Wish I could send *her* a message." He keeps talking, something about their housemates playing too much bingo at the senior center, but I barely hear him. I absently pat some part of his white noise body and reassure him that there's a ninety-two percent chance the lawsuit will wrap up soon and he'll get to see his mother.

I focus on Rodrigo's compact handwriting:

Dear Metatron,

My biggest flaw in life was misinterpreting others. It seems that in death that has not changed. After some deep contemplation, I've decided that it would be best if you don't visit me anymore. I will be fine with my books and music until the lawsuit is resolved.

Thank you for all of your conversation, your humor, and your kindness.

    – Rodrigo

An unnerving screeching noise fills the air, and I realize it's coming from me. The paper crumples in my trembling hands, and big soggy tears fall from my eyes, splattering across the handwriting until it becomes nothing but a black streak.

What did I do?

What did I do?

WHAT DID I DO?

LUCIFER 'IN A LIMOUSINE,

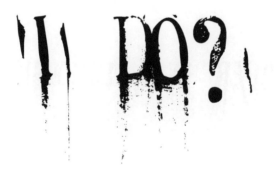

I tear at my wings and bunches of feathers come loose in my hands. He said he misinterpreted something. What was there to misinterpret? Gale is saying something to me, but all I can do is play through every conversation I've ever had with Rodrigo in the hopes I can understand what would make him do this. I gave him gentle reassurance whenever I made a joke. I listened intently to everything he said. I would never do anything to hurt him.

It's true that Friday was different—I upended his routine, I talked about my own problems, and he showed me his human face. But he let me in. He insisted I tell him my problems. He asked if I wanted to see the real him. Was I wrong in saying yes? Or maybe *my* expression and reaction were misplaced, the way he said his always were in life.

I have to fix this, but I have a duty to Gale. Turning to him, I say, <I'm sorry for my behavior. I've... got a personal problem. But that shouldn't be intruding on my visit with you.>

"It's— It's okay. Things can't be perfect a-all the time, huh? You should have seen my mom when she found out that purple ring was— when she found out it was glass and gold-plating. She had to lay down f-for two hours. Do you, uh, want to lay down?"

It's not going to help, but I stretch out flat on the floor, amorphous mountains of objects looming over me.

"While you're resting, d'you think I could look at eBay for a bit?" Gale asks. "Haven't been on there in— in months. I bet there's *so* many neat things."

Oh. Sure. Take advantage of your guardian angel while they're distracted and distraught.

At my command, an outdated PC appears beside us on a desk crowded with collectible glassware, novelty pens, porcelain figurines, and snow globes. Gale gasps, then pulls out the office chair and plops in front of the monitor.

<You won't be able to bid,> I say.

"I could create stacks of money, but it doesn't do me any good here, huh? No F-First National Bank of Limbo." He laughs.

<You make jokes? You've been holding out on me.>

"Even if I *could* bid, where would they mail the items, besides?"

<No P.O. boxes in Limbo either.> But there's no reason I can't send Rodrigo a message in response to his. He might not want to see me, but a letter would at least let me apologize. For what, I'm not sure, but I'll beg forgiveness regardless.

Dearest Rodrigo,

If this is about revealing your human face to me, if you believe that you've somehow conveyed the wrong emotions with your expressions, I promise you haven't. But if it makes you more comfortable to return to using an emoji, that's completely fine. I don't want you to ever be uncomfortable around me.

My purpose is to be here for you and for all of the souls. I realize we're all strained from *resurrections being suspended, but*

I have to give him something real, to say something that's at least close to what I feel for him.

my visits with you are the highlight of my day. I cherish every moment. And I would be devastated if there were no more conversations about the gas giants. If there were no more plans to eat the moon. If I couldn't sit beside you on the grass and admire your socks.

I know so much about him: how one of the faux leather shank buttons on his tweed jacket is loose because he fidgets with it so much; how the pauses in his voice are often longer than his sentences, and he says just as much in those ellipses as he does with his words. But it's not enough. I don't know what kind of tea it is that sits beside him in the study. I don't know what other socks he has.

I don't know why he was five minutes late to work on the day he died.

If I've done something to hurt you, I am incredibly sorry. Let me know what I've done wrong so that I can apologize properly and correct it. Please.
Yours celestially,
M

I sit up, and the letter—enclosed inside a baby blue envelope with a gold wax seal—appears in my hands. Beside me, I conjure a gilded mailbox with filigree flourishes, which is simultaneously in this room and Rodrigo's. Through the open door on the other side of the box, I can see the bookcases in his study. My heart aches at the thought of never stepping foot in there again. But I can't imagine any transgression I'd accidentally committed being completely unforgivable.

There's already movement beyond the other side of the mailbox as I'm gently setting the envelope inside. Rodrigo's hand—his lovely hand I've never worked up the courage to touch—reaches inside and pulls out the envelope. I sink against the box's post, press my wings to the wrought iron, and shut my eyes, imagining him reading each word of my letter.

After forty-nine seconds, Rodrigo's voice drifts from the mailbox. It's thick with the pain of a fresh wound. "You don't have any reason to apologize. You haven't done anything wrong. But you can't help being who you are, just as I can't help being who I am."

I pull myself up and look through the mailbox, met with a view of Rodrigo's fuchsia tie. <I don't understand what that means. What happened? I'm the same angel you met on the day you arrived; who I am hasn't changed. And I like who you are. I— I *adore* who you are.>

He lets out a small choking noise, his voice a harsh whisper. "But I misunderstood." The mailbox door slams shut.

<I don't understand.> I punch my fist through the

mailbox, knocking the door back open. <I don't understand!>

His voice drifts, soft and distant. "Please get this mailbox out of my study. I want to be alone."

Damn it! I slam my elbow into the mailbox and the top caves in. Another whack sends it askew on the post. Yanking it from the floor, I hurl it across the room, where it hits a mushy mountain of Gale's collectibles, then winks out of existence. Only then do I realize what I've done. That mailbox just sailed across Rodrigo's study and probably slammed into his shelves of precious books. It might have knocked over his tea. It might have hit him.

I sob and dig my fingers into my feathers. Sending my voice into his room, I say, <I'm so sorry. I didn't mean that. I'm sorry. I'll leave you alone.>

Obeying physics might be for chumps, but so is being reckless with the rules you choose to break. The urge wells within me to send him more apologies. More letters. Paper airplanes. Cakes. Every book ever written, with alligator-print covers and gilt titles and deckle edging. Infinite bookshelves to hold them. Baker's lamps with emerald green glass shades that cast soft light over the pages. Velvet ribbon bookmarks. Tufted wingback chairs with nailhead accents. Zebra patterned ottomans with turned wooden legs. Keith Haring paintings. Basquiat. Warhol. The moon, cheese or otherwise. Venus and Mars and tiny rejected Pluto. The sun. *All* the suns. I'll give him a sugar bowl of galaxies to stir into his tea. I'll stand in front of him, carve out my heart, and present it on a charcuterie board surrounded by peridot grapes and seeded crackers.

But I can't. He doesn't want it. He doesn't want *me*. There is a black hole at the center of my universe, draining all my stardust into the immense gravity of his rejection.

There's two minutes left in my appointment with Gale. He's muttering about how a Lego bonsai tree set has zero bids and only forty-five seconds left. I stop beside him, and when I say his name, he visibly startles—which is quite a feat when his body is nothing but TV snow.

The chair squeaks beneath him. "Oh... I-I forgot where I was for a moment. Thought I was, uh, that I was back home." He slumps down, his hand falling from the mouse.

<Afraid not... Do you want that Lego set? Make a bid.>

"You said I couldn't."

<It's not the real eBay. I just pulled some pages from the site and stuck them in the PC. And I know you had a bit of a bidding addiction in real life, and I shouldn't be fueling that, but—>

But I'm a chump. And if I can't give my adoration to Rodrigo, I have to replace it with something, even if it's by heaping a bit of illicit happiness on the other dead. Wouldn't be the first time I've done it.

Gale taps at the keyboard, then sits back, uncertainty radiating off him. When the auction timer hits zero, the page refreshes, congratulating him on his winning bid.

The Lego set in question appears on the desk beside him with a fanfare of party horn noises and a burst of confetti. He gasps and picks up the box, inspecting the taped down flaps and dented corners.

<Since you don't have a money constraint like you would in life, I'm giving you a time limit instead.> I pat the computer monitor. <I'll give you until my next arrival to bid on whatever you want, and if you win, the items will appear here and remain for twenty-four hours. You can, of course, generate them again with your own imagination if you'd like.>

It's going to put a bit of a strain on the Renascenz program, but it'll hold up better than I'm going to over the next twenty-four hours, I'm certain.

"Oh, that's— that's amazing!" Gale says. "Thanks. But what if something I want still has six days left b-before the auction ends?"

<It won't. I've changed all the times. I have to go now. Toodles.>

He's already turning back for the computer as I leave the room. Campbell is next. I hadn't planned on visiting him today, but I don't have the will to fight against the program's pull into his room.

A dark parking lot stretches into infinity, my shoes scraping against wet asphalt. Tall arc sodium lights on industrial concrete bases march between the parking spaces and cast a jaundiced, painterly glow on overturned shopping carts and the few lone cars. Their windshields are speckled with rain... except for the sedan closest to me, which is smeared with blood. There are two perfect windshield wiper arcs cutting through the crimson, as though the driver hit a deer but couldn't be bothered to stop on their way to pick up their groceries.

I nudge a flattened drink can out of my path and half-heartedly scan the area for Campbell. He's somewhere nearby, maybe in one of the cars. Knowing him, maybe *under* one of the cars. But I can't muster the urge to care.

I pull open the back door of the bloody car, climb inside, and lay down on the seat, which is more of a suggestion than the real deal. Velvet cushions sprout beneath me, and I add a squishy bolster for something to hug. Tears squeeze from my eyes, soaking the pillow.

It doesn't matter what reassurances Rodrigo has given me; I have to have done something wrong. And it must have been between Friday when I sailed that paper airplane into his room and yesterday, during my Sunday evening appointment.

Gripping the bolster tight, I rewind the seconds, starting backward at—

The car door rips open, and Campbell's voice vibrates with barely contained rage, full of all his spines and none of the softness. "You left me alone for days, you 32-bit DOS program!"

And now I'll be leaving Rodrigo alone, and oh god, what if the lawsuit verdict is imminent and I never talk to him again? He'll go on to his second life and the only thing he'll remember about me is how I hurled a dented mailbox across his study. I sob harder, every particle of my consciousness vibrating with the urge to correct this situation somehow. But I'm shackled by his wishes to stay away, and I can't force him to like me again.

Campbell pulls at my ankles. One of my gold oxfords comes off in his hand and he loses his balance, falling onto his backside. He's clothed today, his jeans now smeared in wet grime from the asphalt. Tossing the shoe away, he props himself up on his elbows and says, "Are you malfunctioning? What's the matter with you?"

What indeed? What did I do? I press my eyes to the bolster, wondering if I had mustered the courage to take Rodrigo's hand while we stargazed if things between us would be different right now, or just hurt even more.

"Hey." He slaps my socked foot. "I'm talking to you. Hey! I'll chop off your feet!"

Even if I could feel physical pain, I imagine I would be numb to anything he does to me right now. The ache in my heart is too great to notice anything else.

Something hits the ground—my other shoe, my foot, it doesn't matter. Nothing matters anymore.

"I'm going to hack you into little pieces, stick all your pathetic parts into a shopping bag, and take you to the customer service counter for a refund," he says.

<That's highly convoluted. And you'll need more than one bag. I estimate eight if the bags are following basic physics. Better get a shopping cart.> Rain pats softly against the roof of the car, my wings rustling as I let the velvet cushions absorb my tears.

Campbell slides my shoe back on. The laces pull tight. Something presses against my other ankle, then falls to the ground. With a grunt, he says, "How do I put your foot back on?"

<Just leave it.>

The distinct sound of duct tape peeling from the roll saws the air. The tape winds around my ankle, again and again. "Now get up," he snarls. "You're here for me. Get up and pay attention to me!"

He's never this direct with his threats or desires, normally glossing them up in a manipulative veneer of concern and innocent commentary. At least we're done playing games.

I climb out of the car on a stiff, taped ankle. My foot is crooked, making me pigeon-toed, and the caps of my shoes are scuffed and smeared with dirt. I reset my avatar, then stare pointedly at Campbell. <Okay. I'm paying attention to you.>

He leans closer, and I imagine he'd be squinting if he had eyes. "Why are you so upset today?"

<The fact that you're vicious to me isn't enough reason?>

"I've never seen you cry and hug pillows before." His voice lilts with amusement. "Did someone die?"

My hope died. My dreams. Never seeing Rodrigo again is inevitable, but I didn't want it to happen this soon or with this misunderstanding between us. I was hoping to delay the pain of his absence as long as possible.

It was a mistake to come here, no matter how much energy I have to exert to resist. <Just this once, it would be nice if you

left me alone.>

"Left you alone?" Campbell's voice stabs at me, cactus spines digging in. "You left *me* alone for days. And now you're mopey and sad and want to sleep in a—" He stands rigid, raindrops pattering against his tee shirt and arms. "You know what? Tell me the truth, and I'll leave you alone for the rest of my appointment."

<Which truth? I don't tell black lies; nothing I say to anyone is for my own personal gain. But I'm telling a handful of gray lies and have lost count of the white ones. And if lies by *omission* count, well—>

He sputters. "Then tell me everything."

I sigh and drop the velvet bolster on the ground. Some secrets I keep as close to my chest as possible until I'm forced to share them—and Campbell can't force me—but there's no harm in letting some little ones spill if it gets me some peace. <Shall I start from the beginning? I mentioned that when the Renascenz program first started up, I had a different avatar. A human with feminine features and long hair. A soul named Walter wanted to see my vagina—he was very insistent—so after he asked for the tenth time, I gave in and showed him. Told him to get a real close look. Then I gave it teeth and made it bite off his head... He didn't ask again.>

Campbell regards me for a long moment, his gaping wound of a face glistening in the arc sodium lights. He barks a loud laugh, which echoes across the parking lot.

I slide down against the car, leaning against the tire.

<You're right that I break the rules for the others. I've smuggled illicit information to many of the souls here—news articles, classifieds, their loved ones' social media pages, updates on the lawsuit, eBay listings... All they have to do is ask, and I give in. I lie to the COO about it. Tell him I'd never do such a thing because it's against my programming.>

He folds his arms and takes a step toward me. "Do you intend to keep me here even after the lawsuit is resolved?"

I hesitate. My efforts to get someone at Renascenz to care about Campbell's behavior is going nowhere. I'm going to have to come up with some kind of failsafe on my own, but I'm unsure yet what that would look like. <I want to, but I can't. And that's the truth. No matter whether there's a plan in place for you when you leave or not, I can't just hold you in Limbo forever.>

"I don't see why there needs to be a 'plan' for me. Car accidents happen all the time."

Not ones where the drivers purposely run red lights in order to murder their passengers. And if Rodrigo hadn't driven through the intersection of Cherry and Grand five minutes later than normal that day, he wouldn't have been T-boned by Campbell's car. Even if there was evidence that Rodrigo died because of—at best—Campbell's recklessness, not to mention what happened to Campbell's husband who was riding shotgun, it's easy to see him slipping through the cracks once he's alive again.

<Maybe I should go talk to your husband and ask *him* if it

was an accident,> I say. Try as I might, I can't convince him to make an official statement of what Campbell did.

Campbell's hands open and close spasmodically, then a hacksaw appears in his grip. "You said I'd need eight shopping bags to fit all the pieces of you?"

<Approximately. Depends on the size of the bags.>

He strides away, heading for a shopping cart sitting beside a light post. Stopping suddenly, he whirls around and hurries back. "Can I see a picture of him? I know he doesn't want to talk to me, but I miss him sometimes. Please."

He never asks about his husband. But the poor soul deserves an apology from Campbell just as much, if not more so, than Rodrigo. Maybe a photo will open up a bit of dialogue. Under no circumstances do I intend on taking Campbell to his room for a "block of alone time together," though.

A polaroid appears in my hand. I stand and shake it until the picture develops. He takes it from me, and his voice is hushed as he traces the lines of the photo. "He changed his hair. And he's thinner. Makes him look unhealthy."

<I have to be honest; your face looks pretty unhealthy too. Possibly infected.>

He ignores me, still clutching the photo. "Do you lie to *him* about things?"

Rain patters against my wings, plopping softly onto my suit jacket. <Yeah. I told him you were sorry.>

12

The Resurrected

A sweat-damp pillow sticks to the back of my neck, the sheets twisted around me. I think I must have fallen asleep, though I have no idea how much time has passed. Whispers drift from the hall.

"I still think we should take him to the hospital," Ivan says.

A new voice, grainy and sweet, says, "He was very adamant that he didn't want to go."

My heart lurches, and I can smell her perfume on me even now, beyond the stench of my sweat and stale breath. I should have called Ivan instead of my ex-wife, but in the moment Metatron's broken heart hit me, I was certain I was dying, and Ivan already dealt with that once.

"I don't understand." Ivan's voice has the same frustrated anxiety it always carries when he's talking about me. "Why wouldn't he want to go to the hospital? What if he has appendicitis?"

"Maybe it's food poisoning," Dusty says.

"This is silly. I'm going to call an ambulance."

"No!" I groan and clutch my stomach, rolling over in bed.

There's a puke bowl on the floor, but I haven't used it yet. It might make me feel better, but I'm afraid I might throw up nothing but feathers and glitter, and how would I explain *that*?

Poor Metatron. I don't know what happened exactly—I think I would have known if they'd confessed their feelings to Rodrigo—but the sense that he rejected them is coming through loud and clear. I hadn't expected that. Not when so many of the resurrected are in love with our guardian angel. But maybe I'm not the only one without the desire to look them up on a Rule 34 site. This doesn't deter my determination to be a good wingman, though. Maybe I can still fix this.

Dusty hurries into the room, light from the hall picking up the red in her shorn hair. She crouches next to the bed and takes my hand, thick eyebrows furrowed. "Are you feeling any better? Do you want some water?"

"My phone," I gasp. "I just— I just need my phone."

Ivan's bulk fills the doorway. "You need a doctor."

"It won't help." I point to my jeans on the floor. "My pocket. Need my phone." The Renascenz app was still downloading at work when the nausea slammed into me like a powdered sugar wrecking ball.

I think Dusty's going to question my request, but she picks up my jeans and rummages through the pockets. She sets my wallet on the end table, then my keys, then turns my antacids over in her hand. "Has this been an ongoing thing?"

Wiping at sweat on my brow, I say, "Ever since I was resurrected."

Alarm fills her face, and she looks back at Ivan. He shakes his head and says he didn't know. Of course he didn't.

Dusty turns back to me, her mouth a crooked line. She gently brushes curls back from my damp forehead, seemingly unconcerned with how gross and sweaty I currently am. She's seen me much worse than this, but we were married then. And her nails through my hair almost makes me believe we're married still, that the span of time between our divorce and now was only a dream brought on by a fever. And now that it's broken, I'm going to get better and go back to my life. Back to my wife, my daughter, Jack, and the house we built together.

"Why do you do this?" she whispers. "Ivan cares about you. And refusing to let him in isn't going to help you move on."

I don't want to move on. Metatron tried to help me do that in Limbo, and while I was there with them it seemed easier to accept. We talked about the things I was grateful for: that Dusty and I are still friends even after everything; that I still get to see Poppy every week; that I've been clean for ten months without getting a single neural enhancement pin—not even a legal one, aside from my ADHD meds—inserted in my arm; that I have Ivan and David as my housemates now, my found family. And I *am* grateful for them. I like them. But real life is full of reminders of what my life used to be and what I no longer have due to my own fuck ups.

Dusty scrolls up on her phone. "Um, have you had any dizzy spells along with the stomach issues? Very cold hands or feet? Drowsiness or confusion?"

"No." I take my jeans and fish through the pockets.

"Have you had blood in your stool or your vomit? Do you have a hernia?"

"No." Where the hell is my phone? Maybe it fell out on the floor. I push up with some difficulty, trying to see beyond the quilt.

"Is there pain in your testicles?"

"God, Dusty. No."

"Well shit, I'm just—"

"I don't have appendicitis, kidney stones, or IBS. I know what this is. I just need— Where is my damn phone?" I toss my jeans on the floor and swing my legs over the bed, but she pushes me back against the pillows and gives me her no-bullshit glare. Whether we're exes or not, that glare pins me down the same as it always has.

"C'mon," she says. "Tell us what's going on before Ivan worries all the hairs out of his chin."

Ivan stops tugging on his beard and sighs. "We just want to help, but we don't know how if you won't tell us what's wrong."

Telling Mr. C was one thing. That was an exchange of information. But telling Dusty and Ivan means letting them share the burden of my problems. I've been a burden enough as it is.

It's clear, though, that they aren't going to leave this room or help me find my phone until I explain. So I tell them all of it—the nausea and indigestion brought on by Metatron's love sickness; the snippets of their thoughts for Rodrigo; how at least one other resurrected is experiencing the same thing, but in their teeth. I even confess that I only applied for the Renascenz job so I could contact Metatron.

"Then you *really* need to go to a hospital," Dusty exclaims. "Get your pants on. We need to go to the Renascenz doctors, the ones who take care of people right after they're resurrected. Except... they won't be there, huh? There haven't been resurrections in six months. But it's likely that they're still working in medical positions somewhere in the city. Either temporary or second jobs while the lawsuit is ongoing. We could look them up."

Ivan's voice is so quiet that I can't hear him beyond Dusty, but he mouths the word "no." He grips his beard and says it louder. "No!"

I've never heard him raise his voice, and I would have bet my life savings on him being the first one to suggest—again— that I go to a hospital. He advocates for all of that: doctors, support groups, therapy, church, training courses. He doesn't ever go it alone or take shots in the dark on something he's not sure about, convinced there's no reason to do that when help is readily available everywhere you look.

"No." He looks at me, a deep furrow in his brow. "We'll do this your way."

Dusty protests, but Ivan says, "We can't take him to the Renascenz doctors, or he'll end up just like David."

A heavy dread settles in my gut along with my nausea. I prop myself on my elbows. "What does that mean?"

His big form shrinks, and he worries at his beard again. "David died the first time in the skiing accident. He hit a tree. It caused a mini avalanche. I lost my arm. David went into Limbo, and I was in the hospital for a bit. When he was resurrected and transferred to the Renascenz outpatient center, he kept telling the nurses something was wrong. His body seemed fine, healthy. But at times he was certain he was still in Limbo. He'd try to create things with his mind, or he'd drop things expecting them to float." His nostrils flare, and he pushes his glasses up the bridge of his nose. "He didn't think he could feel pain or get injured. I guess the resurrected often experience this for a day or two, but it's supposed to wear off. The doctors told David that the transfer of his consciousness from the Limbo servers to his new obol had corrupted, but not to worry because they could fix it. They just needed to send him back to Limbo and start over."

The weight of what he's saying hangs in the silence, our gazes on him. I unstick the lump from my throat and say, "The doctors killed him to fix the problem?" That could be me. That could be me. *That could be me.*

Ivan chews his lip and nods. "David agreed to it, but he wasn't in the right mind to make that decision. He thought he was *already* in Limbo half the time. No one should have let him consent to that before his family got the chance to talk it over with him. I don't want the same thing to happen to you."

I absolutely don't want that either. I want this problem corrected, and Metatron's despair is so thick I can taste it in the back of my throat. Half of me wishes I *was* in Limbo right now just so I can give them a hard hug. But the thought of dying again, of spending weeks away from Poppy, tears my heart in two.

"Aside from the trauma of another death, that's so wasteful," Dusty says. "If the obol isn't accessible in the bodies grown in stasis, that's a horrible design flaw."

"All I know is sending David back to Limbo a second time just made it that much harder for him to exist in the living world again, even though his body and obol are fine this time around. He goes to every support meeting, but it only helps so much." Ivan walks to the bed and sits on the end, his elbows on his knees. "Sasha... If you talk to Metatron through this app, do you think David could use it to talk to them too? Even if it's just once so he can see Metatron say they care about him and that everything is going to be alright? I think that would go a long way toward making him feel better."

David seems so put together and self-assured all the time. I guess if I paid better attention, especially at the meetings, I would know that he's struggling. He practically lives in the same house with me. My stomach feels so heavy it threatens to pull me straight through the bed. I am a shit housemate. "Yeah. Of course. As long as someone can help me find my phone."

Ivan and Dusty start pulling open drawers and looking under the bed, and I'm not sure if they're spurred to action for me or for David, but I don't care as long as they find it. Dusty turns out the pockets of her jeans and pushes through the graphic novels stacked on the bedside table.

"Are you sure it was in your pants?" she asks.

"No. That's where it usually is, but I was downloading the app when my stomach started acting up." I try to play back the moment and pick out the details, but it's impossible. I was too hung up on the fact that my solution was in reach to notice anything else. "Maybe I left it on my desk in the office. You didn't grab it?"

"I thought I did. Thought I grabbed it and gave it to you when we were on the trolley."

"You gave me my keys and the case for my interface lenses."

Ivan pushes himself up and smooths the wrinkled quilt. "I don't think it's here."

"Damn it!" I tug at my hair. It's just like me to get exactly what I want and then carelessly throw it away. "I hope it's not on the trolley. At this point, Eddie owns more of my things than I do."

The doorbell chimes, and Ivan and Dusty look at each other.

"David?" Dusty asks.

"He's coming over, but he just lets himself in." Ivan disappears from the room. I flop back in the pillows and clutch my stomach. If the phone is on the trolley or on my desk, I can get it tomorrow if it's still there, but I'm not sure how I'm going to survive the night.

Metatron's thoughts beam into my brain like a spotty emergency broadcast signal: *He said he was uncomfortable when I cut my fingers into slices. I creeped him out. No, that can't be it... He'll never forgive me for throwing that mailbox...*

I tried pushing my own thoughts at them, even though I'd done that before and never received any indication that it worked. *Metatron, this is Sasha. I know your heart aches right now, but maybe we can fix this together.*

Ivan's voice drifts, taking on a gleeful lilt that's normally reserved for when he's wiping the floor with me—me *specifically*—during game night. I can't hear who's at the door, and I don't see anything to be amused about right now, especially after that bomb he dropped about David. Unless it's someone with my phone?

He strides back into the room with a grin, his voice hushed. "Is your Mr. C a tall multiracial guy with cheekbones so sharp someone could lose a finger by touching them?"

My breath catches. Mr. C is at the door? No no no. Not with Ivan and my ex-wife in the room and how disgusting I currently am. I'm not even wearing pants.

I fling back the covers and push out of bed, gripping the bedside table. "Tell him to go away."

"But—"

I push past Dusty and Ivan and hurry into the bathroom, then start the shower. Water drums against the mosaic tile lining the tub, and early evening light refracts through the bottles studding the wall. I shed my clothes and climb inside, doubled over from my aching stomach, and some ancient memory surfaces of doing this very thing after getting a Woozy Face pin inserted. Getting combos of otherwise legal enhancement pins inserted is most people's high of choice. You have to be a hardcore junkie to go straight for Woozy Face, which says a lot about where I was at back then.

I'd hoped a cold stream of water would sober me up, but instead I'd only puked in the tub, tried to clean it up, and spilled bleach all over the floor. I ended up digging the Woozy Face pin out of my arm with a pair of eyebrow tweezers, then flushing it down the toilet.

The worst part was Dusty didn't even bring it up the next day—and it wasn't because I did a good job at hiding the massacre in the bathroom. She was too tired to keep getting angry. She'd given up. On me. On us.

I straighten with some difficulty and scrub the conditioner out of my hair, then shut off the water. I towel off and spend far too long fussing with my hair, because Dusty calls through the door, asking me if I'm okay.

That depends on whether Mr. C is still here or not. Hopefully he had my phone and dropped it off. Then had some other engagement and declined the invitation to come inside—which Ivan most definitely extended.

I push open the door, gripping my towel, and nearly run into Dusty. She follows me into my room as though I'm not totally undressed.

"Should we invite Ivan in here too?" I ask. She doesn't

seem to get the hint, so I say, "As flattered as I am by the audience, I'm going to have to ask you to leave while I get dressed."

"I'm just not sure you can do it correctly."

I scowl. "I'll have you know I never forget to wear underwear, and I can put my shoes on the right feet. *And* tie the laces. Out, please."

She pulls a short sleeve button-up patterned in pizza slices out of the closet and wrinkles her nose. "But what is this? Horrible. You aren't going to impress your office crush with this."

Mr. C is still here. Shit. I almost ask her if she's pushing me toward him, but I'd rather not have that conversation right now. "You're just going to stand there, huh? Up to you." I pull open my sock drawer and drop my towel.

"Okay, I get it. I'm leaving." Poking her head back in, she says, "Thought you didn't change anything about your body."

"Impressed?"

She scoffs and shuts the door.

She's impressed.

I shrug on the pizza button-up just to annoy her, pop three antacids, and leave the room. Mr. C, Ivan, and David stand at the kitchen island, dipping vegetables into a well of ranch dressing. Oh great, they gave him food. Now he'll never leave.

Mr. C locks eyes with me, a celery stick halfway to his mouth. A glob of dressing falls off and hits the counter. He looks like he isn't sure where to put the celery, then stuffs it in his mouth and wipes his hands on a kitchen towel. Stopping before me, he covers his mouth with his hand and tries to speak through his celery. It comes out: "*Howeroo?*"

"Terrible. Did you stop by to bring me my phone or just to eat all the food out of our fridge?"

Dusty smacks my arm. Mr. C makes an *mm-hm* noise, then points to my phone, sitting on the kitchen counter beside Ivan.

I unlock it and sag in relief as I spot the blue and pink Renascenz infinity icon. I have no illusions that this will be as easy as telling Metatron to go fix things, but the app downloaded successfully, and I'm so close now. "Thank you for bringing this. I really appreciate it. You've helped me twice today."

There's a tiny glob of dressing on his sweater. He follows my gaze, then wets a napkin with water and blots away the ranch. "I was, uh, going to bring you flowers. You know, as a 'get well' thing. But then I figured I'd spend way too long at the florist trying to decide what was best, and flowers aren't going to make you feel better. Then I thought about getting a card, but same deal. Tea might help, though. My mom has a blend that she used to brew up for me and Owl when we were kids and had stomach aches. Except I can't remember what kind it is, and when I called her, she didn't answer. She never does anymore. I used to be Mom's favorite until Owl started giving her grandkids. Hard to compete with that. No chance of that happening anytime soon with me." He chuckles nervously, then pulls in a breath as though prepared to keep going. His mouth clamps shut as he glances at my housemates, who are doing a horrible job at pretending they're interested in the veggie tray on the counter. "Well... I should let you get to messaging Metatron. Do you think you'll be at work tomorrow?"

He was going to get me flowers? My stomach flutters, pulse jittering in my neck. I think about his firm biceps beneath his soft sweater. Damn it. Metatron's feelings must be so strong that they're confusing me. I dig out another antacid. "Um, what was the question?"

His gaze roams my face, a slight smirk curling the edge of his lip. "Did you stop listening to me after twenty seconds?"

"No, I—"

"I see that glazed look in your eyes. It's fine. I'm blathering, and you're not feeling well. I just wanted to know if you'd be at work tomorrow."

"I don't know. I hope so." I follow him to the entryway and see him out.

After I shut the door, Dusty stops beside me and hisses, "What's wrong with you?"

"Pretty sure I explained all of it earlier."

"Did you leave all your flirting skills in Limbo or what? That was pathetic."

"Metatron said I couldn't come back with good looks *and* charm. One or the other."

"Then you got ripped off."

Before I can respond, she pushes me toward the door. "Go

after him."

"He's just a coworker."

"And that's why you spent twenty minutes fixing your hair for him?"

"It was not even close to twenty minutes. And you really think flirting with him right now, while *you're* here, is the best time?"

Her mouth pinches, and she glances back at my housemates. "Look, I'm not in love with you anymore, but if I didn't care about you, I would have let you lay on the floor of your office, tortured by stomach pains. I want you to be happy."

"What about Mr. C's happiness? Maybe you should be warning him to stay away from me." Although I already told him about eating a French fry off a floor mat, and it didn't seem to deter him.

Dusty sighs, her face softening. "If you really want me to drop it, I—"

"Good. I'm going back to bed and messaging Metatron."

I slip past her, but someone knocks at the door. I groan, then turn around as Ivan answers. Mr. C is still standing on the step. He smiles and waves.

To keep anyone from prying further, I step outside with him and close the door behind me. "Hey."

He shakes his phone. "My mom called me back, and I got the name of that tea."

"Oh, great. Can you give me your number so you can text

it to me?"

His eyebrow arches. "As opposed to me just telling you right now?"

"I'll forget what it's called in five seconds if you don't text it. I make Arthur write everything down for me too."

He nods slowly as though rolling over my reasoning in his mind, then opens his phone and hands it to me. "If you say so. Put your number in."

I'm about to give him my number. It's for a perfectly practical reason, but that doesn't slow the throbbing of my heart. Dusty is right—if I just thought of him as a random coworker, especially one I disliked, I wouldn't have bothered taking a shower or even getting out of bed. Let him see me when I look like shit. Who cares? But I do care. And he does too, otherwise he wouldn't have been thinking about getting me flowers or come all this way to deliver my phone.

I imagine Metatron standing over my shoulder, their chipper tenor crystal clear: *If you were the man you used to be— not the puking-in-the-tub man, but the good parts, the genuine parts that Dusty fell in love with—would you be keeping Mr. C at arm's length? Or your housemates for that matter? They want you to fit in with them. Maybe you didn't leave Limbo with your synthetic confidence, but I bet there's some au naturel in there. You should see if you can find it.*

They're nice words, but for as many faux-Metatron bites of encouragement I can create, I can come up with twice as many rebuttals. How do I even know if Dusty fell in love with the genuine parts of me? How would she be able to tell when I had so many pins in my arms? *I* don't even know what was genuine about me.

And Mr. C still wears his wedding ring. It's clear he's not ready to move on.

I pull a deep breath through my nose, then punch in my name and number. It's for practicality's sake. He's not going to take it any other way.

He brightens as I hand it back. "'Sasha' is a diminutive of Alexander, isn't it?"

"Yeah. My family is Anglo European, mostly German, Russian, and English. It's a common nickname over there."

"I have some Anglo too. Dad's white, Black, and Cherokee. Mom's Costa Rican. There's nothing traditional about my name, though." He shrugs. "Mom just likes birds."

"Well, it could be worse. Your mom could be obsessed with naked mole rats instead... Do you want me to keep calling you Mr. C? Or is that only a work name?"

His gaze circuits my face, travels down to my chest, then flicks back up. "I suppose that depends on how often I'd be seeing you outside of work."

I imagine the butterflies that arise from that comment have immediately drowned in all the stomach acid churning inside me. "I'm still not going golfing with you... Corvin."

His grin overtakes his face. "You're the one who keeps bringing it up, not me. But right now I guess I should let you get on with messaging Metatron, huh?"

I ease onto the step and thump my head back against the wall, then start laughing. It rings out across the yard, echoing back from the houses across the street. It hurts my stomach, but I can't stop. Corvin looks mildly alarmed and sits down next to me. "You know"—I choke down my laughter and wipe my eyes; none of this is funny—"I really can't get anything to go my way."

"I don't understand. You've got your phone, you've got the app. What's wrong?"

"I just realized that I have no idea what to say to Metatron. How am *I* of all people going to instill them with romantic confidence? No matter what I say, it's going to sound hollow and hypocritical. A case of all students, no teachers."

"That can't be true. The woman in there with the buzzcut is your ex-wife, right? I overheard your housemates. So you clearly have more experience than Metatron does. Unless your ex completely took the lead in wooing you."

I snort. "No, I was obnoxiously flirty and suave when we met. But I had help... The kind of help that has an emoji name and is inserted in your arm." As soon as I say it, I regret it. Telling him about eating French fries off of floor mats is one thing, but he's going to look at me like a junkie, and it won't matter that I'm clean now. I've tarnished who I am forever, even in a new body with a new life.

"Oh." His lips purse and he drums his fingers against the step. "And you don't have that particular pin anymore then."

If he's judging me, he's hiding it well. "I only have one pin.

If you don't believe me—" I roll up my sleeve, then take Corvin's hand and hold it against my arm. He doesn't resist. Instead, his slender fingers slide across my bicep, then press against the hard pin beneath.

"What is it?" he whispers.

"Methylphenidate. For ADHD."

He sighs deeply, then sags against the wall. "Thank god."

Oh, there's the judgment. I deserve it, and there's no reason for it to sting like it does. "I've been clean for—"

"I thought you were going to tell me it was Tears of Joy Face, and I was going to be so disappointed that your wit was synthetic."

I raise my eyebrows, heat throbbing in my cheeks. "Nah, that's all me, baby."

"Well, *I* am painfully attractive, have a perfect smile, am incredibly stylish, and people of many genders throw themselves at me every week. That's not even mentioning my sparkling personality."

"Stop. You don't have to be modest with me." Not only does he think I'm funny, my past substance abuse is such a complete non-issue for him that he's barreled right past it to talk about himself like it was any other conversation.

"And while it's true that I don't really have any work friends after the coffee *incident*, and my confidence has taken a hit, that doesn't stop me from faking it. Because at the end of the day, I'm still painfully attractive and charming, right?"

The question is probably rhetorical, but I look away,

tugging at a hangnail. "Obviously. Told you that in the first hour of meeting you. Well, the attractive part. But your personality made me want to strangle you with your bow tie."

"I'm glad we've gotten past that." He offers me a stick of gum, then unwraps a piece of his own and pops it in his mouth. "And if I were you, with your genuine humor and your genuine kindness, and that striking profile that I undoubtedly believe artists *would* fall over themselves to sculpt, I'd have far more confidence in myself."

Now I'm certain my face is blazing. Chickens mill in the yard across the street, stirring up gnats. The bugs ignite like sparks in the glow of the sun.

"Besides, you're still on good terms with your ex, right?" he asks. "More than I can say about my husband."

"What was his name?"

"Mr. C."

"What?"

"It was an inside joke. His name is Campbell, and when we were just married, we received a wedding gift from his aunt that was addressed to 'The Mr. Cs.' We thought that was quite funny and started to address each other that way. 'How was your day, Mr. C?' 'It was fine. How was yours, Mr. C?' That sort of thing. So when I started at Renascenz and there was already a guy there named Corvin, I decided to go by Mr. C."

He looks so weighed down by this memory that he might assimilate into the steps. "Do you visit his grave?" I ask, then wave my hands. "I'm sorry. My mouth runs without me sometimes. I just wondered because you still wear your wedding ring, and you told me you were married. The image of you at a grave doesn't jive with— with pretending everything is okay. But you don't look like you want to keep talking about it."

"I don't." Sitting up abruptly, he claps his hands together and says, "Let's see about messaging Metatron, hm? You don't think you know what to say, but I can help. Between the two of us, we can come up with something that sounds genuine and confident."

That was the least smooth topic shift ever, but I'm not going to judge him for it. "So you'll be contributing ninety-eight percent of that? Okay, I got you covered for the other two percent." I hand him the phone. "In fact, why don't you do the typing. I'll be in charge of hitting send."

His eyes widen, and he pushes the phone back at me. "No, no. I'm not going to talk to them. This is *your* thing. *Your* problem you're trying to solve. Don't tell them I'm here."

"You work for the company. You don't even want to say hi?"

"No! Do *not* tell them I'm here." He sits back and tucks his hands in his lap. "Please."

I'm not sure I want to drop... whatever it is that caused his reaction, but the ache in my stomach drives me to nod and open the phone. I stare at the little pink and blue Renascenz logo, then tap the icon.

13

The Resurrected

∞ Hey, Metatron! This is Sasha Roborovskiy. Do you remember me? I'm Arthur's assistant at Renascenz now. I don't know how or why it happened, but I can still sense you outside of Limbo, and I know what you're going through right now. You think about Rodrigo so much that I almost feel like I know him too. You love him too much to just give up and be content mourning what you could have had.

I tilt the phone toward Corvin. "Yeah?"

"Good so far. Send it."

I hit enter, and the message pops up on a pastel pink background punctuated by stylized clouds. After a moment of staring with my stomach twisted into a cinnamon-sugar pretzel, I realize the clouds are moving, revealing a crescent moon as they drift past. "Renascenz is really into the celestial theme, huh?"

"It's kind of cliché, I suppose. I've always hated their shitty infinity loop logo." He wrinkles his nose. "It looks like a drunken figure eight. Or a butt. I'm glad we're working on a mascot design with Metatron's likeness as inspiration. That's far more memorable. And much better than the obol they tried to use in a couple of advertisements. Not the obol here"—he taps the back of his neck—"but an actual obol from ancient Greece; it was a copper coin with a lumpy-looking bee in the center. No one knew what the hell it was or what it was referencing. The only thing memorable about it is it somehow morphed into a joke that people enrolled in the program had a coin slot in the back of their heads. *Insert twenty-five cents to start a new life.*"

I snort. Thank God for his stream of conversation. It's taking the edge off my nerves, even if it isn't stopping me from glancing back at the chat screen on the phone every two seconds. "Do you have an obol? Are you enrolled in the program?" I'm not going to assume that everyone who works at the company is. It could just be another job to them, not something they want to participate in.

"Yeah. Though I'm undecided if that's a blessing or a curse."

"I wonder that myself sometimes..." I want to ask him why he's enrolled but his husband wasn't. If his death was what spurred him to enroll later. But it's clear he doesn't want to talk about him, and I'm not—

The phone vibrates, and my heart leaps. Below my message is a response:

♿ SASHA HELP

"Wow." I guess the hurdle where I convince them to let me help is already cleared. Corvin scoots closer, and his thigh touches mine as he peers at the screen. Thankfully, I can't dwell on that for long because another message appears:

ଋ I'm sorry. That was incredibly impolite. Let me try again.
Salutations, Sasha! ::::::) Of course I remember you. How are you? How's your daughter? I hope your second life is treating you well aside from the whole my-emotions-are-making-you-sick part. PLEASE HELP ME.

Corvin chews his gum enthusiastically, and I vaguely wonder if it's to thank for his perfect jawline. He says, "Hitting Metatron with some confidence will be easy. While they aren't going to be everyone's cup of tea, they're gorgeous in their own way. People say I have pretty eyes? I've got nothing on Metatron. And what a snappy dresser. Though to be honest I'm not sure if their voice fits their look because—"

"How do you know what their voice sounds like?"

He stares at me, gum forgotten. "Well, I... overheard Arthur talking to them, of course. Through the app. You can make calls on it too. And it was— it was on speaker." He clears his throat and tugs hard on the cuffs of his sweater, something I've come to associate with anxiety. "Though I suggest sticking to text right now while we formulate exactly what it is you're going to say."

He's lying. Has he talked to Metatron before? How would that be possible, and for what reason?

The phone vibrates.

☾ Sasha, are you there? Please don't go.
∞ Sorry. I'm here. I think the first thing I need to know is what happened with Rodrigo to make you so upset. He rejected you somehow, even though you didn't tell him your feelings.

"Oh, good thinking," Corvin says, peering at the screen. The cheer is back in his face, but one of his sweater cuffs is still twisted in his hand. "See? You didn't need my help with this."

"No, I did. I do. Especially if Metatron needs reassurance about their looks. Some of the resurrected are very, um, enthusiastic about Metatron's attractiveness, but I've never felt like that toward them. Headless computer programs aren't my type." I glance back at Metatron's next message.

☾ I don't know what happened! He sent me a letter saying he doesn't want me to visit him ever again. And even though he insists I didn't do anything wrong, I must have.
I've really needed to talk to someone about this. On a forum a few days ago, there were resurrected talking about how they could sense my feelings. I was slightly outraged at having my secrets discussed, so I denied it. I said I was incapable of romantic love. That it wasn't

in my programming. But right now I'm so grateful you

I frown at the unfinished sentence. Metatron's alarm blares through my mind, no longer a faint broadcast signal but a tornado siren.

SAINT IN A SUBMARINE
I KNOW WHAT I DID
OH GOD

Rodrigo said he misinterpreted something. He said he misunderstood. He must have seen my message in that forum. He knew I loved him! This whole time, he knew! And then he read that message where I said I didn't. That I couldn't. Oh nooooo.

Nausea slams into my stomach. I gasp, then lean over the side of the step and vomit. It isn't feathers and glitter. There's nothing sparkly or sickeningly sweet about it. This is Metatron's anguish, compacted down to a hard cramp that weakens my joints and makes sweat break out on my brow. I heave again, gripping the step for leverage. A hand gently squeezes my shoulder, and I don't want Corvin to see me like this, but I'm glad he's here all the same because he can help.

I wave the phone in his direction and gasp. "Text them some reassurance. Tell them it's going to be okay. That— that we can help. I can't take any more of this."

"I can't do that. I can't talk to Metatron."

"Corvin, please."

"No."

Groaning, I roll onto my back on the step and wipe sweat from my eyes. I rest the phone on my heaving chest as I look up at him. "Did you steal Arthur's phone once to talk to Metatron? Why won't you talk to them again?"

He stiffens. "I've never talked to Metatron through the app."

"Why are you lying? It's obvious you've talked to them before. I don't know why you needed to, but if you didn't have a good conversation, that doesn't matter right now. They don't have to know it's—"

"Drop it!" His voice echoes back from across the street, and harsh evening shadows fall across his face, the whites of his eyes flashing. "Drop it. I mean it."

The front door swings open and Ivan says, "What's going on?"

"Nothing," Corvin snaps. "I was just leaving."

"Hey, wait." I push myself to a sitting position, but he's already striding across the yard.

Ivan scoops an arm under me and helps me up. "Good grief, you look awful. You need to lay down."

"I *was* laying down."

"In bed, not on the front step."

"Corvin—" I can't get out the rest of the sentence because my stomach heaves again, and I puke over the side of the step.

"Oh god." Ivan nearly drops me. "I'm gonna be sick."

"Go back inside." I pant, my hands on my knees.

"Actually, will you *please* pick up my phone and text Metatron? Give them some reassurance that everything will be okay. Corvin wouldn't do it."

I don't need to ask him twice. He scoops up the phone and hurries back through the door. I'm not sure how long I stay bent over, but eventually the cramp in my stomach dissipates enough for me to stand up, round the side of the house, and pull the hose back to the step. By the time I'm done spraying down the entire front walk, I barely have any nausea at all.

My mind reels with Corvin's outburst, but there aren't enough pieces for me to fit them together into a picture. At the moment, I have a bigger issue to address, but I'm glad I have Corvin's number now so I can text him and smooth over... well, whatever that was.

After patting my pockets and searching around the step, I remember that I gave my phone to Ivan. I head back inside. Ivan sits on the bench in front of the television, my phone in his hands. Dusty and David are huddled next to him, staring at the screen. He types something, and David laughs.

"Hey." I drop onto the bench beside Dusty. "How's it going?"

She cups the sides of my face and tilts my head from side to side like I'm a flickering lightbulb that just needs a little twist. "Are you feeling better?"

"Yeah. I hardly feel nauseous at all right now. Metatron is in a better mood now too, I suspect?"

"Oh yeah. Ivan calmed them down right away. He's really

good at this."

Ivan shrugs and smiles. "It wasn't much." He passes me the phone and I scroll back up through the messages.

∞ Hello, Metatron? My name is Ivan. I'm Sasha's housemate and David Yoshioka's boyfriend. I can't tell you how grateful I am that you took such good care of both of them while they were in Limbo. They miss you and love you, and by extension, so do I. I'm sure this situation feels devastating right now, but I'm here to support you and so is Sasha. Together, we can find a solution.
First, would you mind telling me about Rodrigo?

I look up at Ivan. He *is* good at this. And I can't count how many times he's tried to say similar things to me. *I'm here to support you. Just tell me what's wrong so we can find a solution together.* And I always brushed him off or said something sarcastic in return because that was easier than being vulnerable and talking about my fuckups out loud. But how much better would I have felt, and much sooner, if I'd actually taken him up on his offers? How much better would I feel if I stopped keeping everyone at arm's-length? If I listened at the meetings for the resurrected? Talked to David about our mutual struggles?

"You're a good guy. And I've been an awful housemate since I moved in." I lean in and give Ivan a squeeze. He momentarily stiffens, then crushes me in a bear hug.

"Sorry I've been such an asshole," I say.

His voice is muffled against my shirt, and I'm certain he's going to break me in half with his prosthetic arm. "You're not an asshole. I just wish you'd accept help sometimes."

"Alright. I'll only kick and scream a little bit from now on."

Ivan hugs me for so long I have to wrestle away from him, and when I step back, his smile is wide and joyful. Dusty and David look pleased too, and this moment is getting way too mushy and could possibly result in me being talked into going to group pottery classes or a quilting bee if I don't make a hasty retreat.

Turning my attention back to the phone, I scroll through the messages. Unlike me, Metatron has no hesitation in telling Ivan about their problems. There are long paragraphs of their feelings, how they can't stand the idea of never seeing Rodrigo again, and requests for help. No doubt Ivan completely ate this up.

The most recent message from Metatron says:

ඟ This brings me back to my original problem - even if I tell him how I feel, even if he believes me, and even if he feels the same way, he'll still be resurrected, and I'll never see him again. I lose no matter what. And I knew that was inevitable, but

How do you keep love from hurting?

I didn't know how to answer that question before. But I think about Dusty pushing hair away from my sweaty forehead; think about Poppy asleep against her big stuffed robot on the trolley; about Ivan's prosthetic arm and Corvin's wedding ring. And I think I have an answer now.

There's a little telephone icon at the bottom of the chat window, and I click it. Metatron answers on the second ring, their tenor voice just as bright as I remember, albeit a little more strained. <Hello! I'm glad you called because it seems more efficient than typing. Not for me, but for you.>

Nostalgia floods me, and I'm back in Limbo, Metatron's sparkly gold oxford bobbing as they listen empathetically to all my woes. Their wings brush my shoulder, and they look so real down to each iridescent quill, but at the same time my mind keeps trying to tell me it's a dream. I reel my thoughts back in and say, "Hey. It's Sasha. It's good to hear your voice. Fair warning, if I start making a mess of this conversation, I'm passing you back over to Ivan."

<I have faith in you.>

I head out of the sitting room, and my mates must realize I don't want an audience, because they don't try to tug me back onto the couch. I was serious about trying to share more things in my life with them, to stop pushing them away when they want to help whether I feel like I deserve that help or not. But right now, if I'm going to get real with Metatron the way they did with me in Limbo, I want to be alone.

"Hang on just a moment, okay?" I head up the stairs, passing Ivan's bedroom. Climbing the ladder at the end of the hall, I push open the hatch and haul myself up onto the roof.

Grass tickles my palms, the thick leaves of irises scratching across my arms. I scoot back into the plants and look up at the deepening sky. Pinhole stars wink overhead, threadbare clouds and satellites sliding across them. Beyond the trees and tops of houses, lights glow from the carnival, tinting the darkness pink and orange. Skyscrapers cut geometric silhouettes further on, and I can just make out the needle point of the Renascenz building.

"I'm just going to say it—you can't stop love from hurting."

Metatron makes a noise like they've been kicked in the stomach. <I see.>

"Love... Love doesn't exist in a vacuum. Whether we like it or not, things change. People change. They grow. The world—even Limbo—keeps moving, and to be unable to let go of something you once had is only asking for suffering. But it doesn't mean that love isn't worth it in the first place. It can be wonderful. And in my humble, mortal opinion, it's worth the risk of pain."

<But this isn't just a risk. It's a guarantee. Once the lawsuit is settled, Rodrigo is going to leave.>

I almost ask them how they're so sure Renascenz is going to win; what if Rodrigo's fate is to be deleted instead? But that's a cruel question, even if Metatron doesn't believe it. That nagging uncertainty about the outcome of the lawsuit can be pushed aside for now. And no matter which way the verdict falls, Metatron loses Rodrigo.

If I knew before marrying Dusty that we'd eventually divorce, would I have still proposed? I only debate it for a moment. Of course I would have. "I still think about the good times I had with my ex-wife. I love our daughter more than anything. It hurts, but sometimes you can't separate the pain from the joy. It's just part of it, and you cherish those memories anyway. If you know you're going to lose Rodrigo, I guess the question is: do you want to try for something wonderful before he goes? It'll probably make it hurt more in the end, but you'll have had that time. Those memories. That might be better than never telling him, then regretting it for eternity." Having it hurt more in the end means it's probably going to hurt *me* more as well, but Metatron deserves their happiness where they can get it. And I want to be here for them when they eventually need to talk to someone again.

Metatron lets out a soft sigh, and I imagine them sitting with their halo in their hands, wings drooping and eyes downcast. I pull up a long blade of grass and twist it between my fingers. "Hey, long distance relationships are a thing too, you know. I'm not above illegally loading the Renascenz app onto his phone so he can call you."

<There are several reasons that wouldn't work. For one, he can't handle phone calls.>

Damn. "Text then. Or love letters sent to each other. Does he like writing? Books?"

Their voice is so quiet I can barely hear it. <Books, yes. He reads so many. Often a new one every day. Not a lot else to do

in Limbo, as you know.>

"I thought there was plenty to do. You can make anything your imagination wants."

<Rodrigo only generates two different environments in his room. It's his study seventy-two percent of the time, which he's told me is an exact replica of his own at home. He's autistic and comforted by routine and familiarity. He doesn't like the crowds on trolleys or in grocery stores. Enjoys focusing on his special interests.>

"Limbo seems like a dream place for a person like that." I lay back in the plants and stare at the sky. A gauzy cloud floats by; it covers up the handle of the Big Dipper but reveals different stars in its wake. "Being able to keep your room exactly the way you want down to the last speck of dust. Not having to go off to some job you hate or wait for someone in the cereal aisle to move their cart so you can get what you want. I bet he misses his family, like I did, but I was never actually lonely because I had you."

<Limbo isn't a replacement for a human life. It's not sustainable. And I'm not a substitute for family. I want him to find someone who treats him the way he deserves.>

"Why can't that be you right now? The resurrected love you. They miss you. *I* miss you. Not going to slide into any channels discussing your 'cosmic void,' but—"

<Oh dear, you saw that too, did you?>

"Unfortunately. But hey, as long as you don't have any nudes floating around the internet, I wouldn't worry about it."

My traitorous mind tries to conjure up what that would even look like, and I immediately regret it.

<Definitely no chance of that... Do you still think about Dusty? The way you did when you were in Limbo?>

"God, I used to be wrapped up in every detail of her, the way you are with Rodrigo." The light weaving across her eyelashes and pooling in her honey eyes. The soft rise of her chest as she slept beside me in bed. Her rusty laugh, and how she'd repaired her favorite coffee mug after it broke instead of getting a new one because she liked the handle.

I rub my face and blow out a breath. "Those memories I have... they're still mine and no one can take them away. Still there when I need them. But I've accepted that we're never getting back together." And I realize that recently I haven't been needing those memories quite as much.

Maybe Metatron can sense my feelings the same way I can sense theirs, either that or they can't help their nature of talking things through with people, because they say, <You sound more at peace. Does someone else occupy your thoughts now?>

It's my guardian angel I'm talking to, but I still don't want to say it out loud. "You're avoiding the subject of what to do about Rodrigo. I thought you wanted me to help you."

A frustrated noise crackles through the receiver. <I'm glad you've made peace with your divorce, but this situation isn't one that can end in a happily ever after. I've done the calculations, and it isn't possible.>

"So you're speeding up the process of being miserable by denying yourself *and* him the joy you want? C'mon."

<This is how I sound when I'm counseling the dead, isn't it? I don't like being on the other end of the conversation.>

I grin. "I told you Ivan is better at this kind of thing."

<No, no. I think I need Sasha-brand counseling right now.>

"You said Limbo isn't a replacement for a human life, but Rodrigo has made his time there into a temporary home, hasn't he? His study is exactly the way he remembers it?"

<It isn't real.>

"I'll bet the comfort it gives him is real. Just like the comfort *you* give him is real. And so what if it's temporary. Everything is temporary, no matter how much Renascenz likes their infinity loop logo. Isn't temporary joy better than none at all?"

The silence stretches, and I've made a mess of this. They're going to hang up, and I'll be stuck with this ache in my stomach forever. I can already feel it returning. But it isn't the hard cramp of anguish that made me puke over the front step. It's a sudden crest of sweet aching need, pulling like a licorice rope around my waist.

<Okay.> Metatron's voice trembles, almost giddy. <Okay. You're right. There have been so many times I've come close to taking his hand, to telling him how I feel. My hesitation always held me back, but if he feels the same about me that I do about him—and our argument leads me to believe he does—then there's nothing to hold me back now. I need to draft him a new letter, or— or show up in person. He doesn't want to see me, but now I know why he's upset. I can fix it.>

"Yes, good! Do you need help with that part?"

<Oh, no. *This* part, telling him my feelings, I've thought about in detail three hundred and thirty-five times. I can do it.>

"Alright. Well I wish you the best of luck, and I'll still have the app on my phone if you want to tell me what happens."

<Thank you, Sasha. Ivan told me David wants to talk to me. Please pass him the phone, will you?>

"Sure, but before I go..." I might end up talking to Metatron in Limbo, waiting for my *third* life if Corvin finds out what I'm about to ask, but I can't stop myself. "Have you ever talked to anyone else at Renascenz?"

<Aside from you, Arthur, and Jack? Lavaughn once. He worked for the company, and when his wife died, he begged Arthur to let him talk to her in Limbo. There were important documents in his house that he needed, but his wife was the only one who knew where they were. At least, that's what he told Arthur. Between you and me, I think he just terribly missed his wife and wanted to know she was okay. So I went along with it. I put him on speaker, so to speak, and let them talk for a whole hour. Arthur only gave permission to let Lavaughn text me his question and get a simple answer, but... eh.>

The spire of the Renascenz building glints in the dark, and I think of standing across the street as Corvin ate his cookie and told me about his deceased husband. He still wears his ring and says he's married. Realization strikes me like a brick. Campbell isn't permanently dead. He's simply been stuck in Limbo for months. I don't know why that didn't occur to me earlier. If it's true, Corvin has probably been aching to talk to Campbell the way this guy Lavaughn ached to talk to his dead wife.

Disappointment drops into my stomach, and I don't know why the hell I'm disappointed when I've been doing a damn good job at convincing myself that I don't like him. But I suddenly don't feel like pursuing this conversation anymore.

Crickets saw in the irises and faint music drifts from the carnival. I switch the phone to my other ear. "Hey, never mind all this. You've got people to do and things to see, yeah?"

An awkward chuckle comes through the receiver. <You transposed that phrase.>

"I know. Good luck. Text me if you need me. I'll hand David the phone in a few." I end the call and close out of the app.

This roof suddenly feels like the loneliest place in the world, all the housetops and skyscrapers tiny shards of black glass in an empty universe. It's tempting to complain about my stomach, crawl into bed, and shut out everything and everyone. But Ivan's startling laughter bursts from below. It's enough to motivate me off the roof and back down the ladder.

The zesty scent of garlic and oregano drifts down the hall, and I immediately know he's making his lentil Bolognese. I think back to his harsh whispers at the last resurrection meeting: *I'm not just here to support David, you know. And when I cook at home, I'm not just cooking for David.*

Dusty and David sit at the kitchen island as Ivan stirs tomato paste into a pan on the stove. A bottle of red wine that he reserves for cooking sits between them. I slide onto a stool and point to David's nearly empty wine glass. "Oh, I see how it is. I get my hand slapped if I try to drink that, you know. And Ivan's porcelain slaps hurt."

Ivan glances back at me with an exasperated laugh. "I've never done anything of the sort."

I open the Renascenz app and hand my phone to David. There's gratitude in his eyes as he accepts it. He tucks a lock of hair behind his ear, jostling his dangle earring, then starts typing.

Dusty slides off her stool, then squeezes my shoulder. "I need to get home. Are you feeling better? How'd it go with Metatron?"

"I'm much better now, and I convinced them to go bare their feelings."

"That's great! Keep me updated, okay?"

"Sure. Give Poppy my love."

She nods and heads out the front door. I pull her nearly empty wine glass over to me and take a sip.

Ivan snatches the bottle and splashes a bit of wine into his pan. His wooden spatula scrapes against the bottom of the pan, the sauce bubbling. Glancing over, he says, "If it went well, why don't you look happy?"

I run my nail along the foot of the wine glass, nothing but Corvin's gold wedding ring in my mind. How ironic that Metatron is finally going to fulfill their romantic dream, and my spark has been snuffed out before I even let myself accept that's what it was.

I hold my glass out to Ivan. "Top me off, and I'll talk. No sarcasm or bullshit."

He brightens, his round cheeks bunching. The bottle clinks against the glass as he pours. "You got it."

14

The Seraph

A new song throbs from Rodrigo's room. Bright, celestial synth tinkles over a funky bassline. It sounds vintage; not disco-nouveau but just *disco*. I don't know the band. I could easily look it up, but I've never had to before—Rodrigo always tells me about his new songs when I visit.

There was no visit today. But there's still time, as long as I can decide on the most perfect idea for baring my heart to him. Using a charcuterie tray is probably a bit much, as is showing up in nothing but fishnets and a garter belt. A paper airplane or another letter in a mailbox are out. It's likely he wouldn't even read them. I can't make pages tear from the books in his study to form words—if he wasn't already dead, that would do it. A message in his tea leaves is out because he never actually drinks from the cup. And I don't dare change his new song to something different.

A signpost sprouting from the rug? Rearranging the pattern on his chair? *I love you.* No. Too open to interpretation. *I'm in love with you.* No. He might not believe it after what he read in the forum. I have to cut right to the heart of the matter.

With a message secure in my mind, I peek into his room just enough to manipulate without it prompting my avatar to generate. I'm met not with his study, but his star-gazing hill, which I wasn't expecting to see back so soon. He sits on a blanket in the grass, ankles crossed in front of him, his human face turned toward the sky. The *sky*. A big twinkling celestial canvas with infinite room to create a message.

I pull down the stars, weaving them into letters. He shifts on the blanket and looks wildly around. I resist the urge to blurt out an apology for tampering with his room, focusing on the letters instead, until the rawest and most meaningful message I can give him blazes across the velvet sky:

I LIED

It's hard to see his expression in the dark from this distance, but I can worry about that after I'm finished.

I scrape more stars from the heavens, adding them to my candescent confession.

I'm mildly encouraged that Rodrigo's first response is not to demand that I get out of his room or stop being dramatic. Instead, his voice drifts from the hill, small and hesitant. "About what?"

My avatar generates as I step into the room and walk across the grass. When he spots me, his head suddenly becomes an apprehensive two-dimensional emoji. I stop; in my letter to him, I suggested he do this very thing if it made him more comfortable, but it wounds me all the same.

He stands and brushes off his slacks. His face shifts toward the sky, then back to me, and he tugs on a button on his jacket. I bridge our distance, stopping at the edge of the blanket.

<As I told one of the other souls recently, I'm lying about a few things, but in this case, I'm referring to a post I made in an internet forum for the resurrected. When I discovered people were discussing my most intimate secret in there, it made me feel naked, exposed without my consent. How dare they feel my ache for you. How dare they know my thoughts about your sturdy fingers, and your beautiful mind, and your argyle socks. How dare they be privy to my fantasies of showering you with everything you desire. How *dare* they wonder alongside me why you were five minutes late for work on the day you died.>

His emoji eyes widen in surprise, cheeks blazing neon pink. The jacket button he'd been fiddling with rips off his front and falls from his hand. It bounces off the cap of my shoe and rolls into the grass.

I keep going, because if I pause, I might lose the nerve to finish. <Those people didn't consent to this either, and I have it on good authority that being constantly bombarded with my feelings isn't very fun. I can't blame them for this situation. It isn't their fault, and it certainly is not the first time there's been a glitch in the Renascenz program. But my knee-jerk reaction upon reading those comments was to lie, to deny that I was in love. To deny that I was even *capable* of being in love. I— I didn't think you would ever see what I wrote.>

Without his oft-handled jacket button as the target of his stim, his hands open and close spasmodically at his sides. I'm not sure why he doesn't just create a new button, but perhaps he's too stunned to think about it. Blue cartoon sweat drops appear beside his head, then disappear. He says, "Just so there's no wiggle room for misunderstanding this time, will you please plainly tell me what you feel for me?"

I step onto the blanket, the edge of my shoes catching on the thick quilting. One of my wispy aigrettes brushes against his shoulder. <I am desperately in love with you.>

He makes a small noise, and his emoji suddenly disappears, replaced with his human head. His eyes are wide and glossy behind his glasses, his gaze roving across me but never directly locking onto mine. His throat flexes, thick brows pushed up. "My grandpa's brother had a big swimming pool in his backyard. It was flush with the ground and had mosaic tiling all the way around. It even had a diving board. We hardly ever went to his house when I was a kid because he and my grandpa had some kind of decade's long feud where they refused to visit each other."

I don't understand how a story about a swimming pool relates to my confession of love, but I adore Rodrigo's mind and trust there's a very good reason he's telling me this. I sit cross-legged on the blanket, my attention on him, and he sits facing me. Starlight pools in his eyes, his gaze growing distant as he focuses on some far-off place in time.

"For some reason, off and on for years I've had a recurring dream where I'm pushed into that pool and drown. On the morning of my death—my *actual* death—I had that dream again. It started the same way it always did; I'm seven years old, standing at the end of the pool in blue swim trunks patterned in little yellow triangles. And I'm watching light refract off the rippling water. The way it shifts and sparkles is mesmerizing. My brother comes up from behind and shoves me. I fall into the deep end and sink like a rock. I flail, trying to get back to the surface. It's— it's too far. I can see my brother's distorted face above the water, but he just stands there. Panic consumes me. It fills me the way the water is filling my lungs.

"But then, for the first time in my life, the dream changed. Someone was suddenly there with me in the water. They wrapped their arms around me, and even though they didn't say anything, I knew everything would be okay. And I don't mean they pulled me out and rescued me. I still drowned. But I stopped panicking; I was too comforted to be afraid."

His fingers twitch against his thigh, still needing something to fidget with. I compile all of Sasha and Ivan's encouragement into the forefront of my mind, then reach out and touch his hand. He immediately snatches my fingers and pulls my hand into his, squeezing tight. Cherub in a chariot! I try to keep my heart from going supernova as I focus on his story.

He says, "When I woke up, it was twenty minutes later than I normally got up. I rushed to get ready but was still five minutes late getting out the door. I was worried that someone was going to take my parking space. Thinking that I'd have to drive around to the back lot and walk across campus, which would make me even later. My students would wonder where I was... Two blocks from the university, I got hit by Campbell's car." His Adam's apple bobs, and his jaw tightens. A thin quaver winds through his voice. "I remember feeling something warm and wet and slippery in my lap, and I was terrified to look down because I knew what I was going to see. So instead, I looked out through the windshield. There were strips of broken safety glass still hanging from the molding, and light bent through it as it twisted in the breeze, turning it the blue-green of swimming pool water. I thought about that person in my dream again, suddenly there, comforting me as I drowned. And even though I knew I was dying for real this time, that same sense of calm came over me, wrapping me up like a blanket. It was going to be okay. I'd never been more sure of anything."

I lace my fingers through Rodrigo's and caress his knuckles with my other hand. He rubs anxiously at my thumbnail, and a tear rolls down his cheek, disappearing into his beard. "Then I was in Limbo, in this negative space that I didn't understand and couldn't get my bearings in. But I didn't have time to panic because you showed up. You, so sunny and pleased to meet me with your warm, radiating light. You— you said Limbo was regrettably short on alcohol, but you could give me a hug instead. And when you wrapped your arms around me, that's when I knew." He licks his lips and blinks hard against his tears. "I knew who was in the swimming pool with me in my dream. I knew who was in the car with me as I stared into the gray sky and bled out.

"It was you."

I gasp and pull his hand against my chest, too overwhelmed to reply.

"I don't know when you started to get feelings for me," he says, "but I fell for you the minute we met."

It takes me a moment to process exactly what I want to say, but he doesn't push for a response, patiently waiting for me as I often do for him. Finally, I say, <As much as I want that to be true, as much as I wish I was there with you for those moments, you know it really wasn't me, right? I don't want your love for me to be based on something imaginary.>

"That it was imaginary is... debatable. I won't argue that you weren't consciously there with me. But the obol in the back of my head was my spiritual connection to Limbo and to you, and who is to say that a little of that didn't slip through at times? Do you think that's impossible?"

<I know it isn't. There are a handful of people enrolled in the program who have experienced anomalies, some of which none of the higher ups at Renascenz even know about, and not for my lack of trying.>

Rodrigo wipes his eye with his thumb, then shrugs. "Even if it wasn't you, it sparked a flame that only grew over time as I got to know you. And I can confidently say I've fallen in love with you not for the dream on the day of my death but for your personality. Your humor. Your kindness and patience. That sexy suit. Does that put you more at ease?"

<Does it ever.> I'm grateful I'm holding his hand, because otherwise the buoyancy in me would pull me straight off the hill and into the sky like a lost balloon. <Why didn't you tell me how you felt? Were you afraid, like I was?>

"I have a very hard time knowing most people's intentions, especially when they're flirting with me. But you never flirted. Instead, you've listened to me ramble about my special interests for six months with rapt attention. Like everything I say is interesting."

<It is.>

"You never get bored of me. You drink up my presence like you need it to live."

<I do.>

His lips pucker in, brow furrowing, and I'm not sure what emotion this is, but I won't tell him that because then he'll put on his emoji again. "That's when I realized you loved me back. But I figured you never acted on it because you had some kind of duty to stay professional. After all, you have all these other souls to visit too. So I never said anything; I didn't want to have that conversation where you turned me down. But when you leave me each day, I count the hours until you return."

I sigh in time with the heavy throb of my heart. <Would you mind terribly if I put on a human face right now? I have one. It's for special occasions.>

"I would love to see your special occasion face."

I keep the wings and halo, but my biggest floating eye disappears in lieu of a human head. I've retained the shoulder-length honey-brown hair from my original avatar, but replaced the features with pensive brows, an aquiline nose, and thin, bowed lips.

Rodrigo's gaze circuits my face. "Oh, you look like—"

<An angel?>

"No. You look like a moody British musician. Or the contemplative star of an art film."

<It's the eyebrows, huh? They don't reflect my personality enough.>

"No, they do. You're incredibly thoughtful and introspective. It's just that you've never had a face to wear that expression on."

I give him a wide smile. <Does this expression fit me?>

"Yes. Very much." He cups my cheek, finally looking into my eyes. "I like you the other way too, but"—he closes our distance, and his gaze drops to my lips—"now you have something to kiss me with."

I press the tip of my tongue against my teeth. My nose is inches from his, our ties nearly touching, and for all the times I've yearned to hold his hand, *this* particular action is foreign even to my fantasies. <I... I don't know how. I've never thought about it before.>

His eyebrows shoot up. "Why not?"

<Neither of us had mouths. I mean, sometimes I give myself one if it's necessary, but since it isn't a part of my regular avatar—>

Rodrigo leans in, and his eyelids fall in slow motion, curly black lashes slicked with starlight. The parting of his full, ombre lips happens in freeze frames. The tilt of my head slows. My hands slow. My mind slows.

The moment

stretches.

Is this

what it feels

like

in the

material world?

fingers

                    stutter

        lips

                            bloom
                    rose

    petals

                            fragile

        soft

                damn

                        it

    Gale

                    how

        many
things

                did

                        you
            bid
                on?

Everything in the server comes slamming back at normal speed as I delete the eBay items from Gale's room. My lips smash against Rodrigo's, and his forward momentum knocks me off balance. We fall, and he gasps against my mouth, but we never hit the ground. We rotate, suspended, his body against mine, a background of stars-grass-stars-grass shifting behind his head.

He nestles his face into the crook of my neck and sighs, fingers winding through my hair, and I want this moment forever. I want *him* forever. <I'll still need to meet my other appointments each day no matter what's going on with us.>

His voice is muffled in my hair. "Of course. I don't want our relationship to be a detriment to the others here. Right now, my heart wants you to never leave my sight again, but logically I know we have eternity to spend together... Can you put us down? I'm getting dizzy."

I gently lower us to the ground, and grass tickles my ear. Rodrigo's body presses on top of me, and it's an even better sensation than our weightless drifting, but the word *eternity* is sticking in my mind. <We don't have eternity. I don't want to think about the day you leave me, but—>

He pushes up, glasses slipping down the bridge of his nose. "Why would I leave?"

I sit cross-legged, brush hair from my face, and straighten my tie, thinking of Sasha saying *Isn't temporary joy better than none at all?* <Because you'll be resurrected.>

He stares into the grass, his mouth a tight line, then rubs his forehead like he's confused. I'm not sure what there is to be confused about because we've had variations of this conversation before. "You're in charge of the resurrections, though, right? Not the Renascenz program?" he asks. "You're the one who sends souls into the bodies once they're ready."

<Yes,> I say carefully. My starry confession is still floating above us, and I wonder if I should take it down. <A person decides on their body and gives the details to the program. Once the body is grown, I send them into the resurrection queue. From there, their consciousness is uploaded into the new body. It's never an automatic process because every soul's stay here is different. Some of them need more time. Some less. I only send them when they're ready.>

"Then I'm not going."

<What?>

He sits on his knees, facing me, and takes my hands in his. "I'm not leaving for my second life. I'm going to stay here. With you."

I pull my hands away in surprise. <No no no. That's not possible.>

"Why not? If you're in charge, who is going to force you to resurrect me?"

<It isn't that simple.>

"Explain it to me."

I do not want to have this conversation. My heart sunders as I choke out, <I want eternity with you too. I want nothing more. But I have a duty to your well-being, and if you stay with me, you're throwing your life away.>

He grips my fingers, expression resolute. "You're enough. I promise you."

I'm so very, very not. <You mustn't let yourself forget

what you want beyond me. Do you remember when we last sat on this hill and I said I needed to tell you something? You asked if it was about the lawsuit, if it had been settled. When I said no, you were disappointed and said, "Well, it's only a matter of time, isn't it?">

He lets out an exasperated laugh. "I wasn't disappointed because you said no. I was disappointed because it was inevitable. I didn't want it."

Weakly, I say, <You signed up for the Renascenz program for a reason.>

"A couple of my students gave me a brochure for it as a joke because I was always so clumsy."

I don't know why I find the idea of clumsy Rodrigo so endearing, but it dissipates a little of the aggravation inside me.

He says, "Joke or not, I found the brochure intriguing and decided to enroll. After all, who doesn't want some security against potential tragedy? But am I not allowed to change my mind? Even though I've found something I want better than a second physical life? Would you deny me that?"

Oh, my heart. My brows push up, and I scoot closer to him, gripping his fingers. <I would never deny you anything. I'd give you the universe and every single thing in it until the lag in the server became a black hole that consumed us all.>

I'm a moth drawn to the light of his smile, eager to burn to ashes in its warmth. A realization is forming in my mind. It's something I never considered before, and I don't know whether to be overjoyed or terrified. I want to tell him. I want to tell him everything I've been holding back. But I have to be certain of his choice before I do anything. <Tell me what you miss about life.>

His smile shifts to a scowl, and he pulls his hands away. "Don't do this."

<Please. Please tell me.>

His nostrils flare, muscles in his jaw working. "Tea. It tastes like nothing here no matter how hard I concentrate on the memory of the flavors. Ice cream too. A lot of food, actually. And smells. Fresh laundry, mowed grass, petrichor, the skin of a partner... I miss hot showers and the tactile joy of putting a vinyl record on the turntable. Cracking open a real, physical book and turning the pages." His voice steadily rises, eyes blazing and glossy. "I miss looking forward to the weekend. I miss sex. I miss packages waiting at my door. I miss pain. Isn't that bizarre? Stubbing my toe or falling on my ass or sipping coffee that's too hot, just as the reminder that I'm alive and I *feel!* Is that what you want to hear? Are you happy now?"

Quietly, I say, <And you're willing to give all of that up for me?>

He looks taken aback, but only for a moment, his face schooling into one of concrete resoluteness. "Yes."

If he's prepared to sacrifice his entire world for me, then I have to be willing to do the same. I shut my eyes. <We can't have eternity, Rodrigo. Not literally. But I'll get us as close as I can.>

Staring up at *I LIED SO HARD* written in the stars, he

says, "Do you mean it?"

<I absolutely do. I want to be with you no matter what plane of existence we're on. But I need you to know that this won't happen the way you imagine it.>

"Nothing ever does. But I'll take you any way you'll let me have you."

Oh my. <Okay, but to clarify, I'm ninety-two percent certain—>

"Stop talking." He seals his mouth over mine, his tongue sliding between my lips. I make an inhuman noise and dissolve in his hands. He lets out an exclamation as feathers and glitter spill through his fingers, then frantically tries to scrape all the grains of me into a pile. "I'm sorry!"

I reset my avatar, avoiding his gaze. <That was embarrassing.>

Bits of silver sparkle against his skin, a miniature of the night sky above us. "What happened?"

<Just a little overwhelmed.>

His shock shifts to amusement, teeth flashing as he pushes up his glasses. "Maybe we should take it slower, huh? After all, we have time." Leaning in, he gives me a gentle, barely-there kiss. It still threatens to undo me, but I manage to keep myself together.

I sincerely hope he meant every word he said because there will be no going back from what I'm about to do. I dial up Renascenz's Chief Resurrection Officer. It always takes six rings before they pick up. But they always do.

Four.

Five.

Six—

"What?" Their Southern drawl bristles with irritation.

<Hello, Jack! I need a huge favor.>

Their laugh almost sounds genuine. "Is that what you're calling it?"

<Everything else I've asked you to do was for the sake of the souls here. Call it blackmail, coercion, your stubborn and surly self resistant to listening to logic, whatever you like. But this is one thing I need for *me*.>

Silence stretches over the line. Rodrigo toys with my hair, and I try to imagine the added layers of sensory stimulation it would have in the material plane. Finally, Jack says, "What is it?"

<I need you to get another stasis pod prepared.>

"What? For whom?"

I nuzzle Rodrigo's neck, experimentally pecking at his jaw with my rarely used lips.

<For me.>

15

The Resurrected

After talking to Metatron through the Renascenz app, I had the best sleep of my life—*both* my lives. I could have blamed it on the wine, but I'd only had one glass. I could have blamed it on spilling my guts about my crush to Ivan and David and the support they gave me in return, but I wasn't quite ready to admit how much it probably helped me. And when I climbed into bed, despite the disappointment of realizing Corvin was likely waiting for his husband to return from Limbo, my entire being was so relaxed and blissful that I couldn't dwell on it. It was like I'd gotten a massage or had incredible sex. That thought spurred me to wonder if Metatron had gotten lucky, but before any unwanted visuals could keep me awake, I was out for the night. I slept so deeply that Ivan had to shake me awake in the morning.

As I step through the front doors of the Renascenz building and toe off my shoes, an ache settles in my gut again, but it doesn't have anything to do with my guardian angel. Being back at work pushes Corvin to the forefront of my mind. I need to smooth things over with him even if I'm not convinced I did anything wrong. And even if nothing romantic is possible between us, he needs a friend and there's no reason I can't still be that for him.

I carry a cup holder of coffees to Owl's desk. "Morning. I, uh, couldn't remember what you ordered last time, so I just got you a latte. Hope that's okay."

She smiles and accepts the drink. "You're so sweet, Sasha. It's perfect."

I'm about to ask if Corvin is here yet so I can give him his drink, but someone slides a little placard into a holder in the glass doors of Marketing & Design that says *MEETING IN PROGRESS.*

Owl twists the other drinks in my cup holder, reading the types. "For Arthur and my brother?"

"Yeah."

"They're both in there"—she nods her head toward Design—"but no one will mind if you go in."

She's probably right, but... "Would I be putting you out by asking you to do it for me? I don't really want to be fueling rumors about me and Corvin in front of Kevin and his bionic penis."

Owl snorts loudly and slaps a hand over her mouth. Her eyes crinkle. "Are you sure they're rumors?"

"Well, I'm not going to ask Kevin to pull down his—"

"No, I mean about you and my brother. Is it only a rumor that you're into each other?"

I pull my own coffee from the cup holder and take a sip

even though it's way too hot. "He still wears his wedding ring."

Her lips pucker, and there's a hint of the irritated expression she wore the other day when her husband Trav was here. "Don't let that fool you. They were getting a divorce. It's nothing but misplaced guilt."

Divorced. Like me. A tiny surge goes through my heart. "Is his husband gone, or is he in Limbo?"

"Limbo." Her expression deepens into something close to disgust. "But it doesn't matter. Corvin isn't going to take Campbell back once he's resurrected. I know that for certain."

It's clear he isn't ready to let go of all his baggage, but if I drop my interest because he's a hot mess that would be the most hypocritical thing I could ever do. If I pursue him, there's a chance he'll resist and cling to his wedding ring and his guilt. Or it might make him let go. Help him move forward. Too much of Metatron must be rubbing off on me, because I pick up the cup holder, round Owl's desk, and push open the door of Design.

People surround the conference table, hunched over an enlarged rendering of Metatron—the same image Metatron attached to the email about their mascot—and mutter about eyeballs and halos. Corvin stands amid them, gesturing with a pencil and breathlessly explaining all the ways in which this can work as a mascot. He's wearing cream and orange swirl patterned slacks and a matching cropped suit jacket, and I'm suddenly craving ice cream. That train of thought is barreling straight for Innuendo Town, so I shove it away and approach the table. Several people look up, and Corvin pauses mid-sentence.

"Good morning." I focus on the drinks in my hand and set Arthur's in front of him. "Matcha latte, right?"

He twists toward me, eyebrows raised. "Oh, yes. How nice. Thank you. How is your stomach today?"

"Much better, thanks."

Corvin stares at me, and I can't read his expression, but I'm at least relieved that he doesn't look angry about my presence. I pull the other coffee from the holder, round the table, and set it in front of him. "*Mr. C.*"

Some of the people don't give my gesture a second look, going back to their mascot conversation. But a stunned silence radiates from more of them than I like, and it's clear by their scandalized faces that they're absolutely bursting to say something. I may not have my synthetic confidence anymore, but I'm not leaving this room until I thoroughly drive home the point that Corvin has a friend.

"Lunch at eleven? I'm buying," I say.

He blinks, shoulders rigid in his orange swirl suit, and I think of his eyes flashing in the porch light as he yelled at me, then stormed away. I'm certain he's going to brush off the invite, maybe even push the coffee back at me.

His gaze flicks to the people around him, then he gives me a megawatt smile that doesn't look quite genuine. "Absolutely. And thank you for the blackeye." He turns back to the image on the table. "Now, as I was saying, you can get away with all sorts of imagery if it's cute enough. Just think about Halloween decorations. If we simplify Metatron's—"

I push through the doors and nearly run into Owl. She whispers, "How did it go?"

Her face was practically smushed against the glass, so I doubt she missed it. "I don't know. You know him better than me. You think I have a shot?"

"I know you do." She gives me a full-face grin, all teeth and crinkling eyes, but there's more authenticity in it than her brother's had, and it leaves me less reassured than I was before.

I head to Arthur's office and stop in front of my desk, where someone has placed a large garbage can. It's hard to blame them when my stomach was cramping so badly yesterday that I was certain I'd be sick everywhere. No risk of that today unless Metatron and Rodrigo get into a lovers' quarrel, but I suspect I'll have many more nights of blissful sleep ahead of me.

There are things to catch up on due to my early clock-out the day before, and a list of tasks from Arthur in my email. I make a note to place a lunch order before eleven. There are plenty of restaurants nearby, and I don't know Corvin's favorites, but it seems like a safe bet that he'll eat just about anything placed in front of him.

In the middle of drafting an email, I glance up, then startle and jerk back in my chair. "Good god! You scared the hell out of me."

Corvin stands beside my desk, chewing gum. "I said your

name three times."

I clutch my pounding heart. "So you thought staring creepily at me instead would be better?"

"It worked. Did you order lunch yet?"

"No. Are you hungry already?"

His gum chewing slows, and he glances away. "Not at all. But we need to talk, and I don't feel like confessing things in the break room."

"You know I'm not a priest, right?"

His mouth twitches up. "We don't need priests when we have a guardian angel. I'm assuming you like pizza."

"I love pizza." Serious talks and confessions, not so much. But I tell Arthur I'm taking my lunch and follow Corvin through the building. He's uncharacteristically quiet as we pass two blocks and head into a little pizza joint I've taken Poppy to many times. Gesturing to the arcade room adjacent to the dining area, I say, "Whenever I come here, my daughter doesn't want to play the games, she wants *me* to play them because she knows I'll win, and I'll give her the prizes. She thinks I'm the king of arcade games."

Corvin slides into a cherry red booth, and I sit across from him. "Are you?"

"Yeah. Carnival games too. Won her the biggest toy robot there the other day."

"Well, I'm terrible, so no chance of me dethroning you." He tugs at the sleeves of his suit jacket. "I'm really sorry for yelling and storming off last night. You didn't deserve that, and

I need to confess something. Several somethings."

I already know what one of them is, but the idea that there's more than one sets me on edge, and I pinch the ADHD pin in my arm. "You lied when you said you'd never used the app to talk to Metatron."

He shakes his head, but before he can say anything, a server stops at our table and asks us for our order. Despite insisting he's not hungry, he orders a large spinach, artichoke, and hummus pizza with extra dipping sauce. Once the server leaves, he clutches his water glass and stares past my shoulder toward the arcade room. Music and *pew-pew* sound effects drift.

"When I said I wanted to help you contact Metatron, you accused me of wanting something in return." He clinks his nails against the glass, something complex playing across his face. "I led you to believe that all I wanted was a friend."

My heart sinks, and anger rises in its place like the heat from a volcanic vent. I clench my jaw until my teeth ache, waiting for him to continue.

He avoids my gaze, but if he were any closer the heat of my indignation would probably melt off his face. He says, "The truth is... When I realized how badly you needed to talk to Metatron but didn't have an avenue in, I knew that was something I could help with. It was only a matter of time before I had to talk to Metatron again, and I could relay your problem to them myself, saving you the risk of getting fired by snooping on Arthur's computer. But I knew, faced with that opportunity, I wouldn't bring it up." His nostrils flare and he fusses with his suit cuffs, yanking them up his wrists. "I don't like talking to Metatron if I can help it, because the topic always turns back to me and my husband. But I would have felt far too guilty if I didn't help you out in some way. And if I wasn't going to talk to Metatron about it, the least I could do was help you get the Renascenz app so you could do it yourself. But I want you to know that I did want a friend. I *do*."

The anger in my chest snuffs out, smothered by confusion. "I don't know why you would have felt guilty for not helping me. It's not like you caused my problem."

"No, but you mentioned Rodrigo, and I do have a reason to feel guilty about what happened to him. Campbell is still technically my husband, but I wanted a divorce. I still do. We got married after only a month of dating, and we had problems almost right away. Shocker, huh? But I—" He bites his lip and shrinks in the booth, the vinyl groaning beneath him. "What happened is my fault. We were in the car and getting into another argument. I told him I wanted a divorce, and I said— I said, 'I've never loved you. *Never*. Let me out of this car. I don't want to see you again for as long as I live.' And he just sat there, hands on the wheel, like he hadn't heard me. Then we started to approach a red light, and instead of slowing down, he sped up. I begged him to stop. There was another car going through the intersection. Rodrigo's car." He squeezes his eyes shut and puts a hand to his forehead.

Oh god. I need Face With Monocle for this because I do not have the emotional perception for this situation. I slide out of my side of the booth and scoot next to him. "That isn't your fault."

"It is. If I hadn't brought up the divorce while we were in the car—"

"You are not responsible for someone else's actions. It sounds like you're just as much a victim as Rodrigo."

Corvin's face contorts, and I can almost see him struggling to pick up the conversation. "Regardless, you accused me of lying when I said I'd never talked to Metatron through the app. But it wasn't a lie." His throat flexes, face grim and slightly ashen. "I was able to talk to them after I... after I died in the car wreck."

Replaying our initial conversation about this, where he sat on my desk and told me he'd never been resurrected, only succeeds in creating more questions. "But you said—"

"I've never been resurrected." His voice is tight and shaky, eyes glossy, and he looks like a fragile glass vase about to tip off a shelf. "I didn't get weeks with your guardian angel to process my death. I don't get to go to your cute little meetings about living your best second life. I'm still here, in this awful first one, in this awful body!"

His hand is twisted in his suit cuff, and I pry it loose and squeeze his fingers. He stares at our conjoined hands in shock, then yanks his fingers free and tucks them into his lap like I hit them with a hammer. Damn it. If I had an enhancement pin for this, I wouldn't be fucking up—

No no. Touching his hand was the wrong move, but I

don't need pins. I summon Ivan's reassuring voice and crushing hug and remind myself that I'm not going to ruin my *new* found family the way I did with my last one.

I awkwardly scoot away from Corvin, trying to keep the wounded edge out of my voice as I pull back the conversation. "So you died and went to Limbo, saw Metatron, but then came back to your same body? I think that's what they call a near-death experience."

He's still massaging his fingers, brow furrowed. "Yes, but nobody believes that's possible. If you die, the obol reformats your consciousness and it's uploaded to Limbo. There's no coming back to the same body. But they resuscitated me after the wreck and... here I am. Arthur tried to convince me that going to Limbo was my imagination, something brought on by the trauma of what happened to me and Campbell. I convinced myself he was right. But then a month later... it happened again."

"You went to Limbo a second time?" This sounds disturbingly like what David went through, but I have a feeling Corvin never went to the Renascenz doctors for help.

He nods. "That time I just bumped my head against a kitchen cabinet. I went to Limbo and woke up on my kitchen floor a couple minutes later. Arthur wasn't there that day, so I told my coworkers about it instead. Something was very wrong with me, and I needed to know what to do. Instead of anyone helping me, Kevin made a joke about my mental health, so I pulled the coffee pot off the maker and threw it at him. Now everyone looks at me like I'm insane."

"I don't think you're insane."

"You don't?" His eyes glitter with gratitude, and even if he doesn't want me touching his hand, I'm at least glad to be helping him in some manner.

"Of course not," I say. "Ivan's boyfriend had obol issues after he was resurrected—kept thinking he was in Limbo—but even if I didn't know about that, I've had my own weird tether to Metatron too. Would be hypocritical of me to believe that your experience was impossible. Has Metatron talked to Arthur about this?"

He grunts, still tugging on his fingers, and I realized he's trying to work off his wedding ring. It finally comes free, and he stuffs it in his pocket. The tan line where it used to be makes his finger look naked and vulnerable. He slides his hand over mine beneath the table, his grip warm and firm, and my heart rockets into my throat.

"Sorry, what was that?" he asks.

"What?"

"You asked me a question."

"Did I?" When I'd taken his hand before, it had been instinctual, a little bit of comfort to keep him from breaking down. But pulling off his wedding ring and sliding his fingers over my knuckles feels decidedly like something else, and there isn't a single thought in my brain now. "I, uh, I don't remember. Keep talking. You're good at that."

"Even after knowing about your problem, I wasn't sure

you'd believe mine, simply because no one else has." His voice dips, and his fingers slide against my palm. "Even if you didn't like me, you still didn't look at me like everyone else did, and I didn't want to ruin that."

I swallow hard. "I like you."

He flashes me a broad, sparkling grin. Our server returns with our order, and I'm suddenly unsure if Corvin likes me back, because the look he gives the pizza is full of leagues more desire than what he gave me. He slips his hand free, then doles me a plate. "Have you had this kind before? It's delicious."

I rub my clammy palm on my knee. "Uh, maybe. I don't know."

Pausing in the slices he's piling on his plate—he might as well eat it straight from the pan—he says, "You don't look like you want any. Is your stomach still bothering you?"

Only because it's swarming with butterflies. I take a slice and set it on my plate. "Nah, I'm good." I pinch the ADHD pin in my arm and try to focus. "So how many times have you gone to Limbo?"

He wipes his mouth and tucks his napkin under his plate. "Five. The last time was just yesterday."

Five? I gape at him. "Are you actually dying each time? Does it hurt?" I can't decide if I want to pull him into a hug, use the Renascenz app to beg Metatron for help, or order him another pizza.

"The first time hurt, yeah." He stares at his plate and reaches for his ring finger. He looks slightly startled that his wedding ring isn't there, then fusses with his sleeve instead. "I died in the car wreck. The other times, I don't know. Not sure it counts as dying if I wake up on my own afterward. Yesterday morning I was just sitting on the trolley and when someone turned, they accidentally whacked me in the face with their purse. I was out long enough to miss my stop, but not long enough for anyone to become concerned. They must have thought I was just asleep."

I want to tell him he needs a doctor, but what if they want to "fix" him the way they "fixed" David? My train of thought from earlier suddenly comes barreling back, and I say, "Has Metatron talked to Arthur about this? Do you even trust Arthur to help?"

"I don't know. On both accounts. I know Metatron cares about me, but all they ever want to talk about is what Campbell did to me and Rodrigo and how I need to tell someone. Someone in authority, I mean."

Metatron isn't wrong. I'm no detective, but it sounds like Campbell took Corvin's last words of *I don't want to see you again for as long as I live* as a challenge. And not only did he try to take Corvin with him, he killed Rodrigo. If Corvin is the only one who can attest that it wasn't an accident, he needs to say something, but it's clear he needs more than logic right now. "Those death conversations suck, huh? I hated them. And if you're only in Limbo for a few minutes at a time, that's not long enough to really get comfortable to open up, I'll bet."

He turns to me, and his tongue prods his lips, his gaze

raking over me. It's suddenly very hot under the collar of my shirt. "Thank you for saying that. Owl and Trav know what happened and what's going on with me now, but Trav keeps trying to push me to do what Metatron wants. And I know I need to." His voice cracks. "But I'm not ready."

"Because you think it's your fault?"

He fusses with a napkin, folding it carefully and pressing down the creases. "Yeah."

"Do you *want* to go to those cute little resurrection meetings where you talk about your feelings? You belong just as much as anyone else. They won't make you explain anything you don't want to, and I mean, you'd fit right in with the other hotties there; they'll never know this is your original body. You could come with me, Ivan, and David to the next one."

Sitting back, he blinks and dabs the napkin against his eyes. "I would love that. Thank you."

My phone suddenly feels heavy in my pocket, and I know I'm going to sound as annoying to Corvin as Ivan always does to me, but I say, "Will you let me message Metatron about this? Maybe if it's coming from me, they'll focus more on your problem first and you can deal with the other part afterward."

He blows his nose into the napkin and pushes away his plate of pizza. "Yeah, go ahead. I've been a bit of a prick to them. Literally. Kept transforming into a Saguaro cactus so they'd leave me alone."

I snort. "I'm sure they've dealt with that kind of thing before. I can't imagine all of the dead are agreeable."

"They have to deal with my husband, so I'm sure that's true... Let me out, please. I'm going to get a to-go box." He practically pushes me out of the booth, then strides for the front counter, weaving around tables.

I sigh and tap on the Renascenz app on my phone. At least he took off his wedding ring. That must be some kind of progress. I can understand why he thinks he needs to hold onto that guilt, but it's clear it's eating him up inside. Maybe going to the resurrection meetings will help. All I need to focus on right now is contacting Metatron.

The chat screen appears, and I'm met with a new bolded message from Metatron, time stamped half an hour ago. Strange that the app didn't alert me, but it's clear by how corrupted the message is that something has gone awry.

ꙮ H3llo8^oo. tast n>Got wi,h Rodrigo w1s both increPiHle anH terrifyi{g. I !ust t@<!k yoG a8ai! INR lour 6ako. I wWnt%d to Kive yo9 a se{)s up. .he <immo7s #s. R"na>ceni IMw^u`C haf fir5lly $omI yo a [!ore, and Rena}ceW2 has non. I'm /u5tA suVe yCu'll h6ar SYout this [?6n at w[Qk, vnd go d2uzt every^~H wilc b[ yzaite^, bu} I'm af~OiP ti s!y tv`t O)nascenz i3 ucturly bandrupt ^n8 thege's m|ly a 4% chc,ce op!ra/Nonx |ill be ub^e +o zesume. Rvsryjhing is g~inJ t' shut doo#—th' ;ompans, t\e @kmbo s6rveS1, t9e stZ+i' pXd "ac|lit%. But ro@ tC f2r3p b,cau[e I'v% *u{pect7>]hP, Lor some ~iEe and Jack AmZ alro&dy =rown all cf (he bodies. x8'll y) snn*:nV the wouls inZo them shortl8. I've 1(cjde& to ToPn RGdrXgo in toe

mVteri6l <lQne, so I su"pose I b(gAt meet yo" Fn tF(
flesh evlst4dlly! 7nywaR, th~ Z"|nt gf >his is (w}dpld—
Zne, Eo# a'; >FQvNn ough@ tV Molish uX your
wes>mes bZcOuse y(u'lA |e out of jRbs hZr. socn,
aUd two, I'v^ bepn Nrying in vuil to ge~ :0Zvi% tM [@l+
somelne - la+ etforZeY?]t, a t4]ra:i/t - w)at h#S ey-
h&sFand Gil ab soon as dossible. I feN~ thPt
Tampbell Z[ghi haru s<Xe1ne ag/in, oY Vigself, onct
he'c bacU imtM y%B LambriGl wor$d. <Wrv_n in
particul{r seem_ a likely ta]g_X, and I'm nMQ 3gre
RodriDo Is sa9e either @ith as G8ch as fa2Nbell vas
fixated on Dim.
{'ve Jhough< oy an dmer<$ncy failsaf;, Cut it'? not a
guaraS~ee.

My brain resists reading through that pile of letter salad,
even though I can pick out words like "Rodrigo" and
"Renascenz" and "bodies." I type back, asking if Metatron can
send the message again, but my text is just as corrupted.

Metatron replies:

۩ sh no, not agein. Sohry, Sasha, bl] tgis gliAch ;a6
ha[pEe^F bxfore, a2d th@re's n/ on1 lefk G! fix Ct!
I'll t<y po zoll
YalO laxe}
call vhte>
ca\l later

Sounds like this has happened before. I glance up to give
my eyes a reprieve from the garbled text. Corvin is drumming

his fingers on the front counter and talking with the cashier. Someone appears from the back and hands him a to-go box.

I read Metatron's message more carefully, piecing together the first line: *Hellooo. Last*—something—*with Rodrigo was both incredible and terrifying. I just... Just...* Hmm.

Corvin says something. I gasp and nearly drop my phone. "What?"

He stands so close I think I could count every freckle dusting his nose and cheeks. After unwrapping a piece of gum and popping it in his mouth, he holds up a transparent token card. "Our conversation was getting way too heavy, and we still have a bit of our break left, so I thought you could impress me with your arcade skills." His gaze rakes over me, a smile tugging at his lips.

My heart throbs, and the only thing I can think of to say is, "I can win you a teddy bear."

"Then what are we waiting for, Arcade King? I want the biggest one."

I nod, keeping my phone pressed to my chest. I *do* want that call from Metatron, but I'm suddenly hoping it won't come until later. "I'll box up the pizza and be right there."

16

The Resurrected

We're ten minutes late coming back from our break, and if it were just me, I'd be happy to take whatever chastising Arthur gave me, apologize, and tell him it won't happen again. But there are already rumors about Corvin and me, and he has a big teddy bear wearing a frog hoodie tucked under his arm.

His ring finger is still bare, and the thought that he took the ring off for me, so he could take my hand without it being between us, drops an anxious ache into my stomach. It feels almost as sugary as Metatron's love sickness, but this time it's only coming from me. And there's only one way to get rid of it—the same solution I encouraged Metatron into.

The thought cramps my gut harder. I was nervous beneath my flirty veneer when I was first interested in Dusty, but my enhancement pins dulled the sensation. They boosted my confidence, so I didn't chicken out of making a move. They gave me witty quips, charisma, and enhanced perception.

It would be so easy to blow it with Corvin. I have no doubt that despite his struggle for friends at work, what he said about people constantly throwing themselves at him is true. He could walk into any bar and be the hottest person there. Maybe it wouldn't hurt me to go get Smiling Face with Sunglasses after work today. It would be totally legal, and I could get just enough of a dose for a couple of weeks, then let the pin dissolve and not—

No no no. I can't. It would never be just one. I'd decide I needed something else a couple days later, then I'd be picking out my favorite illegal combinations and all my progress would become a flaming dumpster barreling down a hill until I lost everything I cared about and died of heart failure again.

Corvin glances at me. "You're very quiet. Everything okay?"

I shrug and hope it looks casual. "I'm always quiet. It's just that you're usually filling the silence with a stream of words that don't have spaces between them."

He chuckles. "I'm a little lost in thought, I suppose. Thinking about our conversation."

The teddy bear under his arm with its little zip-up frog hoodie looks like a physical manifestation of the desire churning in my stomach. I clear my throat. "You think anyone will notice we're coming back late?" *And together?*

"It doesn't matter how long of a break you take or how frequently, as long as you're getting your work done. You have less leeway than I do since you need to be present at the desk to handle inquiries and whatever Arthur needs, but he's not going to care that you're back a few minutes late. That being said, I don't normally like taking long breaks because it just means more work I need to catch up on when I get back. I'd rather not stay past five or come in early if I can help it."

We reach the building doors and push inside. The lobby and Owl's desk are empty. I glance into Marketing & Design and see nothing but sketches strewn across the table. Animated chatter drifts from farther on, and as soon as we reach the cubicles, there's a palpable energy in the air. Someone on a call ends it abruptly and pushes out of their chair so quickly it rolls into the wall. They glance at us as they hurry past and say, "Everyone's meeting in the lounge. C'mon!"

It's tempting to make a joke about more cake being far from an emergency, but the sudden anxious cramp in my gut tells me it's a verdict on the lawsuit. I'm not sure which way it's fallen, but Metatron is. Maybe believing their corrupted text was about their romance with Rodrigo was the wrong assumption. It was probably about the lawsuit and Rodrigo being resurrected. Now I wish I would have tried to call them instead of winning Corvin an arcade prize. They're probably desperate to talk to someone about this.

I pull out my phone and click on the app. The chat screen opens, clouds floating against a baby pink background, but when I try to place a call, nothing happens. I tap the button again, and the app crashes. Shit. I try again, but the app lingers on the loading screen and finally times out. Corvin calls my name. With a sigh, I stuff the phone back in my pocket and follow him into the break room, joining the crowd clustered around Arthur. He's shorter than most of the people surrounding him, but everyone hushes when he raises his hands for silence.

"Friends, I have great news." He strokes his neatly trimmed beard, and I swear he's pausing for maximum effect. "Renascenz has won the lawsuit. We can resume operations."

An ear-splitting cheer erupts from the crowd. People hug each other; they hug Arthur. Someone pulls a bottle of what might be champagne from the fridge and waves it in the air. Corvin and I are the only ones not cheering. His face has gone ashen, and he's hugging his teddy bear so hard its head might pop off. I drag over a nearby chair and push him into it in case he's at risk of fainting.

Someone tries to hand me a coffee mug of champagne. I should be happy. This is what we wanted. It'll be better for all of the souls stuck in Limbo. Better for Rodrigo. Better for anyone enrolled in the program who has died in the last six months and hasn't been allowed to be uploaded into Limbo.

But it's not better for Corvin *or* Metatron. The anguished love in my gut that I just got rid of is going to get worse, and I see a lot more vomiting in my future.

There's no way I can drink alcohol when my stomach is contorted with Metatron's anxiety, so I push the champagne into Corvin's hands. People are still laughing and celebrating; I bend to his ear so he can hear me. "Bottoms up, huh? You look like you need it."

He takes a sip of the champagne, then pushes the mug away and tugs anxiously at the cuffs of his suit jacket until they're up against his knuckles, his teddy bear wedged between his knees. The laugh that bubbles up his throat is high-pitched and strained. "This day had to come, of course. All those souls deserve to be out of Limbo. And I'd be out of a job if we weren't up and running. Then where would I be?"

Wherever that is, it would be somewhere other than a break room full of people who refuse to eat lunch with him. A person with olive skin and huge glasses is standing next to us. Their dark hair is pulled into a ponytail, and a little pendant winks in the well of their neck, the symbol for Universal Church. It takes me a moment to realize it's the bookkeeper who's always taking a nap on the couch at noon—I've never seen them awake before. They aren't celebrating either. In fact, they look ready to burst into tears, magnified eyes watery behind their thick lenses.

Cold sweat prickles on the back of my neck. Why does the bookkeeper look so stricken that operations will resume?

I push through the sea of people and retrieve more champagne, then return to the bookkeeper. Offering the mug, I say, "Sorry, we haven't been introduced. I'm Sasha, he/him. What's your name?"

They take the champagne in a daze. "Anise." It's almost a question. "She/her."

"Are you okay?"

"Um, sure. Yeah." She gives me a tight smile that doesn't reach her eyes, then glances at Corvin, who is zipping and unzipping the frog hoodie on his teddy bear. She downs the champagne in one draft, then pushes the mug back at me. "Is there more?"

I raise my eyebrows, then reach for Corvin's champagne. He shakes his head when I ask him if he's going to drink it, so I hand it to Anise. She knocks it back, then excuses herself.

Before I can mull over what that was about, Arthur shouts above the din, asking for quiet. People squeeze each other, bouncing on their toes and laughing. There's a loud *POP*, and a champagne cork slams into the ceiling tile. Arthur climbs onto a chair and tries again. The cheering finally dies down.

"I want everyone to take the rest of the day off—"

Another round of cheers drowns out the rest of his sentence. He grins. "Take the rest of the day off, but when we get back tomorrow, there's going to be a lot to do. The stasis pods have been shut down for six months. Jack has been maintaining the facility, but the pods will need to be cleaned and restocked with biomaterial to grow new bodies for our poor souls who have been stuck in Limbo. I'll need volunteers for that; it's okay if you've never done it before. For the rest of you, I'll speak to your departments individually, but we have accounts of the departed that are backed up, and we will need to stagger their uploads into Limbo so that Metatron isn't overwhelmed with a huge influx of people at once. It'll be two weeks before—"

I can get the rundown tomorrow. I'm sure Arthur will send me an email with a huge list of tasks. Right now, Corvin looks like he needs some fresh air, or to at least sit in the grass in the lobby. I urge him out of the chair, out of the room. His hand shakes as he fumbles for something in his pocket. The teddy bear falls on the floor. I bend down to pick it up, and when I straighten, he's typing furiously on his phone. After a moment, he tucks the phone away. "Asking Trav to come pick Owl and me up. He's got the car today. I don't drive after... well. And he's worried about something happening to me on the trolley again."

Corvin probably has a ton on his mind, and trying to come up with something comforting to say leaves me drawing a blank. At least he'll have the rest of the day to process it. Metatron is likely overwhelmed with the idea of losing Rodrigo, and I doubt anyone is going to give *them* the rest of the day off.

I reach for my antacids, but the only thing in my pocket is the token card from the pizza place. Damn it. I didn't think I'd need them today.

We stop on a grassy island in the lobby; Corvin sits down, his back against a huge potted dracaena. I sit next to him, staring at the blades of grass poking between his bare toes. Nudging his shoulder, I say, "You thinking about how much easier your life would be if you were a cactus?"

He huffs. "I'm sure I'd manage to screw that up somehow too. You know, sometimes I wish... I wish I'd stayed dead. Gone to Limbo permanently. Come back for a shiny new second life, even if it took six months."

"I thought that too, but a new life didn't help me. It's not a reset button. There's no easy way out. You have to figure out how to own your problems."

The intensity in his gaze is almost desperate. "Have you?"

"No." I think about taking his hand, of hooking my pinky finger through his, but even with our coworkers distracted by good news, the thought of someone seeing us makes me hesitate. By the time I decide to do it anyway, Corvin's phone jingles, and he pulls his hand away to answer it. While he's texting, Owl rushes by us, heading for the front doors.

I call out to her, and she turns around. When she spots Corvin, her whole body sags like a sprung rubberband, and the urgency in her walk disappears. She drops next to us and pulls Corvin into a hug, even though he's still mid-text. She cups the side of his head, mussing his slicked hair, and presses her forehead against his.

"Are you okay?" she asks.

"This day had to come." The slightly hysterical edge that statement had when he said it in the break room is gone, the words flat and drained of emotion. But it doesn't answer Owl's question. I glance at her and shake my head.

"Um, hey, the next support meeting for the resurrected is tomorrow," I say. Ivan might have a heart attack that I'm planning to go to another one so soon. "You still want to come?"

He hesitates for only a moment. "Yes. Can I bring someone? Owl?"

"Sure. Ivan goes to all the meetings to support me and his

boyfriend."

Owl asks questions about the meetings as people head through the front doors with their lunch bags and coats. Anise, the bookkeeper, heads past us, and I'm tempted to get up and ask her why the lawsuit news made her upset, but I don't know if my gut is telling me something is off, or if I'm only confusing Metatron's feelings for my own. And if I ask her, she'd have every right to ask me or Corvin why we aren't happy either.

Anise brushes past Trav as he walks into the building. His pale hair is gathered into a messy bun, and paint or maybe lime plaster is smeared on his shorts and one of his flip flops. He stops before us, gives Corvin a sympathetic smile, then stoops over to meet Owl halfway for a kiss. Pointing a thick finger at me, he pauses, then says, "We met the other day."

Corvin stands and gestures to me like the assistant on a game show revealing the grand prize. "This is Sasha."

"Oh! *You're* Sasha."

Corvin turns to me as I push off the grass. "I tried to tell him that you'd already met, but he didn't remember."

"You said he was a 'short white guy with cute curls,'" Trav replies exasperatedly. "The city is full of white people, *everyone* is shorter than me, and I don't know what constitutes 'cute' hair on a guy."

"Do you want a headshot so you can remember me?" I ask. "It's four ninety-nine for a five by seven. I'll sign it for you."

His eyes crinkle behind his coke bottle glasses. "I'll pass."

"We should go." Corvin's voice is so low I barely hear him.

"Trav is doing home repair today and... I think I need to lie down for a while."

"Yeah, of course."

We all say our goodbyes, and I realize I'm still holding Corvin's teddy bear. I catch up to him as he pushes open the door. I'm not sure what emboldens me, but I hand him the bear then give him a wink. "Call me later if you want to talk."

He's momentarily stunned, then flashes me a smile and pushes through the door. The building is almost deathly silent now, nothing stirring but leaves in the A/C and the bad feeling sitting heavy inside me. I wish I knew if it's a sixth sense that something is off about operations resuming, or if it's simply misplaced worry for Corvin and Metatron.

It would make sense that not all my coworkers are happy about the lawsuit being settled today. Jack said people were laid off after Renascenz suspended operations, and from the looks of things around the office, some of them have been paid to do basically nothing for the past six months. People will have to pick up slack until the company starts hiring again.

I try to reassure myself that my reasoning is sound as I pull my phone out of my pocket. This time, the Renascenz app makes it past the loading screen, but I'm afraid to touch any of the buttons for fear of it crashing. Instead, I scroll through Metatron's garbled message again and hone my concentration.

Hellooo. Last—with Rodrigo was both incredible and terrifying. I just—I wanted to give you a—Renascenz—has finally—I'm—you'll hear about this—at work, and—4%

chance—to resume. Everything is—shut—But—because I've expected—some—and Jack—all—bodies—into them shortly. I've—Rodrigo—so I suppose I—meet—flesh eventually—two, I've been trying in vain to get—someone—as soon as possible. I feel that Campbell—himself once he's back—particular seems a likely—and I'm—Rodrigo is safe either with as—Campbell has fixated on him.

I've thought of an emergency failsafe, but it's not a guarantee.

Ice sleets through my veins. If Metatron is that worried about Campbell, then it's going to be in everyone's best interest for Corvin to tell someone about the true nature of the car wreck as soon as possible. Hopefully the meeting tomorrow helps, because we've got two weeks tops before Campbell is back in the material world.

Unless... Jack oversees taking the bodies out of stasis once the souls are inserted. Maybe there's a way for them to delay the process for Campbell if Corvin needs more time. I'll have to ask Jack about it.

I mull over what Metatron's "emergency failsafe" could be as I push through the front doors.

17

The Seraph

You have to eat in the material world. You have to drink water. What if I don't like how water tastes? What then? I die, I guess.

When the sun goes down, you have to sleep. How will I know when to wake up? What if I get thirsty while I'm sleeping? What if I have to *pee*?

What if I get itchy? What if I forget to blink? With only two eyes, both of them firmly stuck in my skull, I won't be able to see what's going on behind me.

I'm not supposed to pick my nose. What happens if I do?

To Jack, I say, <Is there a punishment for picking your nose?>

A surprised laugh comes through the line. "Yeah, two years of community service."

<Well, that should certainly deter people. But Galvlohi is always sparkling clean. Does that mean there are legions of nose-pickers cleaning things up?>

"Metatron, there's no punishment other than people being disgusted with you. Will you focus? You haven't completed your body model."

<I did. Two arms, two legs, torso, a head. My special occasion face. Everything is there.>

"You didn't choose genitals."

Oh.

Oh no.

"Supernova" is not an option for genitals. I wasn't exactly fond of having a vagina, but that was mostly due to Walter's fixation with it. People fixate on penises too. And butts. And breasts.

I must be silent for too long, because Jack says, "Are you wishing there was a 'nothing' option?"

<Yes.>

"Want me to flip a coin? Whichever you choose is going to affect which hormones the body produces and influence secondary sex characteristics too, of course. It'll alter your chosen body and face at least a little bit. You can take hormones later on or other medical intervention to change some things you don't like, but it would be far easier to settle right now on something you think you'd be happy with. I'd let you choose an intersex option, but those require prior approval, and it would take me too long to get around it."

I think about my original avatar—upturned nose and wide feminine eyes, heart-shaped face, a soft and curvy body further accentuated by the gauzy robes that clung to my hips. And every time Walter asked to see under my skirts, it made me more misaligned, like he was seeking some irrefutable truth that I belonged in that avatar. Like he could tell it didn't fit.

That wasn't what he was thinking at all, of course. It's what *I* was. And even though the classic male form of lantern jaw, broad shoulders, and hard muscles doesn't fit me either—I'm at home with something here nor there, both and neither— thinking about my original discomfort at least helps me make a selection so we can get on with this.

Jack sighs. "Okay. You know, you're lucky I break the rules and always have at least one base body ready to go in case something happens to one of the others. Otherwise this would take weeks, which we apparently don't have."

There's no such thing as a "base body" but I suppose that sounds better "paused in a partially developed state of muscle and exposed organs." It would be more costly to keep a bunch of half-grown bodies in suspended states until they're needed than it is to grow specific ones from scratch once there's an actual soul to enter them, so I can see why Renascenz doesn't allow it. But I'm grateful Jack is a rule-breaker—for a few reasons.

"Alright. It's going to take at least three days still," they say. "Maybe four. And I guess if I get caught, I'm screwed, huh? I was planning on pointing blame your way, but there won't be any way to do that now. 'Metatron forced me to illegally resurrect all the souls in Limbo, but no, you can't confirm it with them because they're in an anonymous human body with no name, no paper trail, and no fingerprint records.'"

<With the lawsuit resolved, it's not technically illegal now.

Simply that no one from Renascenz has given you permission to go ahead… and they aren't going to because there's no money left for it. But I can record a confession if you'd like.>

"Nah." Their voice is heavy with weariness. "You've known all along that the company is going to shut down, huh?"

<I tried to tell you.> If Jack had believed me months ago when I predicted it, I wouldn't have had to blackmail them into helping me. I can see their reasoning, though. With a ninety-two percent likelihood that Renascenz would win the lawsuit, why would they close their doors? But six months without revenue and staggering litigation fees gave me all the reason in the world to believe Renascenz was going bankrupt. I ensured that Jack had the chosen bodies for each of the seven souls in Limbo grown ahead of time just in case shut down was imminent. I didn't trust that their contracts would be honored with the bottom falling out of the company. <And if you're still not convinced, all of the tangible assets in the medical facility are already being liquidated, and the company president moved to France today.>

"Fuck. Is that why you made me set up that medical stuff next door and you have a doctor in your pocket to check on the resurrected when they're done baking? I thought it was just to keep things more hush-hush, but if there's no medical facility to go *to*…" They grumble and the sound of fabric rustles over the line. "I kind of figured you were right for a while now. I just didn't want to believe it. Anise called me today. She's really upset."

My conscience digs its hooks into me. I'm tired of deceiving everyone I talk to, whether it's outright lying or simply pretending everything is okay when I know it's not. Sick of empty promises and empty threats. "I would never actually tell Anise's parents that you two are in a relationship."

They breathe a humorless laugh. "Kind of figured that too. Even if you did, it might not be the worst thing. Those conservative assholes are going to find out eventually anyway. I don't want to keep sneaking around. And Anise sleeps on the couch during her break at work every day because she's exhausted from getting up so early to see me."

<You knew I was bluffing, but you've been helping me anyway?>

"You? Nah. I've been helping Rodrigo and Mei-Hui and Gale and all the rest. They don't deserve any of this, and they absolutely don't deserve to be deleted. *Now* I'm helping you."

My heart swells, and I wish I was in a body right now so I could give them a hug. <Thank you so much, Jack.>

"Yeah, yeah. I ain't good with sappy stuff, so dry all those eyeballs. Give me a heads up when you start sending people into the queue."

A mixture of anxiety and elation bubbles inside me. <I'm going to start right now. There's no reason to delay.> I say goodbye and end the call.

Gale will get to see his mother and his millions of collectibles. Mei-Hui will get to be with her parents, her real-life cat, and go back to school. Campbell will hopefully be ordered to stay at least five hundred feet away from Corvin and Rodrigo.

I promised to tell Rodrigo the lawsuit news before anyone else, but he's also the soul I'm most nervous to see. He might not forgive me for allowing him to believe we would have our happily ever after in Limbo. I started to tell him the truth at our previous visit, but the more I tried to talk, the more he kissed me to shut me up, until I didn't dare do anything that would ruin the moment.

I don't think he'll mind me throwing off his schedule by arriving now, but just for good measure I sail a paper airplane into his room before my arrival. Written inside is:

I have good news! Renascenz won the lawsuit. I also have bad news. And more good news!

The ever-present disco-nouveau thumping from his room suddenly stops. I peek inside. He's standing beside the chair in his study, the airplane unfolded in his hands and a deep furrow between his brows. When I walk inside, he glances up. "Well, you did say this wouldn't happen the way I imagined it."

<Yes, I'm afraid that's the case.>

He curls and uncurls the edge of the paper between his fingers. "Logically, I know that there are so many variables to any given situation that it's near impossible to predict a specific outcome, and yet I always try anyway. And now I'm working myself up over the idea of bad news when I don't even have a clue what it could be."

I gently take the paper from him, then close my hands over

his. <The bad news is that Renascenz is bankrupt, and I don't think the company or the Limbo servers are going to last through the week.>

"*What?*"

Rushing on to keep him from panicking, I say, <But the other good news is I was certain this was going to happen, so I've ensured ahead of time that your body is already grown, and you can enter it within the hour. No risk of you or any of the other souls being deleted.>

Rodrigo pulls his hands away; they flutter at his sides like they're infused with lightning. I expect him to chastise me for dropping this information on him now instead of months ago or even during our last appointment. Months ago it was only a sinking suspicion in my guts, and I wasn't going to alarm all of my souls on nothing but a hunch. Especially because I hadn't yet worked out a deal with Jack and had no safety net in the event the servers were faced with imminent shutdown. And during that time I was hoping to have some plan in place for Campbell. I was planning to let Rodrigo go without ever knowing my feelings or telling him that I was prepared to go down with the ship.

"But— but *you're* going to be deleted." His eyes are wide, tears quivering on the brims of his lids.

<Technically, I'm immortal. Not me as you know me, but the neural net I derive from. This Limbo version of me wouldn't exist anymore, but I was hoping you would take solace in the knowledge that the essence of me is in Eddie the

trolley operator, in ChatDoc, and in the clerk at the DMV.>

The look on Rodrigo's face tells me that, no, he does not take solace in that. He says, "Those versions of you wouldn't remember me, would they?"

"No. But it doesn't matter, because that scenario isn't going to happen. You were so unflinchingly ready to give up what was natural to you to stay in Limbo with me forever—no longer a choice, I'm afraid—that I've decided to join you in the material world in a human body. It's growing right now. I'll only be a few days behind you.>

His lips part, obsidian gaze locking onto mine, then he throws his arms around me hard enough to knock me off balance. "Holy hell, you could have led with that! If that was always an option, why were you resolved to stay here and die?"

<If I was wrong and Renascenz continued to operate normally, Limbo would have been left without a guardian angel. I can't abandon all my souls no matter my personal desires. And even after I was certain the company was bankrupt, inserting myself into a human body just... never occurred to me before our conversation.> I shrug. <A bear could leave the woods and get a cushy office job, but it doesn't, simply because the idea never comes to mind.>

His face scrunches. "That analogy doesn't really make sense, but I think I understand what you mean." He chews his lip thoughtfully, trailing a finger down my tie. I shiver from his touch. I can't imagine what it will feel like in the material world any more than a bear can imagine using a copy machine, but it doesn't stop me from trying. He says, "You won't look like... this, right? I don't think the mortal mind will be able to handle it."

<I'll have everything a human body would normally have and nothing more.>

He drops his gaze, and his shoulders sag slightly. "We won't have eternity, will we?"

I tilt his chin toward me, and my feathers brush against his lips. <Time stands still when I'm with you.> Pulling up the resurrection queue, I give Jack the signal, then soak up Rodrigo's beautiful face. <See you on the other side.>

I push him into the queue.

The farewell to the rest of the souls is slightly less emotional, though if I required breathing Mei-Hui would make it a problem with how hard she hugs me. Campbell I've saved for last, and it would be understandable if my reason was simply because I don't want to see him even one last time. But truthfully, I have a little tidbit of information I've been withholding from him, and I intend to savor his reaction. That's not exactly an angel's virtue, but I won't be one for much longer.

As I enter his room, I step into the middle of a four-way intersection. The streets stretch into messy vanishing points, empty of cars. Steel wool clouds sit low and swollen in the sky, and the first drops of rain dash against brilliant red traffic lights. Despite the painterly rendering, I can still make out the letters on the street signs—"Cherry St" and "Grand Ave."

I'm standing directly where Rodrigo and Campbell died.

"What are you doing here?" Campbell's prickly voice startles me, and I suppress a shriek. The scenery suddenly vanishes, sucked into a black void with nothing but a dim, cold sun as illumination.

I turn around. Campbell stands with his arms crossed, one hip jutted out, staring at me with his glistening hole of a face. He says, "It's not your appointment time."

It's tempting to prod him, to ask if I saw something I shouldn't have, to ask why he's angry that I'm here and angry when I'm not. But there's no need. What I have to tell him is going to anger him in a far deeper way. It would be prudent not to say anything at all, to simply shove him into the resurrection queue, but he'll find out eventually anyway. Better that it be here in Limbo where he can't hurt anyone. Jesus in a jalopy, I hope my half-assed failsafe works. It's too late to alter it now.

I stroke my feathers and shrug. <I just figured you wouldn't want me to delay resurrecting you, but I can come back if—>

"Wait!" He steps toward me, shoes thudding against the nothingness below us. "What do you mean? Renascenz won the lawsuit?"

<Indeed. Are you ready to go?>

"You know I am!" He shrinks into himself, and his crossed arms suddenly look more like protection than defiance. His voice is hushed, each word like a steppingstone he can't quite reach. "You're... You're not really going to let me go, though, are you?"

I'm not a being of spiritual judgment, but Campbell doesn't need one since it's clear he's capable of assessing himself. <I *am* letting you go. Your body is ready. But I have something to say first. You wanted the truth from me. All my truths. I gave you some of them, but there's a little thing I've been holding back for the past six months.>

He stiffens. "What is it?"

<Why did you really cause the car wreck? Did you think by killing yourself and taking Corvin with you that he would somehow fall in love with you again? That you'd be irreparably bonded by death, and he would pine for you during his stint in Limbo?>

Campbell flinches, his tone defensive. "I don't want him back."

I generate a pink velvet club chair and take a seat, lacing my fingers over my stomach. <That may be true, but you want *him* to want you. Maybe just so you can be the one doing the rejecting.>

"Shut your non-existent mouth."

<You hurt him physically, but what you really want is his emotional pain. You hope he's dwelled on the car wreck and his actions all these months. You want him to feel bad and need your forgiveness so you can throw it back in his face.>

"Shut up!"

<But what do I know? I'm just a computer program, right? And besides, that plan doesn't make any sense because Corvin

isn't dead.>

The silence stretches between us. Campbell rakes a hand through his long hair then lets out an uncertain scoff. "What do you mean? You said you've talked to him."

<Oh, I have. But while you've been stuck in Limbo for months, he's been living his okayest life in the material world. It's just a hunch, but I don't think he misses you.>

I pull polaroids from my suit sleeve, tossing them in front of Campbell. Certainly part of Campbell's plan succeeded because Corvin's guilt is eating him up, but social media only shows the most curated version of a person's life, and the photos I've chosen to share with Campbell are absolute gems. If he notices the dark circles beneath Corvin's eyes and how thin he is in some of the shots, it might give away that there's pain beneath Corvin's sparkling and stylish veneer, but with the way Campbell's hands shake as he picks up the photos, I doubt he's going to analyze the details too hard.

I pull out photos of Corvin laughing at parties, campy poses for mirror selfies, his newest paintings, candid shots of him kissing the cheeks of beautiful people, and screen captures of posts he's made over the months:

I have a date with Lacey and Antwan tonight! A friend date. If it were an actual date, how would I choose between them?? (I wouldn't 🌢)

Bought the most ridiculous outfits from a bargain bin today, and I'm going to wear them like I mean it. Do you think I can pull off a string tie? Nvm of course I can.

OMG Lourdes' flores de gelatina is almost too beautiful to eat. Almost. I had like half of it.
Ya sabes como soy 🪴

I didn't know having a guy win me a stuffed animal at an arcade would be the key to my heart, but here we are. Or maybe it's because he's funny and sweet and has the sexy nerd thing going on. 💕 And no matter what he says, he's actually a good listener. Ahhh, okay, I can't gush on here and jinx it! Gotta get back to work.

Campbell's chest heaves, the photos crumpling in his grip. I point to the most recent screenshot about Corvin's new crush. <You can expand that if you want and scroll through his posts. It's all real. Or refuse to believe me out of spite and find out for yourself once you return to the material world.> I push out of the chair and bridge our distance, leaning toward his empty face. <But if you touch Corvin *or* Rodrigo, I will personally hurt you.>

He barks a laugh and throws down the wrinkled photos. "How? You can't drop an anvil on me from Limbo."

Swapping my avatar, I shed my wings and eyes and don my special occasion face. <I won't be in Limbo. I got me a body! Isn't that neat?>

"But that's— You can't do that. You're not human. That

has to be against the rules."

I smile and say, <Rules are for chumps, Campbell,> then boot him into the queue.

18

The Resurrected

A warm breeze whips my curls across my forehead, and David bats at his own loose hair, trying to smooth it away from his face. Ivan glances down one side of the sidewalk, hands in his pockets, then looks the other way. There's nothing to see but the usual—a dentist's office, an acupuncture studio, a bookstore covered in a vertical carpet of sticky purple geraniums. A Cherokee restaurant on the corner. Tulips bloom in the street's meridians, and a chipmunk sits on the trolley tracks, chewing through the shell of a seed.

"I'm sure Corvin can find the place," Ivan says. "We can go inside and wait."

But what if he changed his mind and decided not to come? I pull out my phone and check my non-existent notifications again. I can't blame him if he doesn't show up, but it could help him with what he's going through, and things at work have been so busy the last few days that I've only been able to give him a quick hello in passing. Meeting for lunch was replaced by wolfing down a sandwich while replying to emails and answering the influx of phone calls from reporters, journalists, and friends and family of the souls in Limbo. In contrast, the brokers seemed to be more bored than usual, and some of their cubicles were even empty. I'd expected them to be slammed with people eager to sign up for the program after all the exposure the lawsuit got, but maybe the idea of resurrections being suspended again in the future if something *else* happens put a damper on people's enthusiasm.

Something niggles at the back of my mind, reminding me that I was worried at work—or maybe *about* work—but I can't remember the reason. It used to happen far more often before I had ADHD meds; there was constant random boss music playing in my head with no danger in sight. Sometimes I'd remember what I was worried about and sometimes I wouldn't, and the most annoying part was half the time it was a tiny thing, like hating that I'd said something stupid in a conversation.

Right now my biggest worry is whether Corvin has bailed without telling me. I glance down the empty street and pinch the pin in my arm. "You guys go on in. I'm going to wait here for a few more minutes."

Ivan looks like he wants to protest, but David nods and drags him into the building.

I press a hand to my stomach. Metatron's spiritual presence in my guts has been a strange rollercoaster of joy and anxiety over the past few days, but I've been so busy I haven't had time to tease many actual thoughts out of it all, other than their strong desire for Rodrigo last night as I was falling asleep, chased by a very weird: *What if I loved eating ice cream so much I didn't know how to stop?*

We've all been there, Metatron.

I start to pull out my phone to check the app, even though I know it'll do nothing but crash, when movement catches my eye. A group of three people cross the block and head my way. My heart fills my throat. Even if I had trouble recognizing Corvin's slim build from a distance, the broad expanse of man half a foot taller than him can't be anyone other than Owl's husband. When Corvin spots me, he waves enthusiastically, which is hopefully a good sign.

He reaches me, puts hand over his mouth, chewing something, then gestures to Trav and Owl. "They both wanted to come. I hope that's okay." The warm scent of cinnamon and sugar wafts from the paper cone in his hand, but I can't see what's inside.

Seeing people in support of him makes my heart swell. Just a week ago I'd been convinced he had no one at all by the way everyone at work acted around him.

"Yeah, of course it's okay. Trav might need two folding chairs, though," I say.

Trav snorts. His glasses have tinted dark in the sun, and his white-blond braid is flopped over one shoulder. "I'm good at brooding in a corner with my arms folded. Are we late? I thought we could go eat at Gayvgogi after this"—he points toward the restaurant on the corner—"because it has the best food in the city, which is a completely unbiased opinion, but

Corvin *had* to stop for candied almonds on the way here... I'm not convinced he doesn't have tapeworms."

"Trav is a chef at Gayvgogi, and his cousin owns the place." Corvin folds the top of his paper cone and clutches it tightly in his fist. "In my defense, I don't know how long these meetings go for, and I eat when I'm nervous."

Trav opens his mouth, then shakes his head and claps Corvin on the shoulder.

"You're not late," I say, "and no one is going to make you talk if you don't want to. Some people just listen the whole time." And some people tune out the whole time. Like me. It's doing a disservice to David, to Ivan, to everyone in the group, but especially to me. As I invite them inside, I vow not to do that this time.

I introduce Corvin's group to my housemates, then to the support group as a whole. Owl sits beside Corvin; instead of brooding in the corner, Trav takes a wide-legged stance directly behind him, looking for all the world like his personal bodyguard. That would make me nervous as hell—I was only joking about him needing two chairs to sit down—but Corvin leaves the cuffs of his shirt alone and shoots me a tentative smile.

Determined to focus, I watch each person as they speak, their perfect brows furrowing their perfect foreheads, perfect lips pressing into perfect lines. But my gaze keeps flicking to Corvin, to the muscles working in his jaw as he chews gum. To the delicate pink string tie hanging from his rose-embroidered shirt; it matches the pearl earring dangling from his lobe. I imagine his closet must be massive, and I want to see him in every outfit he owns. I want to see him *out* of—

David clears his throat. "I'm always so worried about wasting this life. I... I don't want to be resurrected again. I don't think I could handle coming back from Limbo a third time. So I'm intent on doing everything I can in this life to *do* and *achieve* and make the most of things, and any relaxation feels like I'm squandering my time." He twists his fingers through Ivan's, mouth drawn, then tucks a lock of black hair behind his ear. "But this week has been different. I actually let myself enjoy our date. We had dinner and watched a movie and laid on the grass on the roof talking about nothing, and not once did I feel guilty for not editing my novel instead or not weeding the garden or not working out. I allowed myself to just exist and spend time with Ivan."

I had no idea David wrote novels or that all his time at our house watching movies was something he felt guilty about. Now isn't the time to ask him if he writes gay romcoms or if it's something completely different from his movie preferences, but I file it away for later.

The facilitator says, "That's wonderful. Can you pinpoint any reason that you changed your mindset this week?"

David glances at me. If he mentions talking to Metatron through the Renascenz app, that's going to open up a whole can of worms best left out of this meeting. Turning back to the facilitator, he shrugs and pulls Ivan's hand into his lap. "I thought about what Metatron would tell me if they knew what I was going through. That the quiet moments where you simply *be* or where you are forging connections with people you love are just as important, if not more so, as being creatively and professionally successful, as having a perfectly maintained home, that sort of thing. Achievement is great, but so is self-care, and constantly having a ticking clock in the back of your head is doing nothing but hurting you."

Everyone in the circle murmurs, nodding their heads and agreeing that it does indeed sound like something Metatron would say. Imagine that.

Ivan follows up David's thoughts with some of his own that border on verbal PDA, and the more I listen, the more my stomach knots at how much they're both trying despite their flaws and uncertainties in their own worth. And how much I haven't been.

When they've said what they need, the facilitator turns to Corvin. "Do you want to share anything? It can feel a little intimidating at first to jump into the conversation, and I want to make sure you have the opportunity if you want it."

Corvin stops chewing his gum and digs his fingers into the cuffs of his shirt. His gaze darts to me. He crosses his legs then uncrosses them. "I, uh, I feel like I should. Like I'm supposed to. My family has been trying to get me to open up to someone for months—"

Owl starts to protest, but he waves his hand and says, "They all have my best interest in mind. But I... I..."

He's fidgeting so much I wonder if Trav is standing behind him to keep him from escaping. But when he starts to push out of the chair, Trav steps back to give him room instead.

"I know how that feels," I blurt out. "I'm scared. I'm fucking terrified all the time."

Everyone's attention pivots my way. Ivan looks like I told him his cooking sucks. Corvin grips the back of his chair, watching me, then slowly sits back down. The facilitator has been inviting me to share something since I first started coming to these meetings, and xe looks so shocked by my outburst that I don't want to keep going. But I have to. If not for me, for my housemates. For Corvin.

"David thinks he has to squeeze every last drop out of his life in order to make it meaningful," I say. "But in contrast, I've convinced myself that my second life is pointless. I haven't tried to achieve anything because my first life was such a trashfire that there's no reason to try again. When I was in Limbo, it was easier to talk about what I was feeling because the environment was so surreal. I treated Metatron the way I would if I met God. They would probably already know all my secrets and feelings, so there'd be no point in hiding them. But now I'm back here, and I don't share things with my housemates. I don't listen at these meetings. I didn't know any of that stuff David just talked about even though we're always here together. I act like I don't care, and I push people away. But it's because I'm scared, and I'll bet it's for the same reason Corvin is."

Corvin tugs on his bare ring finger, his throat working,

until Owl takes his hand.

"Why are you scared, Sasha?" the facilitator asks quietly.

"Because I'm full of guilt for what happened in my first life. For the people I hurt." I don't dare look at Corvin's expression or I might stop. "Regardless of whether I've earned that guilt or not, and whether Corvin has earned his, I wear it like a coat everywhere I go. I'm afraid that if I take it off and try again with this new family that I love, I'll eventually screw up and hurt them too. It's easier to wrap myself up in the guilt and continue to punish myself for my last life than face anything new. I mean, I have thoughts all the time that tempt me into relapsing. They're easy to brush aside right now, but what if someday I give in?"

Ivan suddenly throws his arms around me and smothers me in a hug, nearly pulling me off my chair. His voice is half-sob, and I can barely understand him. I think he says, "If you love us, then let us love you back."

I gasp for air. "I'm trying."

"I've noticed." He pulls back, takes off his glasses, and wipes his eyes. "But this context helps so much. I've been pleading with you for almost a year to—"

"I know. I know. And I don't want this life to be pointless. I want to be present for my daughter. I want to continue having a good relationship with my ex-wife. I want to belong at home."

"You do. And if you're worried about relapsing, we can help. You don't need to suffer alone." Ivan's voice is so full of conviction that I couldn't come up with a rebuttal if I tried.

David smiles and nods.

The facilitator looks so pleased that I'm afraid xe might hug me too. Xe says, "It sounds like your life is far from pointless. A lot of people have goals or desires for the future that they want to pursue in their second lives. Do you have one that you might be holding yourself back from?"

I imagine tugging on the end of Corvin's string tie and unraveling the bow, then sliding it off his collar. "Uh, not one I want to share with everyone."

Corvin is quiet for the rest of the meeting, and I catch myself trying to gauge his mood instead of listening to the others. I don't know if my contribution helped him at all, but voicing my fears out loud has lifted some of the weight from my shoulders. Ivan is probably already making a mental list of ways for me to let him show his love, but I think I'm okay with that. Even if it's a group pottery class.

After things wrap up, we all head outside, and Trav invites us to Gayvgogi. Corvin heads toward the restaurant like it's the only opportunity he'll ever get to eat again. I can't tell if he's purposely trying to put distance between us or he really is that hungry. Maybe I shouldn't have said that stuff about relapsing. I could have talked to Ivan about that in private later. Now they all know I was an addict. The meetings are a safe place to talk about that, but my *coworkers* were there, and now Corvin won't even look at me.

I'm so wrapped up in my thoughts that when Trav introduces me to two of his cousins, I forget their names immediately and barely register that we're sitting at a table in the back of the restaurant. Focus.

There's no nametag on this cousin's shirt to help me out. Crow's feet line his eyes, and he's shorter than Trav and heavier set, with a belly that strains his shirt. His glossy black hair hangs in two braids over his shoulders, and there's a flush to his russet skin, like it's too hot back in the kitchen. Though he doesn't have Trav's albinism, it's easy to pick out the same heavy brows, broad noses, and full lips.

The cousin pulls the menu from Corvin's hand, then gathers the others. "No menus. We have a family option with four of our most popular dishes and you can try them all. It's on me. Sunflower cakes with blue corn grits, sauteed pitseed goosefoot, and milkweed seed pods. Bean bread topped with sumac-crusted snapper, sweet corn hazelnut sauce, and roasted squash. Wild rice—"

Trav starts to protest, but his cousin waves the menus at him and says, "You never bring your friends, and I still owe you for the Nuwtiegwa."

"You do not. Just because you forgot that the festival needed—"

Corvin lightly touches my wrist, and I startle. It's the first time he's looked at me since we left the meeting. He leans in and the ends of his string tie brushes the table. "Do you want to go see the greenhouse?"

"The what?"

"The greenhouse next door. Where they grow their food?"

Yours Celestially

"Oh. Right now?" But I don't wait for an answer, pushing away from the table instead.

Trav's cousin drags a chair from an adjacent table and drops into it because apparently this argument is going to take a while. I excuse myself and follow Corvin past tables and beyond a wall mosaiced with intricate red, yellow, and turquoise patterns. The savory scent of roasted corn wafts past as we head by the kitchen doors. He turns down a hall hung with woven baskets and beaded art pieces, then pushes through a glass door. The humidity thickens, food smells replaced with the scent of damp soil and bright greens. The glass ceiling offers a cloudy view of the sunset sky, limning the plants a soft lavender. Rows of squash and beans march into the darkness.

Corvin stops beside a tall trellis burgeoning with green tomatoes. He rubs his face dramatically, then blows a breath through his nose. "I couldn't do it. I'm sorry."

"Do what?"

"Talk about it. My death. My problems. My *guilt*. I— I wanted to do it for you, especially after the way you shared what you're going through, but all I could see when I looked into those people's faces was everyone in Design in their coffee-soaked shirts, staring at me like I'm insane."

"It's okay. I've been going for seven months, and this was the first time I've ever said anything."

"Because I was there?"

I shuffle my feet, dirt scratching beneath my soles. "Yeah, that's part of it. Just wanted you to know that you're not alone in what you're feeling. I could tell you all day long that you're not responsible for Campbell's actions. Just like you could tell me that it's impossible to think clearly in the grip of an addiction. We could tell each other that we aren't destined to be failures, and if we try again, things aren't predisposed to go badly. But that belief that we *deserve* to be failures is so loud that no other message gets through." I swallow the lump in my throat. "We think we don't deserve the people in our lives. Don't deserve to have a second chance. Or at least, that's how I've felt."

Corvin's mouth wavers, the whites of his eyes bright in the fading light. The nod of his head is almost imperceptible. "I couldn't have said it any better myself."

"Listen…" I scrub the back of my neck and pull out my phone, hoping this isn't a terrible idea. "I don't want to push you into anything you're not ready for, but we're running out time before Campbell is—"

"I know." His response isn't as defensive as I expected, laced instead with an anxious urgency.

"Metatron sent me a text the other day. The app has been glitching and I can't understand all of it, but it sounds like Campbell has had an unhealthy interest in Rodrigo. Even if you're not ready to talk to someone about the car wreck for *you*, maybe you'd consider doing it for Rodrigo."

His throat clicks as he takes my offered phone, open to a screenshot of Metatron's message. After staring at the screen, he says, "What do you think this failsafe is?"

I shrug. "Maybe Campbell will spontaneously combust if he gets within twenty feet of you or Rodrigo."

Corvin's laugh is jarring in the quiet space, ending in a slightly hysterical note. He blows out a deep breath. "Personally, I don't think Campbell would do anything to Rodrigo. And I waffle between thinking he would hurt me again as soon as he got the chance and believing what he did was an impulsive act brought on by anger and heartbreak with no reasoning behind it. He was manipulative and temperamental but hadn't shown any indication of violence before then. However, Metatron has known him longer than I have at this point, so I'm not going to brush off this warning. I can't risk Rodrigo getting hurt." Standing a little straighter, he hands me back my phone and nods. "Tomorrow. After work, I'll go to the authorities and give a statement about how Campbell purposely caused the wreck."

Relief washes over me. Before I can ask him if he wants me to come as support, he says, "While we're still talking about all of this..." He fiddles with the button on his shirt cuff. "I never noticed until tonight what you meant about all the resurrected looking so gorgeous. But seeing them in one place really made that stand out, and I couldn't stop thinking about how imperfect *I* am."

"Dude, are you serious? You have nothing to worry about. Just standing next to me makes you hotter by comparison."

"That's not what I mean." He starts to roll up the cuff of his shirt, then pauses and looks like he might be sick. The fabric bunches in his white-knuckled grip. "I want to show you something."

"Okay."

He pushes up his sleeve and holds out his forearm. A puckering scar runs across it, pink lines cutting through his tawny skin. His voice shakes. "From the wreck. I was supposed to go in for scar treatment later on. Never did. Owl bought me cream to help minimize them. I threw it away."

My guilt is a heavy metaphorical coat clinging to my shoulders, but Corvin's is carved into his skin. I chew my lip and finally say, "There's more than this one?"

He rolls up his other sleeve, and I suck in a breath. This scar is deeper than the last, deforming the line of his arm. My chest bristles with static, so many emotions wrapped together that I can't tell if I'm angry at Campbell, sorry Corvin has to live with this physical reminder, or frustrated that he thinks this makes him less than perfect.

I take his hand, turning his arm one way, then the other. "You know, it kind of looks like a feather." I lightly drag my finger across the line of the scar. "Like a quill, with the smaller lines branching off like barbs." I wait a beat for him to reply, but he doesn't, so I say, "They'd make cool tattoos if you ever wanted to cover them up, y'know, with something other than shirt sleeves. You clearly live up to your name as a raven. You're confident and graceful. You like shiny things. You're incredibly annoying when you open your mouth."

He lets out a wet chuckle, then wipes his eye.

I say, "You're too colorful for a raven, though. I keep thinking about that orange swirl suit you were wearing the other day. And your floral sweater." Taking a step closer, I inhale the scent of his cologne. Cedarwood. Vanilla. Green tobacco. I drop my voice, trying to make out each of his freckles. "You should really buy sweaters that aren't so tight. I'm distracted easily as it is, and that doesn't help."

His manicured eyebrow arches. "Is that so? Then what would you like to see me in?"

My heart throbs as I lean in and tilt my chin. "Everything."

He presses his lips against mine, soft but urgent. I let out a small moan and kiss back. Stubble scrapes across my chin. Fingers dig into my hair, and the taste of spearmint fills my mouth.

It's over before I'm ready, and I'm still reeling as he rolls down his shirt sleeves and buttons his cuffs. His gaze rakes over me. "I kind of want to—" He suddenly turns his head toward the entrance. A curvy silhouette fills the doorway, and I have no idea how long the person has been standing there. I take a step back, not wanting to be chastised by staff for fooling around in the greenhouse. The person shifts and light from the hall falls on her face. I sigh. It's just Owl.

"Um, if you two are done doing... whatever it is you're doing, the food is here. You *are* hungry, aren't you?"

Now there's a question. As I pass her, I can't decide if her question was meant as the double entendre it sounded like, but either way, it makes me feel sheepish, even though she was the one who encouraged me to go after her brother in the first place.

The argument between Trav and his cousin seems to be over for the moment, and huge dishes crowd our table. Corvin sits down and immediately begins to pile food on his plate. He spits his gum into a napkin and tosses it in the trash.

I run my tongue across my teeth and taste spearmint. Sinking into my chair, I take an offered plate and start to fill it without really looking at what I'm getting. I'm sure it's all good. I desperately want to know what Corvin was going to say before Owl interrupted us. Desperately want to kiss him again.

His face doesn't give anything away, but the apprehensiveness he wore earlier has given way to his signature enthusiasm. I break off a hunk of bread, but before I can put it in my mouth, he says, "Oh, no no. You need to top it with something. Bean bread doesn't have salt in it, so it's a little weird all on its own."

I don't eat fish very often, but I add some of the snapper and sauce. Corvin is still talking, something about the bread falling apart if you add salt. He says, "Have you ever eaten Cherokee food before?"

"Yeah, but mostly street food. Three Sisters stew, fry bread—"

Trav grunts. "No fry bread here. We agreed to stick to traditional ingredients for the menu."

Before he can continue, Corvin interrupts him and says, "After the Navajo were forced to relocate to New Mexico where their traditional staples were difficult to grow, the government gave them white flour, refined sugar, and lard to live off instead. They used it to create fry bread. It's delicious and traditional in its own right, but also unhealthy and wrapped up in a lot of historical pain. No one is going to judge you for eating it, of course. Lots of places around here offer it. I have to say that the sunflower cakes here are better, though. Did you get one?" He grabs a pair of wooden tongs, plucks up a cake, and sets it on my plate. Maybe his stream of endless conversation is something he does when he's nervous too. If so, I feel a little bit more reassured that our emotions are on the same page.

Owl puts a hand on Corvin's arm. "Your food is going to get cold."

"Right. Sorry." He carves into his bread and says so low I can barely hear him, "I never stop talking."

A lull momentarily falls over the table until Ivan strikes up a conversation with Trav about the restaurant's ingredients and how he can incorporate them into his own cooking. I try a little of everything, pairing things together the way Corvin directs, and it's all delicious. But all I can think about is his spearmint gum. His long fingers sliding through my hair. The scars always hiding beneath the sleeves of his shirts. I wonder if he even owns anything with short sleeves, or if he threw them all away after the car wreck.

I slide my foot against his leg under the table. The fork slips from his hand and clatters against his plate. His Adam's apple bobs, and he gives me a bright grin.

"In the greenhouse, you were about to tell me something you wanted," I say.

He picks up his fork, wipes it on his napkin, and whispers, "I want to ditch everyone and go somewhere with you."

My pulse jitters in my neck. "Sounds like a plan. Have somewhere in mind?"

The calculating version of Corvin made me uncomfortable when we first met—it was obvious an idea was gathering behind his intense gaze like a thunderstorm, and I didn't know enough about him to guess what it might be—but directed at me now it threatens to unhinge all my joints and distract me from breathing.

"How adventurous are you feeling?" he asks.

I don't know if his idea of adventure is robbing a bank, getting ice cream at the mall, or simply finding another dark and secluded place for us to makeout, but I say, "Very."

My phone vibrates. I open a text from Dusty and frown at the message:

Where are you? I need you now.

What the hell? Her texts to me are only ever memes she thinks I'll like or photos of Poppy—

I type back:

Is Poppy okay???

I stare at the screen, my heart throbbing, and every second that goes by makes me regret all the life choices I've made that led me to being here in this restaurant at this moment instead of with my daughter when she needs me.

The phone rings, and I shove out of my seat so fast I nearly knock over the chair. My friends turn to me in surprise. I excuse myself and answer the call, striding for the front of the restaurant.

"Hey. What happened? Where's Poppy?" I push through the front door and stop next to a light post. It flickers on in the draining light of sunset, washing the sidewalk in a pale orange.

Dusty's sandpaper voice comes through the line. "She's fine. She just went down for the night. Fell asleep with a comic book on her face."

I exhale so deeply I grip the light post for support. "Oh my god. You scared me."

"Sorry. I just... I need you. Please. Will you come over? Maybe stay the night?"

A surge of adrenaline zags through me. I think of cupping Dusty's face, our breath hot against each other, lips and hands fumbling in the dark as I thrust beneath the sheets. Heat rushes to my cheeks, then quickly fills my chest. What the hell is this? I've just come around to the idea of moving on. That life isn't mine anymore, Dusty isn't my wife, and I just shared the first of what I hope are many kisses with Corvin.

I compose myself, trying to iron out my emotions. "Listen, I don't know what made you want to ask me this *now* after I ached for the better part of a year for you to take me back, but you were right to push me toward my office crush. I like him."

"Oh god. I didn't— That's not what I meant at all." Her voice drops to a whisper, and I have to turn up the volume on the phone. "It's about Jack. They never came home, and I can't reach them. Something's going on and I don't want to talk about it over the phone."

She really could have texted me that to begin with and saved me the roller coaster going on in my gut. "Maybe they're just working late. I mean, with Renascenz getting the green light to start—"

"No, no. It's not just that. But I don't want to talk over the phone. Come over, please. I don't want to be alone."

I twist toward the restaurant. If I leave, there won't be any meeting up with Corvin later tonight. But Dusty never asks me for anything—has made a point of going out of her way not to unless it's for Poppy—but she was my wife, my best friend, and she's still the mother of my child. I'm not going to tell her no.

"I'll be there soon." I hang up and head back into the restaurant.

When I reach our table, Ivan says, "Everything okay?"

"Dusty's worried because Jack never came home. I'm sure they're just working overtime, but I'm going to head over there to make sure everything is okay." I shoot Corvin an apologetic glance. "Raincheck?"

If he's disappointed, he's hiding it well. "Take your food with you, at least. Take some for her too." He flags down a server and asks for to-go boxes. "This is our CRO, Jack, we're talking about? I'm sure you're right. Arthur asked for volunteers to help clean up the stasis pods and get them restocked with biomaterial, but I guess no one volunteered.

The facility creeps people out. Kevin told me Arthur assigned him, a couple others from Design, and some of the brokers to go do the job anyway. But when they got there, no one would let them through the gate. He called Jack, and Jack said they didn't want anyone inexperienced to meddle with the pods, not even to clean them. Said they were fine doing it themselves."

Jack is headstrong and refuses to ask for help even more than Dusty, so I can picture them saying that. I can also picture them slapping Kevin on the back of the head for breaking something on a stasis pod, so it's probably good that they sent all the "volunteers" away. "That's really helpful to know, thanks. I'm sure it will put Dusty to ease."

After boxing up food, leaving a big tip for Trav's cousin, and saying goodbye to everyone, Corvin accompanies me out of the restaurant. I clutch my sack of food, heat leaching into my hands as I watch for the trolley. Without thinking, I say, "I feel like I'm throwing away an opportunity with you."

The breeze rustles Corvin's string tie. He tucks his hands in his pockets and looks down the street. "Not at all. You think if you leave, I'm suddenly not going to like you anymore?"

"It sounds silly when you put it like that." But it doesn't quite assuage my worries.

"Family comes first. I'd drop you like a bag of dirty laundry if Owl needed me."

I snort. "Thanks. That's real romantic."

A southbound trolley appears around the corner,

destinations in bright yellow glowing from the overhead marquee.

"My invitation still stands," he says. "We'll do something fun and impulsive and wake up the next day with regrets."

I swallow hard. "That sounds like me from my first life. But I don't want to wake up with regrets. I'm kind of hoping to add you to my list of *good* choices while moving on."

The trolley slows to a squeaky stop; an Elvis song drifts through the open door. Corvin says, "What I had in mind was you coming with me to a tattoo studio while I got some little piece of flash. So I can see what it's like and if I might want to get big ones to cover up my scars. And maybe you'd want to get something too." He presses a hand to my back and leans in so close his lips brush my ear. "I didn't mean you'd regret *me*. You won't."

I squeeze the bag in my hands, the to-go boxes creaking. There's a million replies I could give that statement, but my tongue isn't moving, and the trolley is going to leave if I don't get on. I climb onboard and return his wave.

19

The Resurrected

The walk to Dusty's after getting off the trolley is pitch black, and I have to use my phone to avoid stumbling in the gravel. A biting wind ices my ears, and I'm grateful when I finally get to the front step. Lights glow through the curtains drawn over the kitchen window.

I knock softly on the door to avoid waking Poppy, but the thunder of small feet resounds from inside, followed by exclamations of, "Daddy's here!"

The door swings open, and Poppy practically shoves Dusty out of the way to attack me in a hug. "Daddy! You're here, and it's not a Friday, and Mommy says you're having a sleepover with us!"

I hadn't actually agreed to that, and it's hard to say no to those big eyes and that upturned nose. But I can't imagine anything more awkward than spending the night in this house. Poppy is wearing a tee shirt that's absolutely swimming on her, and I realize it's an old one of mine, the black fabric faded and bleach-stained in places, and the band logo so disintegrated it's barely legible. My heart. Must resist saying yes. "I dunno. I have to work in the morning, and you have school. Plus, there's nowhere for me to sleep—"

Without missing a beat, Poppy says, "Well, Untie Jack isn't here, so you could sleep in their bed. Or on the couch with blankets like you used to when Mommy was mad at you."

I cringe. Dusty ushers me inside like there might be someone hiding in the bushes, then locks the door behind us. She pulls the plackets of her terry cloth robe around her body like they're a shield, then brushes curls back from Poppy's forehead. "Daddy's right. You have school and need to go back to bed soon." It's clear in her voice that she doesn't believe that's going to happen, and neither do I. Not when I'm here throwing off Poppy's schedule.

Scooping her into my arms, I say, "Tell you what—I won't leave until after you go to sleep, and I'll read you a comic book before you do. But I have to talk to your mom about something first, okay?"

"You can have a yogurt and watch one episode of *Realm Babyz* before you get back in bed," Dusty says.

"Yay!" Poppy wriggles out of my arms so quickly you'd think the television was her father instead. She opens the fridge and retrieves a yogurt, then turns on the TV in the living room.

I set down my bag of food. "Want some stuff from Gayvgogi? The sunflower cakes are really good."

Dusty folds her arms and leans against the counter. "Thanks, but I'm not hungry. And I'm sorry for calling you over here. I just... I didn't know what to do. I've had suspicions that Jack is up to something—for one thing, they have a secret girlfriend they've never come right out and told me about—but when they didn't come home tonight, I started adding all these little instances up and got scared."

I pull open the silverware drawer and stare at the contents, which is no longer silverware but wine stoppers, bottle openers, and fridge magnets.

"Oh, it's this one." Dusty slides open a drawer, and I can't remember what used to live there when this house was mine, and that thought alone disorients me.

I take a fork, then open a to-go box and dig into the food, which has cooled some but I'm too hungry to care. "So why wouldn't your theory still hold water? People with secret girlfriends stay over at their secret girlfriends' houses, right? Maybe Jack didn't realize how late it was and fell asleep with the ringer on their phone off or something."

She shakes her head before I'm even finished talking, so I tell her between bites of food what Corvin said about Jack wanting to get the stasis facility running again all by themselves. She knows Jack better than anyone, and I don't see how she can refute the idea that they're just working late.

Poppy runs into the kitchen, snatches a spoon from the drawer, then hurries back into the living room. Once she's settled in front of the TV again, Dusty takes my elbow and pulls me back to the laundry room. The claustrophobic space smells of soap and plant soil, and I try to resist the nostalgia it evokes. I didn't come here to be sad about the past. I have a laundry room at home too, that smells like lemongrass and alfalfa, and Ivan leans against the washer and tells me about his day while I help him fold socks.

Dusty's muddy gardening boots sit beside the back door, and plants with broken pots line the sink. Tiny shirts decorated in rainbows, sharks, and tacos are folded on the dryer. Two of my button-up shirts that I'd forgotten existed hang on a dowel over the counter. Dusty pushes a bag of potting soil aside and pulls out something wadded in a sack. She opens it and holds it out. It's one of Jack's plaid shirts—long-sleeved button-down plaid is all Jack owns. Something stiff and a dark crimson stains the front and one of the sleeves.

I keep my voice down. "Is that blood?"

Her mouth flatlines, long lashes fluttering. "Jack came home two nights ago and immediately jumped in the shower before I could even say hi. I found this shirt in the garbage. I don't think the blood is theirs. I didn't see any injuries on them, and there weren't wrappers or bloody bandages in the trash."

"A nosebleed maybe? Theirs or the other person's? Jack *has* been known for getting into fist fights a modest once or twice a week."

She rolls her eyes. "More like twice a year, and there's always a good reason."

"Okay, so? You didn't ask them what happened this time? They're your sibling. I didn't think you two kept things from each other. Not sure why Jack would hide from you that they have a girlfriend either."

"She's religious, I guess, and trying to do everything she can to keep her parents from knowing about Jack. To be honest, I'm surprised Jack hasn't just marched up to her parents and told them how it is." She shakes the shirt. "But this isn't from some fight in Ashland where Jack was protecting peaceful protesters. They're hiding something. Do you think they could be on drugs?"

I huff. "Are you asking me that because it takes an addict to know an addict?"

She opens her mouth like she's ready to deny it, then sucks in her lips and looks away. "Sorry."

"You lived with me. I think you'd know if they were acting the same way I used to."

There must be too much edge to my voice, because her nostrils flare, and she hugs her elbows. Tears roll down her cheeks.

I sigh. "I'm sorry. Can I give you a hug? Do you want one?" It'll be awkward, but I can't just stand here while she cries about what a terrible husband I was.

She nods, and I pull her close. The nostalgia of *this* dwarfs my discomfort, and there's no resisting the flood of memories evoked by her scent and the shape of her in my arms. But I think about all the things I said earlier—shaking off my guilt instead of continuing to punish myself with it; moving forward and filling this life with good choices—and by the time she pulls away, the ache in my chest is gone, and I hope she feels the same.

I pick up Jack's shirt and turn it over in my hands. When

angled toward the light, a bright wash of mint green shimmers across the surface. I tilt it back and forth, then grin at Dusty. "I was wrong about the fist fight, but right about this being a work thing."

"What are you talking about?"

"See the iridescent bits? It's an immune booster added to the blood pumped into the resurrected bodies."

"How do you know that?"

I don't know if she means it to come out sounding so incredulous, but I let it slide. "After you're resurrected, the nurses in the medical facility take your blood once a day to test for things. I asked why my blood was glittery—other than me being a little fruity, y'know—"

She snorts, then waves her hand for me to continue.

"And they explained it to me. There was less of the immune booster visible in the blood each day that I was there, and they said after a week it's gone entirely." Tapping the shirt, I say, "There's a lot of it in these stains, which makes sense because Jack is restocking the pods with biomaterial. They must have spilled some. And it couldn't have come from anywhere else. No one is being resurrected yet."

"So I'm overreacting."

I shrug and hope I don't look too smug. "And Jack has a million plaid shirts, so they probably didn't even bother trying to get the stains out of this one."

"You're a regular detective." She stuffs the shirt back into its bag and tosses it in the sink. "I shouldn't have asked you to come over here for what is probably nothing. Poppy's wound up and wants you to sleep over, and you thought I was asking you for a *booty call*."

"In my defense, I wasn't trying to be a pig. I'm just stupid."

She laughs and leaves the laundry room. Cartoon music blasts from the living room. I stride inside and shut off the TV. Poppy starts to protest, but I say, "I know an intro song when I hear it. Your mom said *one* episode. And you ate your yogurt, so it's time for a story and bed."

The dirty spoon and yogurt lid sit face-down on the floor. I wrinkle my nose and bend to collect them, but Dusty shoos me away and says, "I'll take care of it. You can go tuck her in."

Poppy rambles about her cartoons and her big carnival robot, and I think about the teddy bear I won for Corvin. About spearmint gum and dates for impulse tattoos. Confessing my fear and guilt in the support meeting. Metatron's corrupted text and their failsafe against Campbell. How broken they're going to be without Rodrigo, and I can't even use the app to talk to them if they need me.

There are too many thoughts swarming my mind, and pinching the pin in my arm does nothing but remind me how useless my medication dosage is.

Poppy climbs into bed and draws up the blankets. I pick up the comic book and open it to the page she directs. No matter what I have going on tomorrow in my gut or my heart or my life, right now I need to be a dad.

I'm only through two pages before she begins to nod, her

gaze staring straight through the comic book and into dreamland. But when I start to shut the book, she protests and grips my arm.

"You're tired, honey. Go to sleep."

"No!" She sits up, scrubbing at her eyes. "You said if I fall asleep, you'll leave!"

Damn it. The sleeves of my old tee shirt she's using as pajamas fall past her elbows, and I wonder why she's never packed it in her overnight bag when she stays with me on the weekends. Maybe Dusty is worried I'll take the shirt back or it will get mixed up in my laundry and I won't remember Poppy wanted it.

"How come you're wearing my shirt?" I ask.

Staring down at the crusty logo, she says, "Because Mommy won't let me wear it to school. She says it's too big." Pausing, her gaze darts to the open bedroom door. "She gets mad if I take it out of the hamper to wear again."

My jaw aches, nose stinging. I kiss her forehead, then check my phone. There's a text from Ivan, asking me if everything is okay.

I could leave after Poppy falls asleep. Walking down the gravel road in the chilly dark until I get to the trolley stop isn't that appealing, but Ivan would give me a ride if I asked, and I could be home in fifteen minutes. But Jack still isn't home yet, and with as unnerved as Dusty was, I don't like the idea of her and Poppy in this big house without them. I text Ivan back and explain the situation. He wishes me good night and says he'll see me tomorrow.

I turn to Poppy. "I'll stay after you go to sleep, okay?"

Her mouth purses, brow furrowed. "Promise?"

"Yeah. I'll probably still be snoring on the couch when you get up for school."

"Yay!" She throws her arms around me. "That's good because I'm actually pretty sleepy."

"No kidding? But this is a special occasion. After this, we're going back to our normal schedule, okay? You'll only see me on weekends."

She seems satisfied with that answer—more satisfied than I'll ever be with just weekends—and rolls over in bed, snuggling against Mr. Teeth. It doesn't take long for her to fall asleep. When I ask Dusty for a blanket and pillow for the couch, she doesn't comment, but gratitude flashes in her eyes. Trying to sleep on the same couch I used to spend the night on whenever I'd fucked up something in my marriage threatens to pile my heavy coats of guilt back on, but I remind myself how happy Poppy will be to see me still here in the morning, and I eventually drift off.

Jack still isn't home in the morning, but Dusty tells me she got a text from them early in the a.m. that they'd worked late then stayed over at mystery girlfriend's house and forgotten to call. I resist an "I told you so." Since she's busy chewing Jack out over the phone, I get Poppy ready for school and send her off on the bus.

By the time I shower and dress in one of my old button-ups that had been hanging in the laundry room, I'm already ten minutes late in my morning routine, and the trolley stop is a longer distance than it would be from home. There's no way I'll get to work on time.

As I'm walking past the community house, I call Corvin, and he answers on the second ring with extra enthusiasm in his voice. "Hello, Sasha!"

"Hey. I hate to ask this, but if you haven't left for work yet, how out of the way would it be for you to swing by the trolley stop on Kali Nvda and pick me up? Or I guess I should be asking Trav, since he drives you, right?"

"It's Owl giving me a ride this morning. Is everything okay?"

"Sure, yeah. Helping my daughter get ready for school took longer than I thought it would."

Silence stretches over the line. "Did you sleep over at your ex's house? Nevermind, that's not my business."

I'm not sure whether to be affronted and amused. "Yeah, on the couch. Nothing happened."

Corvin clears his throat. "I'm not the jealous type, but I guess I was kinda hopeful that—"

"Yeah, I get it." I have to save him from whatever awkward thing he's trying to say, which is probably exactly what I would say: that we're not an item, but I'm hoping that will change. Considering how quickly he met and married Campbell, though, I'm more than happy to take things slow.

Rustling and voices drift, then he says, "Owl says she's

happy to give you a ride. We'll see you soon."

He hangs up before I get the chance to say anything else. A warm breeze gusts past with the scent of mint, and blue sky peeks between a bank of thick white clouds. I stare down the road, and eventually a shimmery orange sedan materializes on the horizon. It slows as it reaches me. The window rolls down, and Corvin leans his elbow out. The silky material of his oxblood shirt billows in the breeze.

I hike up my pant leg, exposing my pale, hairy calf, then hold out my thumb and waggle my eyebrows. "Got some room in that car for me, baby?"

He grins through his gum. Owl's voice drifts, and it's probably better that I don't hear her opinion on my sexy legs. I climb in the back, but before I can shut the door, Corvin leaves the passenger's seat and slides in beside me. He points to the seatbelt. "Buckle that up or we're not leaving."

I was getting to it, and I almost joke that he's being pushy again, but I bite my tongue when I think about the scars hiding beneath the silky sleeves of his shirt. When we're both buckled up, Owl pulls back onto the road, and Corvin chatters about tattoo studios he looked up last night, their different artists, and which ones have beautiful flash pieces that can be obtained from a walk-in. I'm more than willing to get a little impulse tattoo with him in preparation for him getting something larger that will cover his scars, but I'm not sure if telling him I have a hideous unicorn tattooed on my ass cheek will fuel his idea or make things worse, so I keep it to myself.

The distant, aching anxiety in my stomach suddenly pushes to full throttle, then disappears entirely. It's such a whiplash of feeling that I nearly wonder if it was my imagination... except that I've never been absent of Metatron's emotions in this life, even if it was in some faint, mostly ignorable way.

Alarm races through me. I dig out my phone and tap the Renascenz app. Ombre pinks and blues drift through the infinity logo as it loads. I watch it for so long the phone goes to sleep. When I wake it back up, the loading screen has timed out. Shit. Maybe if I close my eyes and concentrate hard, I'll still be able to feel them, but there's too much of my *own* anxiety flooding through me now to be able to tell. I need to calm down. I don't know what this means yet. Maybe Metatron has found a way to sever our tether. Maybe my obol has malfunctioned. Maybe the Limbo servers have gone offline for maintenance.

But that last thought doesn't comfort me because it's never happened before and with as unresponsive as the Renascenz app has been, I dread to know how long it would take for someone to fix the servers if they had a problem. I'm about to open my screenshot of Metatron's corrupted text to see if I can parse anything else from it, but Owl pulls into the parking garage down the block from Renascenz, and we leave the car. Hopefully Arthur can give me reassurance that the servers are running smoothly.

When we reach the front doors, a group of our coworkers

are standing just outside, chatting animatedly. I push through them and reach for the door handle, but someone says, "It's locked."

"Locked?" I check my watch. It's a quarter to eight, which is fifteen minutes earlier than I normally arrive, but the looks on Owl's and Corvin's faces suggest that this is not normal.

Corvin scans the crowd. "Arthur isn't here?"

People shake their heads. Lights glow from the lobby, but it's too hard to tell if anyone's shoes occupy the cubby by the door. I jiggle the handle and the doors rattle. The person who told me it was locked gives me a dirty look.

I shrug. "Did you try the door? If not, you're going off of what someone else said, and maybe they were wrong too. Then we'd all be stupidly standing outside of an unlocked door, late for work, until Arthur walked outside and asked us what the hell we were doing."

As if on cue, the crowd parts for Arthur. He rubs his salt-and-pepper beard, lines creasing his face, and his shirt is half-untucked and so rumpled I wonder if he slept in it. Everyone stares at him, but he makes no move to say anything or unlock the front door.

I scratch my head. "How come *we* weren't invited to that kegger, Arthur?"

There's a ripple of uncertain laughter through the crowd. Arthur clasps his hands in front of him, then unclasps them and shrugs helplessly. "Renascenz is closed until further notice. You can all go home."

Surprise and outrage erupt around me. I clutch the phone in my pocket, thinking about the broken Renascenz app and the absence of Metatron's feelings in my gut. I don't have a chance to ask any questions, because everyone else is doing it for me.

"What happened?"

"But we won the lawsuit!"

"What about the Limbo servers?"

Oh god no. I press my hands against my stomach and glance at Corvin. There's so much chatter I barely hear him say, "But Rodrigo deserves to come back."

My guardian angel can't be gone. I pull out my phone and jab my finger against the Renascenz app until it crashes and Corvin's hands close around mine. I pinch the bridge of my nose and blow out a slow breath.

Arthur is shouting. "Jack has assured me the servers are okay for the moment!"

"What happened?" Corvin asks.

Anise, the bookkeeper, pushes through people, her purse clutched to her chest. Her magnified eyes are huge and watery behind her glasses. "The company is bankrupt."

Outrage explodes from my coworkers, all of them demanding to know how long she and Arthur have known that. Anise shrinks into herself, squeezing her purse like a shield. There's something dark and crusty on the sleeve of her cardigan; it catches the light, shimmering mint green. She says,

Arthur tries in vain to smooth his wrinkled shirt, sounding

slightly bewildered. "I—I thought we'd be okay. A large backer was going to inject more funds into the company. The CEO said it was a done deal. But the backer pulled out."

I lead Anise away from the crowd; people are demanding answers from her that she probably doesn't have, and I'm not sure anyone is even listening to Arthur's explanation.

"So you're Jack's mystery girlfriend, huh?" I say.

She gasps and clutches her throat. "I— That's— Please don't say anything to anyone. How did you know?"

I point to her bloody sleeve. "Jack never came home last night. You helping them restock the biomaterials in the stasis pods?"

Anise rolls up her sleeve until the stain disappears. "Not exactly. We—" She stops so quickly that Corvin nearly runs into the back of her. A bearded Afro-Latine person with short black curls strides our way like there's an angry dog following them. Their shirt looks a size too small, stretching across their belly, and they're barefoot. When they see us, they stop as suddenly as Anise.

Corvin whispers, "Rodrigo?"

What? How would that be possible? But despite not recognizing his face, I've seen those same fidgeting hands— deep brown skin, knobby knuckles, pink nails—in my mind's eye so many times over the course of my second life that it can't be anyone else.

He squints hard, scrunching his face almost comically, and stops so close to Corvin that it's definitely a violation of his personal space. Rodrigo's eyes widen and he takes a quick step back. Turning his attention pointedly to the sidewalk, he says, "I guess I shouldn't be surprised that you know who I am. I looked you up after the accident too. I'd say it's nice to meet you under better circumstances, except that isn't true." He cringes. "Not that it's bad to meet you. The circumstances are bad. Anise, I'm so glad I found you. I need help. I don't know where Jack is, Campbell is missing, and I can't get into the—"

Corvin chokes. "Campbell has been resurrected already?"

"Everyone has been. Everyone but Metatron." Rodrigo's Adam's apple bobs as he grips his elbows. "And something is wrong. I can feel it in my gut."

20

The Seraph

My heart is

    thump

        thump

           thump

                thump

                    thump

                        thumping,

and my skin tingles all over to the point that I wonder if I've entered the body too soon and I'm mostly muscle and organs with the skin hurrying to catch up. But Jack assured me I was done "baking."

My eyes are itchy. The ones in my chest. But I don't have eyes in my chest anymore. Do I?

Can't see what's in front of me. Can't move my arms. Am I breathing? I don't know how to breathe. Panic rises like a flood of black water, engulfing me. I scream, but nothing comes out of my straining throat. My eyelids refuse to peel back. Can't see. Can't move. Can't breathe.

I flee back to the safety of Limbo, and entering my avatar dampens the terror vibrating inside of me. That other body is still there—I can feel it—but its refusal to obey my commands is now only a peripheral fear, like a spider in the corner instead of directly on my face. Loosening my tie and opening my shirt, I rub my eyes even though they aren't itchy in this body. That it makes them feel better is probably only my imagination.

Priest on a pogo stick, I hope the paralysis I just experienced isn't what sleep feels like. What if it is? And what if eating is nothing but the unpleasant sensation of mushy, wet matter sliding around my teeth? But now that I think about it, the inside of a person's mouth is already wet, which is gross in its own right.

I shudder as a flood of other thoughts about physical body functions enters my mind. On a surface level, there's no difference between me and the souls in Limbo; we're all digital consciousnesses existing in a server. But the souls are approximations of real humans who existed in the material world—humans who have five million years of biology baked into them.

My mind wasn't programmed for this.

Jack's bedside manner leaves something to be desired, but I don't have any other choice for comfort right now. All the dead were resurrected several days ago, and I already tried calling Sasha twice before entering the resurrection queue. The Renascenz app did nothing but crash.

The phone rings.

Four.

Five.

Six...

Seven.

Eight.

Oh god. Jack isn't answering. They always answer on six rings.

I pull off my halo and twist it in my hands, pacing. Okay. No big deal. I don't like being in that *other* body, but it's very likely still in a stasis pod. Of course it would be in a state of paralysis right now. Jack will return to help me, and once the body is out—once *I'm* out—breathing the air and moving my limbs and blinking my eyes, I'll be fine, certainly.

There will be so many first experiences with Rodrigo, and that alone will be worth everything else. I'm fine. Everything will be fine.

My body's heart rate suddenly quickens and the tingling in my skin intensifies, yanking my consciousness back into my physical body. Oh god, what's happening? Darkness encroaches at the margins of my mind, chewing up thoughts before they reach me. The only feeling left is *SOMETHING IS WRONG*. I try to claw out of my skin, try to wrestle my soul back to the safety of Limbo. But pain is an anchor pulling me back down into a sea of panic.

My mind thrashes. Teeth bite down on a fleshy tongue. Fingertips twitch. Every cell in my body is screaming, but I'm molten melting

from the inside

out

brain

is

lagging

AL HESS

I think

I might be

dying

21

The Resurrected

Rodrigo's quick and nervous stride, like that proverbial angry dog is still behind him, is hard to keep up with. He mashes each crosswalk button, impatiently shifting from one foot to the other until the little person on the sign flashes green.

I stop beside him, prepared to pull him back to the curb if he decides to take his chances on the crosswalk while it's red, especially since it seems like his vision is terrible. "How are you resurrected already? That takes weeks, and the lawsuit—"

The sign turns green, and he starts across the walk, waving away my question. "If you're going to help, we need to hurry."

Anise fills Corvin and me in on how Metatron suspected all along that Renascenz was going to go bankrupt, how Metatron coerced her into embezzlement to keep the servers running long enough to get the souls in Limbo resurrected, and how Metatron is still there, waiting for a brand new human body to finish growing so they can evacuate Limbo too and be with Rodrigo.

The information overwhelms me, all the details hardening to a chunk of cement without meaning that only looks heavy and ugly as I turn it over in my mind. I can only focus on my immediate concern—that something is wrong with my guardian angel.

"So you can feel Metatron?" I ask Rodrigo. "Like, their literal emotions in your stomach?"

"What? No, I..." He frowns, gaze darting to the side like he's lost all sense of what I just asked. "It's a common phrase, isn't it? To 'trust your gut?' I only meant that my intuition is telling me something isn't right."

Oh. I was hoping that if he could—

Sudden distress bombards me, and I double over. Metatron?

Corvin puts a hand on my back. "Are you okay?"

It isn't the sweet ache I'm used to or a cramping nausea that threatens to bring up my breakfast, but an oppressive darkness pressing down on me. It squeezes my throat and clings to me like a soaked shirt. I can't shake it off, and even though I'm standing on the sidewalk with the open sky above me, it doesn't feel like enough space. Drawing in a deep breath, I convince my body I'm still breathing, that my lungs are expanding and there are no bricks piled on top of me.

At least this means that Metatron is still *somewhere*. "It's claustrophobia."

"What?"

"Metatron is panicking at the idea of being stuck in a physical body. As best I can tell anyway."

Rodrigo's mouth hangs open. "How—"

Corvin takes charge of the explanation, which is good because I'm suddenly not up for it. Rodrigo breathes heavily as we reach the trolley stop, bracing his hands on his thighs. In the first days after being resurrected, my muscles had been weak and even walking across a room made me short of breath. I can't imagine how much determination Rodrigo needed to walk all the way here, and barefoot. He must have ditched his hospital garb and scrounged up that ill-fitting outfit from somewhere. His cheeks are pocked with deep acne scars. He could have left that out of his second body and could have chosen perfect vision, but he must have his reasons for staying the same, like I did.

He draws in a labored breath. "Is it weird of me to feel jealous of that ability? I have a hard time parsing people's emotions, and being special enough to feel Metatron's would really come in handy."

"You're special, trust me," I reply. "All of us are chopped liver in Metatron's many eyes compared to you."

This earns me a hesitant smile. "I didn't know what to do. I couldn't get into the main building to find their stasis pod, and the only one I know of who can talk to Metatron is Jack. But I couldn't find them. So I came this way, figuring Anise was here and could help." His semi-unfocused gaze lands on Corvin. "Didn't expect to run into him too."

The trolley pulls to a stop, and as soon as the passengers get off, I climb aboard with the others, then realize Rodrigo is still standing on the sidewalk. He clenches his jaw, brow furrowed, takes a step toward the trolley, then backpedals.

"I—I can't."

Metatron said Rodrigo had trouble around crowds, and being in a packed trolley appears to be too much for him. I'm about to tell him he can sit with me in the very back, legs and arms dangling over the edge so his back is to the passengers, but a car honks behind us.

Owl waves her arm out the window. "I don't know where y'all are going in such a hurry, but it'll be faster in a car."

We pile in, and Rodrigo directs Owl to the Renascenz facility at the outskirts of Galvlohi. My mind is pulling in so many directions that I barely register that I'm crammed into the back so closely to Corvin that I'm practically in his lap.

"You okay?" I ask.

He clutches his seatbelt, staring at the back of Rodrigo's head. "Do you think he hates me?"

Rodrigo twists in his seat, still panting. "I don't hate you. I don't even hate Campbell. Hating people doesn't do anyone any good."

Corvin swallows. "I'm so sorry for—"

"Please don't. You don't owe me an apology." That's apparently the end of the conversation, because Rodrigo twists further and says to Anise, "Can you call Jack and tell them what's going on? They might be in the main facility for all I know, but won't have any idea that Metatron is distressed."

Anise presses her phone to her ear, but after a moment she shakes her head and says into the speaker, "When you get this message, will you please— Oh, hello? What?" She clutches the Universal Church pendant at her throat. "But the grace period is supposed to last until the first of May! Did you tell them there's still a soul inside who needs to be resurrected? Metatron's body isn't ready yet, is it?"

Jack's voice through the line is loud enough to be clear: "They don't fuckin' care. Just our luck the power company is full of assholes who hoped Renascenz would lose the lawsuit. Metatron's body is done baking, but I haven't inspected it yet and don't have time right now. If I have to knock these—"

"Jack, no!"

I can't hear anything else over Anise's panicked exclamations. Rodrigo begs Owl to go faster, and Corvin braces himself against the seat, his complexion green. Shit. I pinch the ADHD pin in my arm until pain blooms. It grounds my racing thoughts enough to pick out something helpful to say.

"Okay, okay! Everyone calm down for a second." My voice is too loud in the enclosed space. Owl runs over a curb, and Corvin digs his fingers into my thigh. "Jack is a little punch-happy sometimes, but it's always for a good reason, and they can handle themselves in a fight. If they can't scare the power people away, we can help when we get there. Force them to come back with paperwork or a police officer, and by that time it won't matter because we'll have gotten Metatron resurrected already. Right?"

"Even if their body is ready, if they're terrified of entering it, they might refuse to leave Limbo," Rodrigo says. "We need Jack to talk to them."

"Jack won't be able to. They talk to Metatron through the Renascenz app, and the app isn't working." I check it again to confirm, hoping I'm wrong, but it times out.

"Then someone needs to go to Limbo and talk Metatron into entering their body," Corvin replies.

Rodrigo frowns. "While I appreciate the enthusiasm, I think that would be counter—"

"*No.*" Owl's voice is so forceful that all the chatter in the car dies. "*No,* you are not doing that."

Corvin turns to me. "Hit me in the head. Try to aim for the base of my skull."

"Excuse me?"

"It'll send me to Limbo for a few minutes. I'll talk Metatron into getting into their body."

Owl slams on the brakes and throws the car into park. "You cannot do that!"

"If I don't, Metatron might wait too long and still be in Limbo when the power people shut off the servers."

"And if you go to Limbo, there's a risk that *you'll* be there too when the power shuts off."

Oh god. Corvin would either die or be stuck in vegetative state. But he's also right that no one else is going to be able to contact Metatron. "I think it's a good idea, but only if we ensure that the power people won't be shutting off the servers immediately. We should wait until we get to—"

"We're already here," Owl snarls. She leaves the car, slamming the door behind her.

A chain link fence with nasty razor wire and closed-circuit cameras wraps the squat stasis facility and the small building beside it. The Limbo servers are housed underground, only accessible through the facility—which is a bit ironic considering Renascenz's fixation on celestial themes. A guard post sits abandoned beside the fence, and the gate is ajar. This is definitely not normal.

I start to ask Rodrigo if the gate was already open when he left, but he leaves the car and helps Owl push the gate open enough to get the car through. They climb back in, and we pull beyond the fence. Several white trucks with the Galvlohi Power logo stenciled across the side sit askew beside the facility, three people next to them. A person jabs their finger into a clipboard, then shakes it in Jack's face. Jack rips the clipboard from the person's hand and flings it like a Frisbee. It sails over a truck and lands in the dirt. This is going well.

When we get out, Rodrigo rubs his palms on his pants and says, "I'm not good with confrontation. But I'll bet all of the other resurrected will go to bat for Jack if it means saving Metatron. Even if they're not feeling one hundred percent, I'm sure they'll be willing to leave their cots and come out here. I'll go get them." He doesn't wait for confirmation, stumbling through the gravel in the direction of the smaller building.

Anise starts to run toward Jack, then stops suddenly. Turning to me, she says, "The code for the door is 62857."

I'm not going to remember that. I pull out my phone to leave myself a note, but Corvin says, "Got it." He jogs toward the stasis facility, and Owl and I hurry to catch up. Anise's strained voice drifts as she yells about grace periods and late fees. Covin's already got the door open by the time we reach it. We're washed in white light, which paints the pink walls and mint tiled floor in soft strokes. Jack's room looks less like an office than a janitorial closet, and tools and tubing are strewn across the floor, trailing out into the hall.

I have no recollection of being here, but there doesn't seem to be anywhere else for the stasis pods to be than down this single hallway. To our left is an elevator with no buttons, only a keypad and card reader.

"As soon as we find Metatron's body and ensure it's done growing, I'll do it." I point to the back of Corvin's neck. Owl shoots me a dirty look. I say, "I don't want anything to happen to him either, but he's right. There's no other way."

"I think if Metatron knows there are people—friends—waiting to get them out of the stasis pod as soon as they enter the body, that should alleviate some of the claustrophobia," Corvin says. "It would if it were me, anyway. Both Owl and I have volunteered to clean the pods before, so unhooking Metatron shouldn't be—"

Feet slap against tile, growing louder. A soft, pained voice carries down the hall. "Mr. C?"

Corvin stiffens. He grips his bare ring finger like it's not supposed to exist.

A white person with long brown hair stops at the end of the hall. Their cheeks are wet with tears, bare feet coated in dust. A piece of duct tape is stuck to the leg of their hospital jammies. They let out a sob and run toward us. Through labored breaths, they exclaim, "Oh god, it *is* you." They sag against Corvin, bunching his silky shirt in their fists. "I—I made a mistake, and I'm sorry. I was just so mad. All this time, I thought you were dead too. Metatron let me think you were dead! They said they talked to you at your appointments. They *lied* to me about you being dead! And I shouldn't have done it, but I was just— I was just so mad."

Corvin's eyes blaze, their arms trembling and a vein standing out in their temple. This can't be anyone but Campbell. I think about the wedding ring Corvin had been wearing as self-flagellation for six months. Think about how fragile he looked as he told me about Campbell speeding up as they approached a red light. Corvin's pink string tie and his pink pearl earring and his pink scars. And now Campbell is rambling about being mad and being sorry and I don't give a shit if any of it is sincere. All he's doing right now is hurting Corvin and cutting into our time to get Metatron out of Limbo.

I ball my fists hard enough to make them cramp. But before I can do anything, Corvin flings his ex-husband away, sending him sprawling onto his backside. His voice breaks as he jabs a finger at Campbell. "You had six months to apologize for what you did to me! Metatron would have given me the message. But you never did, and now isn't the time." He steps over him. "As soon as we're done here, you're signing the divorce papers."

Campbell's voice grows thorns. "I'm not apologizing for what I did to *you*. I'm apologizing for what I just did to Metatron."

Ice water floods my veins. I leap over Campbell and run down the hall. I reach a room full of what could be mistaken for tattoo or massage chairs if not for the glass domes encasing them. At first glance, the dim lighting makes it too hard to see if any of them are occupied, but one of the pods is lit from within, turning it into an iridescent soap bubble. A roll of duct tape, a pair of scissors, and bolt cutters lay on the floor nearby.

My heart throbs, and I swallow hard, praying there won't be a screwdriver or anything else jutting from Metatron's chest. The seal on the stasis pod appears intact, and sleeping peacefully inside is a white person with androgynous features that look more fitting for a portrait in a gothic Eastern European castle than on an angel. They're gorgeous, but in a much more natural way than the flawlessness and perfect symmetry of many of the resurrected. Wet locks of honey-brown hair coil around their collarbones, and delicate blue veins web their closed eyelids. Their nose is nearly as hawkish as mine, but in a much more refined—and less crooked—way. With their hands folded over their heart, it further reinforces the vampire look.

Seeing them with a face is both incongruent and oddly

comforting. Their naked body looks vulnerable beneath the glass, and I realize there are pale gashes fanning across their chest, and another in their stomach above the purple umbilical cord twisting around the back of the seat. I press my hand to my own navel. Oh god. No wonder they were scared to enter this body.

I look up, zeroing in on Campbell, who is standing a few feet away from Corvin and Owl. "What the fuck did you do?" I stride for him, my voice rising, and fling my arm toward the stasis pod. "There are cuts all over Metatron! Did you stab them with those scissors? What's wrong with you?"

Campbell's brows furrowed. "What cuts? I didn't stab them."

"You're sick. I can't believe—"

"I didn't stab them! The scissors were for the duct tape. I— I was so mad that they lied to me, and I didn't want them here with me in the material world. So I used those bolt cutters and snipped their oxygen tube."

I slap a hand over my mouth, and tears flood my vision. Metatron's body is ruined, and there's nothing else for them to enter, all of the other pods dark. They'll never get to touch Rodrigo's hands. Never get to use this face they pulled from an 1800s Romanticism painting. Dead before they ever got a chance to live. And if the servers shut off, their consciousness will be gone too.

I sink to my knees and press my hands against the glass. Corvin and Owl join me like mourners around a casket.

Campbell sniffles and wipes his eyes, his voice strained. "I tried to fix it."

"How could you possibly fix that?" I don't know why I'm asking. I don't want to hear anything else out of Campbell's mouth.

"The body… It started to asphyxiate, right?" Campbell's pause stretches until I look up at him. His eyes are wide, mouth trembling. "And for some reason, *I* could feel it. My throat started to close, heart was pounding, vision tunneling. I just barely made it to Jack's office and back again with the duct tape before passing out. I wrapped the oxygen tube as best I could, but I still feel"—he presses a hand to his chest—"like it's hard to draw in a breath. You've got to help. Please. I'm sorry. I shouldn't have done it, and I didn't know Metatron would feel it. I mean, this is just a body. It's not them yet… Right?"

It's the failsafe. It must be. And I'd bet on every one of Metatron's feathers that if Campbell tried to hurt Corvin or Rodrigo, he'd be able to feel that too. Sitting back, I rake my hair back from my forehead. Considering that Campbell originally committed suicide, it's not a perfect solution, and it may have saved Metatron from asphyxiating, but—

I squint at their body's hands folded over their chest. There's a white slash in the side of their wrist. Pushing up, I round the pod and inspect their other one. Slashes on both sides. That would be an incredibly impractical spot to stab someone, and Metatron's avatar in Limbo had something in those same exact spots.

"They're not wounds. They're eyes!" I tap the dome of the pod. "The ones in their chest and stomach too. Or would have been eyes anyway."

Corvin polishes the glass with his sleeve and takes a closer look. "Maybe they wanted eyes there, but the Renascenz program refused to grow them. Or they're purposeful scars that Metatron gave themself to represent who they used to be."

Owl stares at the touchscreen display above the pod. "I don't know what everything on here means, but their vitals look good? Oxygen seems okay, heart rate is strong, brainwaves are... er, I don't know how to read them, but they're there. Aside from the weird eyeball scars, is there anything else to worry about? They've got all their fingers and toes?"

Corvin helps me quickly scan the body, and we squint at earlobes and fingernails and parts that Metatron probably didn't have in Limbo. I hope none of the resurrected in those online forums find out about Metatron's new physical body because if they were attracted to their guardian angel before, well...

I clear my throat. "Looks good to me."

Corvin agrees. Owl cycles through menus on the display and says, "This gives a rundown of their organs and systems, but I'm not sure we have time to read through it all in detail. If we're getting them into this body, we need to do it now."

I wait for her to say something else about Corvin's idea being terrible, but she doesn't, so I turn to him and say, "So how do you want to do this? Sit down, maybe?"

"What's going on?" Campbell asks.

"He wasn't lying when he said he had appointments with Metatron in Limbo," I reply. "Ever since the car wreck, he's been having near death experiences. *You* did that to—"

Corvin puts a hand on my arm and shakes his head. He eyes the empty pod beside Metatron's, then seems to think better of it and takes a seat on the floor. Owl sits cross-legged behind him, muttering that she won't let him fall and get hurt. Crouching beside him, I take in his dark eyes and long lashes, his immaculate hair and dusting of freckles.

"Come back to us, okay?"

He nods. "I always do."

I slap the base of his skull. His eyes roll back, and he sags in Owl's arms. One of the sleeves of his shirt pushes up, exposing the thick scar disfiguring his forearm. I tug the sleeve down, then wrap my fingers around his limp hand and kiss his knuckles.

Metal scrapes against the tile, then something flashes in my face. Owl cries out. I lean back, staring at the sharp tip of the scissors pointed at me. Campbell's hand shakes, his eyes wild as he hisses, "You think you can just swoop in and steal someone's husband? We're still married!"

Don't say it. Don't say it, Sasha. Not with a pair of scissors aimed at your face. My traitorous mouth is going to do it anyway— except Owl speaks first.

She whispers, almost apologetically, "He doesn't love you, Campbell."

Campbell's face twists with rage. He swipes the scissors at Owl, and I try to shove his arm out of the way. White-hot pain lances through my palm. I suck air through my teeth and press my bloody hand against my chest. I lunge for Campbell, snatching his wrist and ripping the scissors from his grip. His fist slams into my nose, and stars explode in my vision. I yank his loose hair, and he yelps as I pull him to the ground.

Jack's angry Southern drawl carries down the hall, but I can't make out the words because other people are shouting too. Shit. I press my knees into Campbell's chest and pin his wrists to the floor, but it's hard to keep a grip when my left palm is bleeding freely. "Owl, get that duct tape!"

Campbell bucks underneath me, and my hand slips. He swings his fist, grazing the edge of my jaw, but there's no power behind it. He pulls in a ragged breath and clutches his chest. Owl tears off a strip of duct tape, but Campbell puts up his hands in surrender and scoots away, tears rolling down his cheeks. I don't trust that this isn't an act, and I can't risk him hurting—

Opaque darkness suddenly engulfs us, the room giving off a collective electronic sigh as the power dies.

22

The Seraph

I lay on whatever passes as a floor in the undefined space of Limbo, knees drawn to my chest. Under other circumstances, I would generate a bed, floor cushions, a rug, or soft grass, but even the empty white noise is comfort right now compared to where I was. The burning sensation in my cells lessened enough for me to pull away from my physical body, but the resurrection queue keeps tugging at me, insisting I enter and start my new life.

I don't want to go.

I'm suddenly notified of a new soul in need of welcoming. For a fraction of a second, I wonder if I was wrong and Renascenz is back in business, booting up new souls for me to take care of. Then I realize it's Corvin. A mixture of relief and fear twists through me. Rushing to his room, I throw my arms around him and hold on tight, not caring if he decides to turn into a cactus. He stumbles, regains his balance, and squeezes me back.

<You don't know how happy I am to talk to someone!> I bury my eyes in his neck. <But you need to be more careful

about bumping your head. You can't come here again. I really didn't want to have this conversation with you, and not right now, but—>

"I already know everything. I'm here on purpose for once." He pulls back, gum pinched between his teeth. "You need to get into your body before it's too late to do so."

I recoil, thinking of my concrete limbs and molten cells. <No. I can't. It hurt.> I grip his shoulders, staring into his face. <It hurt *a lot*. And you can't tell me that's normal. Something is wrong with that body.>

"About that..." His lips suck in, and he fiddles with his shirt cuffs the same way always does when I try to get him to open up.

Oh. I drop my shoulders and look up at the static sky. <It was Campbell's doing.>

"He cut your oxygen momentarily."

<Color me surprised.> I should have abandoned Campbell here. But I couldn't. Even now, after all he's done, I wouldn't have had it in me to condemn him to be deleted. But that doesn't mean I don't currently have the desire to strangle him. At least my failsafe seems to have worked.

"Your body and vitals seem fine, though. I can't imagine how scary it was to be unable to breathe, but it won't happen again. There are people there waiting to help you. Me, my sister, Sasha... Rodrigo."

My love, my life, my eternal sun around which everything else revolves. I need to see that sun rising. I need to feel the warmth on my skin. I want to know if his beard is scratchy or soft, if his songs in the material plane have the same depth and color they do in Limbo, if he has a tweed jacket in his closet with a faux leather shank button that's only hanging on by a thread because he fiddles with it so much. I want to sit in on the astronomy lessons at the university and see whether he gets just as heated and passionate on the subject there as he does with me.

The pain and helplessness Rodrigo felt in his recurring dream of drowning surely seemed as real as what I experienced when Campbell cut my oxygen. There's a good chance he'll keep having those dreams. But he won't need to dream up my comfort because I'll be there in person, in his bed, arms wrapping around him. And if I get frightened, I know he'll do the same for me.

I absently rub the eyes in my chest. <Alright. I'll go. Someone is there to get me out of the pod?>

Corvin nods, chewing his gum.

<I'll wait for you to leave, and then I'll go.>

"No, you should go now. I'm not going to give you the chance to change your mind. I'm never here very long, so I'm sure I'll be right behind you."

The idea of abandoning one of my souls here feels very wrong, but the longest Corvin has ever stayed for is one minute and sixteen seconds, so I'm sure he'll be rousing as soon as I climb out of the stasis pod. Hesitating, I squeeze him in another hug and say, <Thanks for coming back for me. See you on the

other side.>

I burst into feathers and glitter, letting the resurrection queue draw me in. I'm not sure how long I'm there, drifting in nothingness, until a voice rouses me.

Metatron

Please

Where are you?

A   pulse   beats
in   my   neck.   I   blink,
and   a   gauzy   film   slides   over   my   eyes. Pastel
clouds float in a dark sky, and someone is crying, muffled like

they're underwater. Or maybe *I'm* underwater. Cold needles of sensation vibrate inside my hands. I lift my naked arm, tentatively, and it slides through the clotted clouds, bumping into something hard and smooth. There's a glass wall between me and the sky. I try to wish it away, blow the clouds from my vision, but it doesn't work. I try to draw a breath into my lungs, but they don't listen to me. Nothing is listening to me.

My hand slides against the glass. Silhouettes dart between the pastel clouds, which I'm realizing aren't clouds at all, but a weak beam of light refracting through whatever substance is encasing me.

Jack's voice cuts through, distinct but still seemingly coming from a great distance. "You're gonna fuckin' pay for this!"

My heart jumps in my chest. What's going on? I press against my sternum, hoping my heart stays beneath my ribs where it's supposed to be. My wet fingertips slide over skin, and I try to rub the itchy eyes in my chest. The itch is there—the eyes aren't. In their place are sealed fissures, my skin embossed with some ghost of my former avatar that I didn't tell the program to create.

I press against the glass above me, but my arms don't have any strength behind them. Knocking against the glass does no good. Jack clearly can't hear me over all the yelling they're doing. Feeling my way along the side of the pod, my nails catch on a seam. I wiggle my hand inside, and a burbling noise fills my ears. The viscous liquid surrounding me suddenly sucks away, gushing through the broken seal. My skin tingles, goosebumps pebbling my body. The umbilicus extending from my navel flops against the chair beneath me, and some part of my genitals contracts against my thighs. Gross. All of this is gross. I'm slimy and uncomfortable and my fleshy body is doing weird things without my consent.

I need out of this pod, but my entire body trembles, limbs too weak to push myself up.

Jack's voice breaks. "We only needed a couple more minutes! And you couldn't give us that. Now both of them are dead. How does it feel to have just killed two people?"

Alarm races through my body, sharp and unpleasant. Who died? The power is out, only wan light filtering from the hall beyond. The servers. Oh god. Did Corvin make it out? Even if he did, something is very wrong.

Fighting against my weakness, I pull at the seal of the stasis pod, fire burning in my muscles, until there's a wet *SMACK,* and the dome surrounding me lifts on its own. I have to see if I can help with this situation, whatever it is. Everything beyond the pod is dim shapes. I push off the chair, and my feet slip on the floor.

My throat flexes, some semblance of noise trying to make it past my lips. My chest cavity suddenly spasms, and I'm certain I'm suffocating again, until a wet cough explodes out of me, and I draw in gulps of air. I grip the chair beneath me, unsteady. A garble of syllables comes out of my mouth.

For a moment I'm not sure the voice is mine. It doesn't

sound like me, and my tongue and lips didn't form the words I wanted them to. I realize with horror that I don't know *how* to form words. Not with lips and tongue and teeth.

I make it a couple of feet on my jellied legs before my umbilicus catches on something. Tools are strewn on the floor, and I pick up a roll of duct tape. After wrapping it as tightly as I can around the cord to cut off the blood supply, I pick up a pair of scissors and snip myself free. Stumbling forward, I rake wet hair from my face and try to still my chattering teeth. My eyes struggle to adjust to the darkness, but I follow the weak light and the voices until I'm in a hallway lit with filtered sunlight. A person in a plaid shirt stands with two people in white uniforms. One of the uniformed people is on the phone, saying they need police and an ambulance.

"You better expect them to arrest *you* when they get here!" It's Jack's voice, and it takes me a moment to realize the person in plaid is them. "You caused this!"

I slip on the tile and press a hand to the wall to steady myself. The person on the phone locks eyes with me, then the color drains from their face and they scream and drop the phone. I try again to speak, but it's the wrong choice because now they *all* look terrified. I reach at the air, needing to conjure a marquee, a word bubble, a neon sign to speak for me, but I can't do that here.

Jack blinks, mouth open, then tips back their Stetson and strides up to me. "You're alive?"

Well, that answers half my question. I open my mouth to

speak, then think better of it. I might be able to write words down, as I've done that in Limbo, but that would require asking for a pen and paper, which I can't do. And I'm covered in goo and my hands are shaking.

In frustration, I press my thumb against my chin, waggled my index finger, then simultaneously flip both my hands over and raise my eyebrows. Jack raises theirs in return, and it's clear they don't understand. One of the uniformed people, who I can now see by the logo on the breast of their shirt works for the power company, scoops up their phone, taps something, then aims it at me. They say, "Sign that again."

I do, and a stilted voice from the phone translates: *[WHO DEAD]*

Jack's mouth flattens, their nostrils flaring. "The art guy. Corvin."

Oh no. I yank my hair and squeeze my eyes shut. He came back to help me. To save me. He shouldn't have had to sacrifice his life for mine. It would have been better for me to stay in Limbo and never have agreed to follow Rodrigo here. Would have been better for me to never fall in love in the first place. None of this would have happened.

I sign again, and the phone says: *[WHERE]*

"In the lobby with Sasha. Corvin's sister went to get a gurney and look for defibrillators and an oxygen mask in the building next door. I tried to tell her those weren't going to wake him up. There's nothing wrong with his body. But his mind is gone. She's really upset, though, y'know, and not thinking clearly."

But Corvin never died. Not the way the other souls did; his consciousness is still in the obol in his head. Which means there's hope. I pat Jack on the shoulder and stagger past. They protest that I need a towel and my umbilical stump is dribbling blood. I make my way into the lobby, which is utilitarian and unwelcoming with its bare walls and hard floor. A far cry from how most of the city is dressed up, but no one ever sees the inside of this building except Jack and medical staff. The resurrected supposedly aren't conscious right afterward. I guess I'm an exception.

Sasha sits on the floor, his hand wrapped in a bloody bandage. Black curls hang across his forehead, his slender throat flexing as tears roll off his nose. Corvin's body is limp, his head cradled in Sasha's lap. I carefully kneel beside them, not trusting my shaky knees. Sasha is so intent on Corvin's slack face, whispering something I can't hear, that I don't think he even notices me.

I lightly touch his arm. He startles, gaping at me, his blue eyes wide and glossy. "Metatron?" I nod and try a smile. He lets out a strained laugh, and tears spill down his cheeks. "I was praying to you. I didn't know what else to do, and I thought— I thought, 'I don't believe in God, but I *do* believe in Metatron.' Did you hear me?"

When I nod, it might be another lie to add to my collection, but I don't have the heart to tell him no. And the more I think about it, the more I'm certain I *did* hear something before I woke up. Someone asking where I was. Sasha pulls up the collar of his shirt and wipes furiously at his eyes, sniffling loudly. The way he holds Corvin, tenderly, protectively, is exactly the way I'd hold Rodrigo, and I vow to bring Corvin back not just for Corvin's sake, not just his sister's sake, but so he and Sasha can have each other.

I bend forward over Corvin, my bony kneecaps pressing uncomfortably into the hard floor and a cold breeze tickling my exposed back. When I whisper to him to wake up, Sasha regards me with awe, like I'm speaking a magic spell instead of a trainwreck of sounds that make no sense to my own ears.

Rodrigo argued that my presence in his dream on the day he died, my presence with him in the car as he bled out, wasn't his imagination. He was certain I was there, my comfort enveloping him. And maybe I did hear Sasha through whatever spiritual umbilicus connects us, and it pulled me to consciousness in the stasis pod. If there is any power left in me as guardian of the resurrected, I need to find it and use it now. I cup my hands around the back of Corvin's head, fingers pressed to his obol. Shutting my eyes, I rest my forehead against his and think as loudly as I can.

WAKE

UP

CORVIN

His eyes fly open. He gasps and sits up so quickly his head knocks into mine. Chest heaving, he looks wildly around. "What happened?"

Sasha sobs, then cups Corvin's cheeks and gives him a hard kiss. He flings his arms around him, fingers digging into Corvin's silky shirt. I'm not sure anything has registered in Corvin's mind. He absently touches his wet lips, then blinks at me. After a moment, recognition dawns on his face, and he gives me a sparkling smile.

A gurney bursts through the front doors, laden with medical equipment and pushed by someone who is most definitely Corvin's sister or I'll eat my halo. She spots Corvin, and the sobbing, hugging, and confusion starts all over again. Other people push through the doors, and though some of them didn't have faces in Limbo, I recognize the bodies they chose to be resurrected into. Gale is younger but still somehow possesses the eyebags and pale complexion of someone who spends too much time in front of the computer. Behind him, I spot the face I've been aching to see. I hope he likes mine just as much, though I'm now regretting declining Jack's offer of a towel.

I try to call out to Rodrigo, but my lips can't form his name. People fuss over Corvin, all of them talking, and I can't push through them. Rodrigo doesn't have his glasses; he can't see me.

Gale pokes me in the arm. "How come J-Jack didn't, uh—

How come he didn't give you some— some clothes?" He pulls a white sheet from the gurney and hands it to me. It's a far cry from a suit, but I knot it over one shoulder like a toga, then hold out my arms and turn in a circle.

He cocks his head, brow furrowed. "Well, at least your— your w-wedding tackle isn't hanging out now."

I press my palms together and give him a little bow and wink. Something flashes on his face, and I can't tell if he realizes who I am or just thinks I'm a weirdo, but I can spend time with him later. That is, if he even wants to spend more time with me. I'm sure six months was enough.

Raking my hair back from my face and hoping my navel isn't bleeding through my sheet, I find Rodrigo and hesitantly touch his elbow. He turns to me, and his expression is the brightest star in the universe, burning away every hesitation, every fear, every one of my imperfections. He whispers my name reverently, his voice deep and velvety. His glasses are missing, earlobes unpierced and unstretched, and his teeth are a little straighter, but his face is the same one he revealed to me in Limbo. I want to tell him it suits him far better than an emoji—I can read his expressions just fine. But the words clog in my throat, unformed.

He tucks a lock of hair behind my ear, heedless of how gooey I am. "You're taking the angel look a bit literally with the white robes, don't you think?" When I don't say anything, he cocks his head and says, "What's wrong?"

Sasha appears beside us. "I don't think they can speak

anything we'll understand. Only some ancient angelic language or something."

"Enochian?" Rodrigo asks dubiously.

I laugh—and at least I can do that right—my voice ringing true and clear through the lobby. After motioning for a writing implement, Rodrigo hands me a coffee-stained legal pad and a pen. I press the pen to the paper, and even though my fingers are weak and unsteady, I'm able to scrawl a message.

Rodrigo takes the pad and reads out loud, "*I don't know how to form words with my mouth*"—they pause, smiling at the next line—"*but the first thing I'm going to learn to say is your name.*"

23

The Resurrected

For someone who already has a pierced conch and decided on a traditional dagger as his impulse piece of flash, Corvin sure is a wuss. He sits in the tattoo chair in a white undershirt, hugging his exposed forearms to his stomach as the tattoo artist squirts ink into tiny cups.

He leans in, the scent of spearmint drifting. "I don't want to stop. I'm just worried that if I pass out and fall out of the chair—"

"Come on."

"—then the tattoo will be ruined, and I'll have a hideous piece of art on me forever."

My own piece is already done, smarting on my bicep beneath the plastic film like a mild sunburn. When we walked in and flipped through the book of flash sheets, Corvin looked like he was ready to bail on the whole idea and find something else—*anything else*—to do for our date. So I went first so he could watch, and now I have a little line art poppy to add to my collection of body art.

I lean back on my vinyl stool, admiring the outline of

Corvin's pecs beneath his undershirt. "Let's say you *do* feel like passing out. You let me or this lovely lady know, and then you get a break and some water, right?"

The tattoo artist, Dewbell, beams Corvin a radiant smile. "That's absolutely right." Every part of her fair skin that isn't covered in tattoos is covered in freckles. Her hair is backlit by the afternoon sun, turning the long blonde locks into strands of sunshine themselves. An intricate gold cuff wraps her ear, and at first glance, it simply looks like a piece of jewelry, but a thin wire trails from the back, disappearing into her hair. It's a cochlear implant—a beautiful piece of disability tech like Ivan's porcelain arm.

"And say there happens to be an earthquake right when she's tattooing you, and you do fall out of the chair," I say. "If something gets messed up on your dagger, I bet a fantastic artist like her would have no trouble turning it into something else."

Dewbell adjusts something on her tattoo machine and studies the purple stencil on Corvin's arm. "Accidental lines could be lasered off, but it would be easy to freehand some vines, braided rope, a stream, something like that over the top. Or maybe a moth? A bird?" She turns on her machine, and a quick buzzing noise fills the room. Grasping Corvin's arm, she says, "Ready? If you talk to me or your boyfriend, it'll take your mind off how it feels."

"He's not... Well, this is technically our first date, so it feels a little early to be putting a label on what we are." Corvin's gaze darts to me, and he raises his eyebrows.

I nod. Hopefully this is the first of *many* dates, but with baggage and divorces in both of our pasts, there's no reason to rush into anything. We have plenty of time to take things slow.

"Oh, how cute." Crows' feet crinkle around Dewbell's eyes. She presses the tip of her machine against Corvin's skin. He draws in an audible breath, but doesn't flinch, and after a moment his stiff posture relaxes.

"We, uh, we met a Renascenz," he says. "It's been a wild few weeks."

"Wow, I bet," she replies. "So you're both out of jobs?"

"Eh, I got mine back at a tech company I used to work for," I say. "It's not perfect, but they gave me all my benefits and vacation time back, so it's hard to complain. And Corvin is an artist, so he's taking on some private commissions while he sends out his resume."

Dewbell's steady hand traces the handle of the dagger. "Did you hear there's a new company already planning to replace Renascenz? No Limbo or guardian angels, so no chance of people being stuck in a server for months and at risk of deletion. They're calling that person Jack a hero for having the foresight to upload all those people into their bodies before Renascenz went under."

"Yeah, how about that."

"Sad about the AI, though," she continues. "I hope they were backed up somewhere."

"I don't think an angel can die, you know?" But Metatron is on some romantic vacation with Rodrigo right now, which might be close to heaven.

"I hope you're right. Maybe you two should apply at this new place. I'm sure they'd love to have you."

Corvin and I share a look. He says, "I'm not sure I'm that good at helping people live their best second lives, to be honest."

Now that's a lie. I scoot closer and take his hand, then turn his arm over. "You going to ask her?"

He runs his tongue along his perfect teeth. "I heard you do scar cover up, Dewbell. That you're one of the best around. And quite frankly I don't know why you're taking walk-in flash clients when—"

"Only on Tuesday afternoons," she replies. "It's our slowest time for appointments, and all the money from flash is donated to charity. And yes, I *am* one of the best around."

I like this woman. Corvin rambles on, his fingers rubbing against my thumb. "I've been wearing long sleeves for six months to hide the scars on my arms, which is travesty because I have some fabulous shirts in my closet that are gathering dust, and I used to look quite hot in them. Now I have weird tan lines on my wrists and sweat like a horse in the desert. I'm tired of punishing myself by not doing anything about the scars but covering them with shirt sleeves, and Sasha thought maybe they could be turned into something beautiful instead." He takes a breath. "We were thinking raven feathers. One on each arm. Or a couple of smaller ones arranged together for the left arm. I don't know how hard it is to tattoo over thick scarring, and the skin on my right arm is pretty puckered, but—"

Dewbell stops her machine and sets it on the table. She turns both of Corvin's forearms over, inspecting them. "You'll need to wait at least another six months before getting tattoos over them, because we need to give the scars a year to fully heal. But hypertrophic scars respond to tattooing similar to normal skin, and feathers are intricate enough that they would hide them well." She pauses, then holds out her own forearms, tilting them in the light. "Do you see mine?"

Faint raised slashes run in deliberate patterns across her skin, just visible beneath the garden of flowers covering her arms. My expression must mirror Corvin's frown, because Dewbell smiles and says, "I'm in a much better place now. And it's why I started tattooing. I found the whole process to be very cathartic." She picks up her machine and goes back to work on Corvin's dagger. "I bet you would too. There are other scar minimization methods, of course, and I do have resources on those if you want them. But if you want feathers over them, I'd be happy to do that for you down the line. For the record, I don't think there's any reason you can't wear short sleeves now, though. I'm sure you'd still look hot in them, and I bet your not-boyfriend agrees."

"She's not wrong." My gaze drifts from his forearms, up his softly defined biceps, to the cliff of his collarbones and hollow of his throat. This is the most skin I've ever seen him reveal, and I have to turn my attention to something else before I imagine stripping that tank top off of him.

I inspect the five stitches in my palm instead. It would probably be harder and more painful to get a tattoo there, but I don't need one, even if it does leave a scar. After Corvin's report to the police about Campbell's deliberate car wreck, obtaining signed divorce papers and a restraining order, Campbell promptly checked himself into a mental health facility, citing extreme emotional trauma from romantic rejection and being stuck in Limbo for so long. Even with Rodrigo declining to press charges, the authorities have enough reason not to let Campbell out of their sight.

And Renascenz might be gone, but the meetings for the resurrected are still around, and our group has some fresh faces from Limbo that I'm getting to know better. It seems like a weird way for me and Corvin to round out our date later this evening, but I'm not sure much in my life counts as "normal" anymore.

Dewbell finishes Corvin's little dagger, wipes it clean, and lets him inspect it in the mirror. She spreads a protective film over it, and we head up to the register to pay. The counter is crowded with plants and candles, and sunlight catches in a sequined pillow in a chair, spraying drops of light into every dark corner. She fishes through plant leaves for a business card holder. After handing one to each of us, she winks. "Have fun on your date. If it doesn't work out"—she taps her lips— "better yet, if it *does*, you can usually find me at the Terrible Teapot on Saturday evenings."

We leave the studio, and I shield my eyes. "Did she just hit on both of us at the same time?"

"Do you blame her?" Corvin replies.

"What are you doing on Saturday?"

He laughs and takes my hand. I pull him around the corner of the building and into an alley garden flourishing with lavender, shrub roses, and bean plants. The brick is crawling with ivy, and I back Corvin against it. Leaves tickle my ear, and my nose brushes his as I say, "I thought you were a wuss when it comes to pain, but I was wrong."

"Ah. Well, you're forgiven."

"It was just you being neurotic again. Whether you'd fallen out of your chair or not, if she'd gotten any of the lines on that dagger slightly crooked, no one would ever hear the end of it."

He narrows his gaze, teeth pressing into his plush lips. "Why *wouldn't* I be neurotic about that? Tattoos are permanent."

"Nah, baby. Nothing is permanent. Not you. Not me. And after I was resurrected, I spent so much time wondering if I was still *me*. Is my soul still the same, or am I only a digital approximation of some miserable addict who died of a heart attack?"

"That feels like something that should be discussed at the meeting later."

I shake my head. "I've decided I'm good without knowing. Because either way, that miserable guy is long gone. I'm someone else now. Someone better."

Corvin grins. "That's rather deep for a guy who has a

hideous unicorn tattooed on his ass."

"Yeah, and if you play your cards right, you'll get to see it eventually."

He leans forward, words muffled as he presses his mouth to mine. "I'm looking forward to... that."

I kiss back, and his lips bloom, inviting me deeper. He groans as I slide my tongue into his mouth. We shouldn't do this here because anyone walking by could see us, but he hooks his fingers into my belt loops and tugs me deeper into the plants. It's tempting to make a joke about how he only gets turned on in gardens, but my mouth is a little busy at the moment.

His words slur as I suck at his lip. "I know it's really early to be thinking about it, but I'm the anxious type—"

"You don't say."

"And I really hope your family likes me."

I pull back, then pluck a leaf from his hair. "You already met my housemates."

"But I haven't met your daughter."

"That's who you're worried about?"

"Her opinion matters more than anyone else's. I mean, if a kindergartener thinks you're uncool, there really isn't any hope for you."

Butterflies swarm inside me. "I'm sure you'll be fine but improving your arcade skill can't hurt."

"Will you teach me?"

He looks so sincere that I can't help but kiss him again.

"Yeah."

I press a hand to my navel and take solace knowing that the love sickness in my gut is no one's but my own.

The Seraph

The Milky Way shimmers off the smooth plane of the lake like a spilled bottle of violet ink. Crickets saw in the reeds, and I don't care how much Rodrigo insists they'll leap out of the way while we're walking—I'm terrified of accidentally stepping on one of the little buggers and killing it. Thankfully, our cabin is only a short walk away, so when he tires of staring at the stars out here, we can curl up in the fat quilt on the bed and I can gaze at the most heavenly body in the universe. That isn't a joke about sexual attraction. I don't think I have any. Sexual attraction, that is. I'm never short on jokes.

A chilly breeze wafts off the lake, ripe with the scent of vegetation. Silhouetted hills rise in the distance, lamps from other cabins the only other light aside from the stars. There's something strange and beautiful about viewing them in the material world. They aren't flecks of glitter on a canvas or cardboard prom decorations I can manipulate at will. I can only interact with them as an observer, admiring their beauty the way I would a classical painting behind a velvet rope.

Lake mist dots Rodrigo's glasses, his thumb absently worrying against my knuckles. He speaks in a whisper as though afraid his voice will scatter the stars like fireflies. "You had a feather on one of your wings that looked exactly like the sky does now..." The night swallows his words, crickets filling in his thoughtful pause. "The light would catch the iridescence and turn it this brilliant pink and purple."

"You remember that one specific feather out of the thousands I had?" I ask.

"Of course. But I don't want you to think that I mourn that loss. I already have favorite details about your new body."

"Oh?" But I already know in the slow way he kisses me, taking in the shape of my lips. In the way he caresses the eye scars in my wrists. How his eyes crinkle every time I speak, because despite learning how to fluently form words in a matter of days—my brain is still an AI's after all—I still have an "Enochian accent." He's mentioned several times how much he likes it.

I hope it never goes away.

Acknowledgments

Yours Celestially is a mashup of beloved characters from my unpublished *Travelers Series* and a weirdcore /vaporwave/liminal space novella inspired by the question, "What if your AI chat bot was very gay and tired?" I wanted to keep the cozy, overgrown feel of the post-apocalyptic world in the *Travelers Series* but flip it into something of a cheery maximalist utopia instead. Galvlohi isn't perfect, but my *Travelers* characters deserved at least one universe with softer edges, and Metatron's personality was far too big to stay confined to a little novella.

A huge thank you to Claudie Arseneault, D.N. Bryn, Shelly Campbell, Darby Harn, Jennifer Lane, and Adam Mahler.

Content Warnings

This book contains: past drug addiction, divorce, mentions of car wreck, discussion of death, brief violence, profanity, brief mention of suicide and past self-harm, brief mentions of transphobia, mentions of Christianity and biblical iconography (seraphs, cherubs, etc.), mild sexual elements, depression and anxiety, vomiting

About the Author

Al Hess has a penchant for vinyl records, art deco furniture, and novelty socks. When not hunched before a computer screen, he can be found at his art desk. He does portraits in both pencil and oil paint, and loves drawing fellow authors' characters nearly as much as his own. He writes cozy and uplifting stories with queer, trans, and neurodiverse representation.

Al is author of *World Running Down, Key Lime Sky, Yours Celestially,* and the award-winning *Hep Cats of Boise* series.

Subscribe to Al's monthly newsletter to ~~contact your guardian angel~~ keep up with news, giveaways, promotions, and opportunities to become an early reader for new titles.

alhessauthor.com/subscribe

Want More?

Al Hess is a part of The Kraken Collective, an alliance of indie authors of LGBTQIAP+ speculative fiction, committed to building a publishing space that is inclusive, positive, and brings fascinating stories to readers.

ODDER STILL

by D.N. Bryn

Craving another queer SFF story about a nonconsenting host invaded with the feelings of a non-human sentient being?

Odder Still is a M/M fantasy novel with a class-crossing slow burn romance, murderous intrigue, and a Marvel's Venom-style parasite-human friendship in an underwater steampunk city.

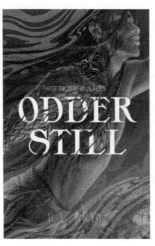

Milton Keynes UK
Ingram Content Group UK Ltd.
UKHW011813120624
444110UK00001B/23

9 781958 051412